# DOWN *the* LINE

# DOWN the LINE

MICHELLE D. ARGYLE

*Down the Line*

Copyright © 2019 Michelle D. Argyle



Summary: "Alex Winzelberg wants to embark on his acting career now that he's graduated high school, but his long-distance relationship with an eccentric girl he's never met threatens everything he's ever thought matters."

This book is a work of fiction. Any resemblance to actual persons, living or dead, events, or locales, is entirely coincidental.

ISBN: 978-1-7342146-0-4

Edited by Diane Dalton

Cover Design, Illustrations, and Typesetting by Melissa Williams Design
New York City Skyline © Greens87, iStock
Boy © OSTILL, iStock

Published by MDA Books
www.mdabooks.com

To all the Supermen who aren't.

# One

## August—1997

---

**From: <winzwarehouse5@hotmail.com>**
**To: <ina.artgirl1979@hotmail.com>**
**Date: August 10, 1997**
**Subject: Ten-Dollar Bill??????**

I might get a dozen spam messages sending this email, but I'll take the chance. Is your name Ina? I used to have a friend named Ina. She was born in 1979. Her name was short for Katrina. The problem is she died when we were kids and your email address is kinda freaking me out.

I guess I want to know why you wrote your email address on a ten-dollar bill??????

—Alex Winzelberg

From: <ina.artgirl1979@hotmail.com>
To: Alex Winzelberg <winzwarehouse5@hotmail.com>
Date: August 28, 1997
Subject: Re: Ten-Dollar Bill??????

I thought nobody would ever notice that address. How far did the bill travel? Where are you at?

I don't know you, so I'm not gonna spill the story of the ten-dollar bill. Yet. But for now, hi. Yes, my name is Ina and I was born in 1979, but I'm not your dead friend. Spooky coincidence, dude.

P.S. "Ina" is a shortened version of my full name too. Don't ask me what it's short for because I'm not telling. I will tell you it's not Katrina.

P.P.S. You don't sell sunglasses, do you?


From: Alex Winzelberg <winzwarehouse5@hotmail.com>
To: Ina <ina.artgirl1979@hotmail.com>
Date: August 28, 1997
Subject: Re: Re: Ten-Dollar Bill??????

Hello, Not Katrina. No, I don't sell sunglasses. Why?

So, yeah, I get that you don't know me, but this is kinda fun, right? I mean, I hardly know anyone else with their own email. I only have one because I work at my family's shipping warehouse. Now there's another reason for me to use it, so that's cool.

I'm in Idaho, by the way. I hope I hear back from you soon and maybe you can tell me where you are?

From: Ina <ina.artgirl1979@hotmail.com>
To: Alex Winzelberg <winzwarehouse5@hotmail.com>
Date: October 7, 1997
Subject: Re: Re: Re: Ten-Dollar Bill??????

Hey Alex,

I wish I had a regular job that let me use their internet. I can only check and send emails at the public library, and I only come here when they have temporary job openings. That's why it takes me forever to answer you. It's a long story and I won't bore you with it.

Anyway, I'm in New York, so the bill went pretty far. What do you do in the shipping warehouse? I've never had a real job like that, just these temp jobs at the library. Peace out.

P.S. I'm not gonna answer the sunglasses thing. Just, yeah…not gonna.


From: Alex Winzelberg <winzwarehouse5@hotmail.com>
To: Ina <ina.artgirl1979@hotmail.com>
Date: October 8, 1997
Subject: Re: Re: Re: Re: Ten-Dollar Bill??????

New York. Wow. That is far. Anyway, that super sucks about not being able to get on the web. I get on all the time since I live where I work and we have three computers. I know you're probably thinking it's weird I live in a warehouse, but I grew up here, so it seems normal to me but sometimes when people find out we live at WFS they're all weirded out about it. I do a little of everything here. Office work, packing up pallets, loading the semis, you name it. It's not very exciting. Your temp jobs at the library sound interesting. What do you do? Does your family live in a house or an apartment? Every time I think of New York, I think of tall buildings covered in graffiti. Is that really what it's like?

P.S. WFS stands for Winzelberg Fulfillment Services, but nobody around here calls it that.

-------------------------

From: Ina <ina.artgirl1979@hotmail.com>
To: Alex Winzelberg <winzwarehouse5@hotmail.com>
Date: October 12, 1997
Subject: Re: Re: Re: Re: Re: Ten-Dollar Bill??????

I'm not weirded out that you live in a warehouse. It sounds cool, but maybe kinda cold. Doesn't it snow a lot there? I've never been outside of New York. It's not all high-rises and graffiti. Dude. No. Come out here and you'll see what I mean.

I'll just give you the straight-up facts so I don't have to explain later. I don't have a family like you probably do. Dad died when I was a kid. Mom's in prison. She embezzled some money or something, but I don't know details because nobody tells me anything and she doesn't really talk to me. She's been in there since I was 11. She's gonna be in there forever and it sucks. But don't feel sorry me. I hate pity more than anything.

My job at the library isn't anything exciting. I'm just helping some of the employees learn the new computer system. They seriously can't wrap their heads around it. Money for me, right?

What about you, Mr. Alex Winzelberg? Got a sad, sappy past you wanna spill? Peace out.

From: Alex Winzelberg <winzwarehouse5@hotmail.com>
To: Ina <ina.artgirl1979@hotmail.com>
Date: October 13, 1997
Subject: Re: Re: Re: Re: Re: Re: Ten-Dollar Bill??????

Really? Your mom's in prison? I'm sorry. That must suck. Is there a reason she doesn't talk to you?

Maybe I shouldn't say this, but sometimes I feel like I'm a prisoner here because I think my parents are going to make me work for them until they die. My sister is twenty-one. She's getting married in six months and my parents are freaking out because she's going to move away and that's one less cheap minion for their work staff. She's so lucky.

I'm kinda curious. If you have no family, where do you live?

P.S. It does snow here, but we don't get cold. We live on an upstairs level that was remodeled into an apartment. I stay warm.


From: Ina <ina.artgirl1979@hotmail.com>
To: Alex Winzelberg <winzwarehouse5@hotmail.com>
Date: October 17, 1997
Subject: Don't Feel Sorry

Dude, do not feel sorry for me. Remember how I said I hate that? I was serious. I'm over the whole Mom-in-prison thing. I don't know why she doesn't like to talk to me. I try not to think about it.

Anyway, how many are in your family? I live in a group home, so I understand feeling like a prisoner. I've had foster parents before, but the older you get, the less people want to take care of you. I've been looking out for myself for a long time. Sometimes people tell me I'm an adult trapped in a teenage body. I'd leave here and go live on my own, but finishing high school and all that shit is kind of important, so I'll ride it out until I finish. Hey, it's free housing, right?

Sorry, gotta go. Someone else wants the computer. Peace out.

6

---

**From: Alex Winzelberg <winzwarehouse5@hotmail.com>**
**To: Ina <ina.artgirl1979@hotmail.com>**
**Date: October 17, 1997**
**Subject: Re: Don't Feel Sorry**

I hope you find out about your mom one day. I've got issues with my parents, but it'd still suck if they never talked to me. We yell at each other a lot. I guess that counts as talking. One day I'm gonna move to New York. I've never told anyone this, but I want to be an actor. On Broadway. Anything you want to do like that?

About my family. There are five of us. That includes my parents. I'm the youngest. I just turned 17 in August.

So, I wasn't going to tell you this, but we've had drama going on here and it's stressing me out. My best friend's been dealing with his own family crap, so I don't want to bother him about mine. I don't feel like any of my other friends would care. They don't really know my sister. Remember how I said she was engaged? Well, her fiancé broke it off and she won't stop crying and I don't know how to help her. It's stressing my mom out ... and then there's my dad ... he's not dealing with it great and I don't know how to help him either. Totally dumping that on you. Sorry. Good luck with whatever you're up to.

From: Ina <ina.artgirl1979@hotmail.com>
To: Alex Winzelberg <winzwarehouse5@hotmail.com>
Date: October 20, 1997
Subject: Me the Painter

If you just turned 17 in August, you're eight months younger than me. For some reason I thought you might be older than me, but it doesn't matter.  That sucks about your sister. All I can say is she probably needs space more than anything. It hurts to get rejected like that. I feel bad for her. I wish we could chat on the phone or in a chat room about it, but I can't. Email is all I've got. Let me know how your sister's doing.

I think it's awesome you want to be an actor. Go for it. Be in plays at school. Or does your town have a community theater program? You gotta have dreams, and maybe if you do move here to get on Broadway we can meet up. I want to meet you.

I think the only thing I've ever wanted to do is paint. Dad was an artist. Mom burned all his paintings before she was thrown in prison. They don't give us art supplies here, so the only place I get them is at school. Sometimes I steal them. I have to or I'll go crazy. I have to paint. I know you won't judge me for that...


From: Alex Winzelberg <winzwarehouse5@hotmail.com>
To: Ina <ina.artgirl1979@hotmail.com>
Date: November 8, 1997
Subject: Re: Me the Painter


My sister is okay now, thanks. She did need space. A lot of space, and if you hadn't said what you said, I might've butted in too much.

We have art supplies here. Do you want me to mail you some? Nobody ever claimed them and they've been here for ages. Most of them are covered in an inch of dust, but I think they're still good. Why would your mom burn your dad's paintings? Lame.

You're right about the dreams thing. Maybe I'll take a drama class and audition for the school play next semester.

From: Ina <ina.artgirl1979@hotmail.com>
To: Alex Winzelberg <winzwarehouse5@hotmail.com>
Date: November 15, 1997
Subject: Get in a play!

Glad to hear your sister's okay.

Your question about my mom…I don't know how to answer that. My dad died when I was little. I have a lot of memories of him, but the best ones are of him painting in his studio. Painting was a huge part of who he was, so it must've hurt my mom a lot every time she looked at his work. I guess she felt like she had to get rid of it and decided to burn it all. Like, she took them all out in the backyard, poured gasoline on them, and lit a match. It scared the hell out of me. I thought our house was going to burn down. Anyway, my theory is she was freaking out because she was sad. Whenever I ask her about it, she finds some way not to answer me.

I hope you auditioned! Or, if you haven't yet, that you will. Seriously, don't be scared. You should care so much about what you want that everyone should be annoyed when you don't shut up about it. That's what a therapist told me once. I thought she was an idiot, but I'm beginning to believe her now.

Thanks for the offer on the dusty art supplies, but somebody gave me new ones yesterday. He's really nice. He's on the Board of Directors for Harmony House (that's my group home). Most of the directors are jerks, but this guy's different. Really different. He's been giving me a lot of stuff. Anyway, gotta go. Peace out.

8

From: Alex Winzelberg <winzwarehouse5@hotmail.com>
To: Ina <ina.artgirl1979@hotmail.com>
Date: November 15, 1997
Subject: Re: Get in a play!

Maybe one day you'll find out about your mom. Do you know when she'll get out of prison? Do you ever visit her?

That's great about the art supplies. If you ever want some from me, let me know. What's it like living in a group home? Just curious because I'd never heard of them until you said you lived in one. And how is this guy really different? What is he giving you?

P.S. I've got my audition tomorrow. I'm nervous. Better get to bed.

From: Ina <ina.artgirl1979@hotmail.com>
To: Alex Winzelberg <winzwarehouse5@hotmail.com>
Date: December 25, 1997
Subject: Christmas already?

I can finally sit down and write to you. Thanks for understanding about my mom. No, I never visit my mom because she told me not to, and every time I call, she ends the conversation as soon as she can. I like to pretend it doesn't hurt, but it does. Still, don't feel sorry for me.

I don't think I told you my birthday is on Christmas, but yeah, I'm 18 today. That sounds young still, maybe because I can't wait to be a real adult. I swear I already am in my head. Jake gave me a laptop. I can email you a lot more now. Well, whenever the staff lets me use it. They have to keep it in the office for me. The only tech-anything we can have in our rooms is a CD player with headphones. I own two CDs: Radiohead's The Bends and Kansas' Point of Know Return. That was Mom's. I stole it. Did I tell you I steal things sometimes? I only do it when I have to. I wouldn't want people stealing stuff from me, y'know? I'll stop. I promise. Look at you judging me.

How was your audition? I've been painting. Maybe I'll show you someday. Maybe we can meet in a chatroom sometime too. It's weird that I think about you all the time. We hardly know each other, but I feel like I know you better than most people. Maybe because I don't know you super well and I can pretend I do. Do you feel that way?

--------

**From: Alex Winzelberg <winzwarehouse5@hotmail.com>**
**To: Ina <ina.artgirl1979@hotmail.com>**
**Date: December 27, 1997**
**Subject: Re: Christmas already?**

Happy birthday! I can't wait to turn 18. I definitely don't feel like an adult. I've always felt younger than my age. It doesn't help that my parents started me in school late, so I'll turn 19 two months after I graduate. It also doesn't help that I've grown up babied by my family. It's hard to break out of that.

I'm not judging you. Promise. I've never stolen anything in my life, but I think if I was in the right circumstance I might.

My audition was great. The play starts next semester. It's Romeo & Juliet. Lame, I know. I'll let you guess who I'm playing. Thanks for nudging me, though. I don't think I would've done it without you.

P.S. I feel like I know you better than most people in my life, too.

P.P.S. Who is Jake?

From: Ina <ina.artgirl1979@hotmail.com>
To: Alex Winzelberg <winzwarehouse5@hotmail.com>
Date: January 1, 1998
Subject: New year

Welcome to 1998! Jake is the man I told you about before. He's on the Board of Directors. I might not answer your emails for a while because he's taking a few of us house members on a skiing retreat with some other Board members. Writing that makes it sound so…I don't know. Important? We never get to do anything. Seriously. Curfews suck. School sucks. We can't even be loud here or we get in trouble. Going to the grocery store with a staff member is like the highlight of our week. So this retreat? I've never been skiing before, but I'm excited.

Are you playing Romeo? I'm trying not to laugh over here if you are. Seriously, though, that would be cool. Lead in a play? Rock on. Peace out.

P.S. Thank you for not judging me. You have no idea what that means to me.


From: Alex Winzelberg <winzwarehouse5@hotmail.com>
To: Ina <ina.artgirl1979@hotmail.com>
Date: January 3, 1998
Subject: Re: New year

Yep. Romeo. It's embarrassing and awesome at the same time. Tell me when you get back from your retreat and maybe we can meet in a chat room.

P.S. Are you ever gonna answer the sunglasses question? I haven't forgotten about it, so I'm still wondering why you asked me that.

From: Alex Winzelberg <winzwarehouse5@hotmail.com>
To: Ina <ina.artgirl.1979@aol.com>
Date: February 19, 1998
Subject: I LOVE ACTING SO MUCH

Hey, I just have to write to you and tell you tonight was opening night for Romeo & Juliet and it was awesome! It felt so good to be on stage like that, after so many rehearsals and feeling like none of it would come together and all of a sudden it just did, and to feel like I nailed it tonight…I seriously want to do this for the rest of my life. Mr. Barringer my theater teacher says I'm a natural. I'm going to audition for the next play too.

Thanks again for nudging me.


From: Alex Winzelberg <winzwarehouse5@hotmail.com>
To: Ina <ina.artgirl.1979@aol.com>
Date: March 8, 1998
Subject: You still there?

I'm a little worried you haven't written in a while. How was your retreat?


From: Alex Winzelberg <winzwarehouse5@hotmail.com>
To: Ina <ina.artgirl1979@hotmail.com>
Date: December 25, 1998
Subject: Hey, I miss you

Hey, if you're out there, happy 19th birthday and Merry Christmas. I miss talking to you. I hope you're okay. Send me a message just to let me know?

—Alex

# Two

June 1999—Alex

"Wake up, Alex. We have three semis to load this morning."

Groaning, Alex buried his head beneath his quilt. Graduation yesterday had almost killed him. Mentally, anyway. There had been too many things to do. Too many expectations. Too much family. Too much noise. But he'd done it all. He'd graduated. He'd been who everyone wanted him to be. Now he felt like he'd been run over by a truck.

"I can't, Mom. Cut me some slack."

His mom gave her signature huff, and Alex imagined her leaning against the doorway as she folded her arms and narrowed her eyes. Her dark blond hair was probably pulled into a crooked ponytail, wisps falling around her face. That was how she always looked when she was working.

"I'm sorry you're not feeling on top of the world, but I need you. *Five* employees quit, even after they promised to stay another month. If you don't help out, I don't know what I'm—"

"Fine, fine!" Alex yelled beneath the quilt. She would just keep going until he gave in anyway. "I'll get up. I'll do my job. Just make me some breakfast. Pleeeease?"

Another huff. "It's too late for that. Eat a Pop-Tart."

With that, she was gone. His head pounding, Alex threw the quilt off his body and sat up in bed. The room started spinning and he closed his eyes. It felt like he had a hangover. He remembered the one time he really did have a hangover a few months ago. His mom had almost killed him, raging about how bad alcohol was for his developing teenage brain. She was probably right, but who could blame him? Getting dumped sucked hard. He'd needed *something* to ease the pain, especially when he knew he'd have to see Jennifer every day at school until graduation. She hadn't given him a solid reason for breaking up with him, but he had a pretty good idea what it was.

Once the room stopped spinning, he got out of bed, threw on some jeans and a T-shirt, and headed down the hallway. He didn't have the energy to brush his hair or shave. Nobody would care, anyway.

The smell of coffee made him stop mid-yawn as he entered the kitchen. He should have known April would be up and about, making him coffee. She was only visiting because of his graduation, but that didn't stop her from jumping right back into her old routine.

She looked up from the coffee machine to smile at him. "Morning! You should've been up an hour ago. Mom's gonna kill you."

Alex slumped into a chair at the table. "Mom's the one who dragged me out of bed. And she told me to eat a Pop-Tart. You're not gonna let that happen, are you?"

"Of course not." April tightened the bow on her apron and opened the refrigerator. "I'm sure I can whip you up something amazing. You deserve it after yesterday." She flipped her long hair over her shoulder and peered into the fridge. "I can make you an omelet. *If* we have enough eggs. When was the last time Mom went to the store?

Sheesh. Look at this bottle of pickles! It's gotta be three years old."

Alex smiled at his sister as she prattled on. She was four years older than him, and two years older than their brother, Aaron, who was currently backpacking across Europe and totally avoiding reality. April wasn't like that. She was working on a culinary arts degree at some fancy school in California. It had always surprised Alex, and pissed him off, that her ex-fiancé had broken off their engagement. Apparently, he couldn't handle the Winzelberg family drama—namely, his future father-in-law's mental issues. That was what Alex suspected had scared off Jennifer too.

"Alex?"

"Huh?" He looked up from the table, not realizing he'd laid his head down and dozed off.

"Your breakfast is ready. Eat up." April sat across from him, a mug of coffee in her hands.

Sitting all the way up, Alex looked down at a plate filled with two cheese omelets folded in thirds, and three slices of cinnamon toast. He grabbed his fork and dug in.

April blew on her coffee. "I'm gonna help out down-stairs today. Mom's about to lose it. She gets so uptight. If she'd just relax, things would be easier. It'd probably help Dad too."

Alex shrugged. "She'll hire more people for the sum-mer. It'll be fine. I can pick up the slack in the meantime."

"I guess so."

"What do you mean?"

"Well, you can't always be here to pick up the slack. You graduated yesterday, remember?"

"Yeah, I remember."

"And?"

Alex lowered his second piece of toast and gave his sister a challenging look. "And what? You think I should up and leave tomorrow? Mom and Dad would freak. Aaron hasn't stuck around, and you've moved on too. I'm all they have left."

"I didn't say *tomorrow*, and Mom and Dad are not helpless. *And* I know you have plans." She set down her mug. "You do have plans, don't you?"

Alex grabbed his own mug of coffee and took a few sips. "I got accepted to The Marion Conservatory of Performing Arts in New York, and I'm supposed to start next month."

April gasped. "That's awesome! Why didn't you tell me earlier?"

"I haven't told anyone except Mr. Barringer."

"Not even your friends?"

"Especially not my friends."

April narrowed her eyes. "What is wrong with you? Nobody is going to judge you for wanting to be on stage. You've been in a bunch of plays now and nobody's given you a hard time."

"That was high school drama. I could pretend it was fulfilling my fine arts credits. But if I choose to do this, nobody's going to understand that. Not here. Last week, Robby was making fun of Steve Adkins for wanting to major in Ballroom Dance. And Carlos was talking about—"

"Alex, this isn't gonna work on me. Your friends are not the reason you've kept this quiet. You couldn't care less if they think acting is lame. Which it is *not*. What's the real reason?"

Alex looked down at the table. "I don't know. Sometimes I feel like I'm in a prison here." Just then, a memory sparked of when he had talked about feeling like a prisoner to Ina, the girl he'd emailed back and forth almost two years ago. She had talked about feeling like a prisoner too. He didn't think about her much anymore, but whenever he did, an uneasy feeling washed over him. He had never solved the mystery of why she'd stopped emailing him.

*"I'm telling you, he's standing right there! Get him off the truck now or I'm gonna call the cops! Fine! . . . I'll get him!"*

Alex dropped his fork at the sound of his father shouting. "Oh no."

April stood up and started untying her apron as she raced out of the kitchen. "You get Dad. I'll get Mom," she called out over her shoulder.

Alex jumped out of his chair and took off behind her, his stomach churning at the prospect of dealing with his father in such a state. It was always an ordeal, and it was always worse if employees were around.

*"Get out of there! He'll get all of us if I don't stop him!"*

April groaned as she and Alex raced down the hallway. Even though their home was separate from WFS, nestled up on the top floor, the walls were not soundproof. That meant warehouse noises carried through their home day and night. Alex had long since grown used to it. He could sleep, eat, and study through anything.

Anything except his father, anyway.

April yanked open the front door and ran down the exposed stairs, Alex hot on her heels. On his way down, he took a moment to survey the situation. The back of the warehouse was an open area, usually filled with stacked pallets ready to be loaded and shipped. There were six bays. At the moment, two of those bays were open to the gaping caverns of half-loaded semitrailers.

Only, everything had stopped because Daniel Winzelberg was causing a scene.

April descended the last step and took off in the direction of the front office as Alex headed for his father. He would never get used to seeing his dad like this, no matter how many times it happened. The main problem was that it was different every single time. He never knew what to expect or how long it would last.

Steeling himself, Alex put on his calm face and reviewed everything he had learned in the past ten years since his dad had been sick. The worst thing anyone could do was panic or try to stop his dad from doing whatever he was set on doing, which was why Alex first had to round up any employees who might make things worse. He spotted a group of three men huddled together, whispering.

"Hey, guys," Alex said casually as he approached them. He thought he remembered their names, but they were recent hires and he didn't want to offend anyone by getting a name wrong. "I need you to clear out of here, okay? Remember training when we told you something like this could happen? Now's the time to leave. You can go into the break room. We'll let you know if we need your help."

One man with a salt-and-pepper beard—Gregory Ostler, Alex remembered—jerked his thumb toward Alex's father, who was currently storming up a ramp into one of the trailers. "We were wondering if we should try to get him outside before he starts breaking stuff or hurts someone. We could handle him. There's four of us and only one of him."

Alex shook his head. "This isn't us against him, okay? I can handle this. Go to the break room, please." He nodded in the direction of the break room, irritated that they were making him repeat himself. He knew they didn't like being bossed around by an eighteen-year-old, especially when their real boss had just snapped out of nowhere, but Alex could fire them on the spot. His mom would back him up if it came to that. He was pretty sure they knew it too. Finally, they headed one by one toward the back of the warehouse.

Relieved, Alex moved on to the other four employees who had gathered to watch Daniel stomping around inside the trailer. He wasn't yelling now, and nobody else was in the trailer, but that didn't mean things couldn't quickly get out of control.

"All of you can take a break," Alex said. "I'll let you know when you can come back out. Sorry. We'll get him calmed down."

"Is he going to be all right?" Maria, the Fulfillment Manager, whispered worriedly. "What if he gets on one of the forklifts again and—"

"He'll be fine, Maria. Help keep everyone together in the break room, yeah?"

"Sure, Alex." She rounded everyone up and soon they were gone.

Feeling more relaxed now that everyone had left, Alex approached the ramp leading up to the trailer. "Hey, Dad?" he called out as casually as he could. "Need any help? I can call someone for you."

His dad stopped peering between the pallets and turned around to face him. He was a big man, which was where Alex got all of his height. He was strong, too, since he worked in the warehouse every day lifting boxes and equipment. One of the things Alex loved about his dad was that buried beneath his physical strength was the kindest, gentlest man he'd ever known. That man was who Alex remembered from his childhood—up until the day he'd started seeing and hearing things that weren't there. That was when everything about him had changed.

"Yeah, call the police," his father said, raking a hand through his thick, graying hair. "This guy's nothing but trouble."

Alex avoided looking directly into his father's frightened eyes, knowing from experience that it might provoke further paranoia. "I'll call them in a minute," he answered. "You wanna come down here? We can sit and talk."

His father flinched. "No, I don't want to talk."

Alex realized for the first time how hard his heart was pounding. He couldn't get Maria's reminder out of his head. Two years ago, his dad had become convinced one of the forklifts was a wild horse that needed to be set free. He'd driven it deep into the warehouse and ended up crashing into some shelving. He'd ended up in the hospital with some cuts and bruises, but nothing major. Still, it had scared the crap out of Alex. It was the first and only time so far that his dad had caused physical damage to anything due to his illness. Dr. Huang had told them they might have to consider "other options" if that kind of stuff started happening all the time. Alex didn't want to think about that.

He kept his voice steady. "I won't argue with you, Dad, but at least come down, okay?"

His dad thought for a moment. "I'm getting an idea. Yeah, yeah. Let's lock him inside the trailer and drive it out to the fields. We can starve him to death. That'll teach him not to try and steal our stuff and hurt our staff, don't ya think?"

Alex grimaced. "The trailer's not hooked up to a truck right now. Let's close it up and keep it here, okay? The driver can take it away later, and he can deal with the guy."

His father sat down in the middle of the trailer, quiet as a mouse. He stared down at the floor of the truck. Maybe if he sat there long enough he'd snap out of it. Alex turned around in time to see April and his mother rushing from the front office. They spotted him and slowed down.

"I was on the phone with Larriatte," Alex's mother explained. "Thank you for handling this."

Alex nodded. Larriatte was one of their biggest accounts. They weren't patient or understanding about anything.

"How is he?" April asked. "Why's he sitting there so quiet now? Is he still angry?"

"No, he's thinking. He wanted to drive the truck out to the fields."

His mom started biting her nails. "This needs to be over. I can't take this right now. April, you're the best with him. Go up there and talk him out."

"No, Mom. It's a confined space. He'll feel trapped if I go up there. Wait for him to come down. You seriously need to chill out. He'll be fine. No wild horses, see? This is nothing."

"Stop joking," their mother snapped.

"I wasn't joking. Just give him a minute, all right?" April slid a worried look to Alex.

Alex looked away, his heart sinking to the floor as he wrapped an arm around his mom's shoulders and pulled her close. She seemed so fragile, like she was going to fall apart any moment. She was usually a strong woman; Alex had always thought of her as his rock. But just as he'd seen a hundred times before, the one thing that could shake her was her husband's illness.

With a heavy sigh, Alex hung his head, a familiar ache growing in his chest. Sometimes it felt like it would never go away.

# Three

"You're looking pretty low for a young man who just got out of this place," Mr. Barringer said as Alex walked through the high school auditorium doors. "Aren't you excited to be moving on?"

Alex looked around the auditorium as the heavy wood doors closed behind him. The familiar musty smell of the room settled around him. "It's just family stuff," he sighed, wanting to forget the past few hours of his life. "Thought I'd get away for a minute." He was still tense from waiting out his father's hallucination. It had gone smoothly, thanks to Dr. Huang showing up with some new medication and his usual therapeutic tactics, but it had taken several hours. After that, his mother had told him to take a break when it was over. So here he was—his favorite escape.

Mr. Barringer walked up the center aisle toward Alex. He was tall, with a receding hairline, thick horn-rimmed glasses, and a brown cardigan he wore every single day. "We just finished rehearsal," he said, nodding toward the stage behind him. A small group of senior citizens were shuffling off the stage. Two high school seniors who had graduated with Alex yesterday were picking up a sofa. They had both been in Alex's drama class, and his heart ached at seeing them on the stage, even if they were just helping old people who couldn't lift heavy things. He'd wanted to be a part of Mr. Barringer's senior theater group in any way he could, but his mother had told him she couldn't spare him while the warehouse was so busy.

"What play are you doing?" Alex asked, looking around the auditorium at the twenty-year-old stained chair cushions and dark red aisle carpet. It felt strange knowing this technically wasn't his school anymore.

Mr. Barringer flashed a smile. "Just a new little play nobody else is allowed to stage yet," he said proudly. "I have connections to the playwright and managed to get permission to perform it here. It's perfect for this group. Has a role I think you'd be brilliant in—although you're a little young for it—but I didn't ask you to audition because the performances are late July." He clapped a hand on Alex's shoulder "You'll be in New York by then!"

Alex's heart sank to the floor. "Yeah," he said, forcing a smile. "I will be."

Mr. Barringer lowered his hand, eyeing Alex carefully. "What's the matter? Family troubles can't have you *this* down."

Alex twisted his hands together, his eyes fixed on the stage. If he didn't go to New York, he would have to find some way to still be involved with theater, even if it was something small, or he would burst. His mom couldn't hold him back from helping out just a little.

He turned his attention back to Mr. Barringer, knowing he didn't have the heart to tell him there was a chance he might not be moving to New York yet. "I thought I might see if I can help you out with the play," he said as nonchalantly as he could. "You know, until I have to leave. I'll do anything you want—lights, sound, props, fly, whatever you need. Like, if one of your crew needs a night off or something."

Mr. Barringer tilted his head. "I thought you said your work schedule wouldn't allow it. It's a lot of time, especially when we get into tech."

"I know." Alex rocked back and forth on the balls of his feet, his whole body itching to get on the stage. "But I . . . I need to be here. You understand, right? I want to be on stage so bad. I want to feel that energy, but if I can't have it right now, then I think just being here will make me feel better." He looked down at his feet. "My family is just . . . the warehouse . . . my job . . . I just need some of *this* world to make *that* world better." He looked up. "Does that sound weird?"

Mr. Barringer laughed as he nudged Alex toward the stage. "I completely understand. It's not weird. Come on, you can help me out right now. We've got some food props that need repairing, and the light board is having issues. Maybe you can figure out what's wrong with it."

Alex smiled. He would make this work. He had to. "Thank you," he said, waving hello to one of his former classmates who was carrying a lamp offstage.

"Anytime, Alex. Let's get to work."

* * *

"There's a mountain of paperwork to get done," Alex's mother said as soon as he got back to the warehouse. She looked at her watch. "And when I told you to take a break, I didn't mean a two-hour break. You know better than that."

Alex gave her a forced look of remorse, but it was edged with anger as he walked past her. Coming in through a side door from the parking lot had been a mistake. It led right into the belly of WFS where his mother was always in the middle of something. Employees zipped around him, carrying boxes and pushing pallets. "I won't do it again," he muttered as his mother followed him to the office.

His mother sighed as she came up beside him. "It's fine, Alex. It's just stress. Think you can get through the paperwork before closing time?"

"I'll try."

"Okay." They stopped at the office door, and his mother took off her orange hardhat so she could swipe a hand across her sweaty brow. She looked exhausted.

"Are you okay?" Alex asked. "Dad's fine, right?"

She nodded. "Yes, yes, it's not that. It's those employees who quit yesterday. It really set things back."

Alex put a hand on her arm, suddenly feeling guilty for running off to the high school for two hours while his mother was here stressing out. "I'll get all the paperwork done," he said gently. "Don't worry."

Nodding, she shoved the hardhat back on her head before going back the way she'd come. Alex went into the office, closing the door behind him. He'd always liked office work. It was usually quiet and nobody bothered him. Sometimes, when he was sure no one out in the noisy warehouse could hear him, he'd turn the radio to a show tunes station and belt out a few songs. The only other place he could do that was alone in his parents' car. Only one of the productions he'd done had been a musical. That was where his heart truly belonged, and one of the reasons Mr. Barringer had pushed him so hard to apply to the Marion Conservatory. Mr. Barringer had even helped him record two Broadway audition pieces for the application, claiming Alex's "natural-born talent" was completely wasted in small-town Anniston, Idaho.

Today, however, Alex was too tired to sing along to even the most sedate show tune. Sitting down at the desk, he cringed at the large pile of invoices and orders. It was going to take him hours to get through it. A knock on the door made him jump. "Yeah?"

"Can I come in?"

"Sure."

The door opened and Alex's father entered. He looked tired, his face pulled down in all the corners. He hovered in the doorway. "I'm sorry about what happened."

Alex knew his father hated being a burden more than anything, and gave him an understanding look. "You don't have to apologize, Dad. None of this is your fault, plus it wasn't that bad. We were just caught off guard."

His dad moved away from the door and walked into the office, stopping at the chair across from the desk. He pushed a hand through his hair. "I thought I was getting better."

Alex waved a hand dismissively and started sorting through the invoices. "You *are* getting better. It's just gonna take time." When he looked up, his father was smiling at him.

"April told me how you handled everything. Thank you."

"You don't have to thank me. I just did what had to be done."

"Yes, but you don't understand." His father leaned forward to look into Alex's eyes, pressing his hands against the desk. His gaze was solid. Real. Present. "I'm lucky, okay? What would I do without you?"

Alex leaned back in his chair. "You know you have April and Aaron too."

"I know, I know. They just aren't around like you are, that's all."

Alex's jaw tightened. His brother and sister were living their lives and he was the one left behind to take care of everything. It wasn't fair. He didn't blame his father, or even his siblings, but it didn't change the facts.

"You okay?" his father asked.

Alex came back to the moment and started shuffling through the invoices again. "Yeah, I just have a lot of work to do."

His dad nodded and started backing up toward the door. "See you at dinner."

"I might not be at dinner," Alex muttered, hoping the announcement wouldn't upset his father. Routine was the best thing for him. "I told Logan I'd meet him at the movie theater after his shift ends. We'll probably go get pizza."

His dad gave him a fleeting smile before opening the office door. "That's okay. We'll miss you, but I'll let your mother know." He slipped into the hallway and was gone.

* * *

"My shift ends in ten minutes," Logan said when Alex entered the movie theater several tedious hours of invoicing later. "I gotta clean up a spill in Theater Two. Be back in a sec." He headed out of the concession stand toward the janitorial closet down the hall.

Alex leaned against the counter to wait. He hated working in his parents' warehouse, but he had to admit it was better than working here. The place was old and smelled like moldy carpet. At least Logan got free movies and popcorn.

Alex knew Logan's main goal was to save enough money to get out of here for good—and not just the theater. As much as Alex wanted his best friend to be happy, he dreaded the day he would be gone forever.

"You guys doing something fun tonight?" Raven Edwards, a friend from Alex's drama classes, asked. She'd worked at the theater as long as Logan and was almost as desperate to get out.

He shook his head. "Nah, just hanging out. You?"

Raven flipped her thick black hair off her shoulder and gave Alex a knowing smile. "We're gonna go clubbing tonight in Boise to celebrate graduating. We know one of the bouncers at that new club and he's gonna let us in. I look twenty-one, right?" She struck a sexy pose.

Alex stifled a laugh. "You might want to lose the bubble gum and change the butter-stained theater polo."

Raven laughed. "Oh, you know I'm gonna! I asked Logan if he wants to come. He could maybe meet someone there. Definitely not anyone his type in this stupid town."

"Well, if he wants to go, I won't stop him," Alex sighed.

"Do *you* wanna come?"

Alex grunted. "Yeah, right. I gotta work tomorrow, and my sister's here from out of town."

The truth was that he'd only been clubbing twice, and he'd hated it both times. He rarely did anything remotely rebellious outside of downing all those beers with Logan the night Jennifer dumped him. A part of it was that he didn't want to be rebellious in the ways most people his age did, but another part of it was that he'd just never had the time. His whole life had been school and work up until now.

A few minutes later, Logan came out of the break room in his street clothes, already looking more relaxed. He was shorter and more built than Alex, with thick blond hair and hazel eyes. Girls were always falling for him, but he had never been interested in them and said he probably never would be. It wasn't something he talked about much.

His closest friends all knew, but in a town like Anniston, some truths were better left unspoken.

"Okay, I'm off the clock," Logan stated. "Let's get out of here." He waved at Raven. "See ya."

"Bye! I'll call you later in case you wanna come."

"Okay, thanks."

Once they were outside in the bright sun, Logan threw on his baseball cap and pulled a pack of cigarettes from his back pocket. "Let's go out to the field. I gotta smoke."

Alex gave him a wary look. "I wish you'd quit, man. You know those are bad for you."

"For the millionth time, I know. Cut me some slack. I've been here all day and my parents had a huge fight last night. Over me. They hate me. They hate everything I do. Nothing is ever good enough."

"What was it this time?" Alex asked as they made their way to the back of the movie theater and the fields beyond. They crunched through dead winter weeds intermixed with the softer green growth of spring. In a few months everything would be brown again. The tangy smell of dirt and rubber drifted up around them.

Logan adjusted his baseball cap. "Stupid stuff," he muttered as they walked to a bunch of old tires. "They think I'm a bad influence on William and they want me to move out." William was Logan's twelve-year-old brother.

"Move out?" Alex asked, blinking in surprise. "Seriously? I mean, I know you were already planning to move out, but they actually told you to leave?"

"Yep." He dumped a cigarette out of the carton and stuck it between his lips, then pushed the carton back in his pocket and pulled out a lighter. "It's like I'm not even their son anymore. They said I gotta be out in two months." He breathed out a puff of smoke. "You should come with me."

Alex leaned back on his hands and looked up at the bright sky. There were no clouds, just an endless stretch of blue. "I really should," he sighed. "Just . . . not yet."

They sat in silence for a long while, both looking up at the sky as Logan finished off his cigarette and leaned down to rub the butt into the soft dirt near his feet. "When do you think you'll be ready to leave, then?" he asked.

Alex shrugged. "I don't know. Not in two months, that's for sure."

Logan stared down at the ground. "Well, I'm out of here way sooner than two months," he mumbled, and gave Alex a guilty, worried look. "I'm thinking about booking a flight in the next two *weeks*."

*Oh, no.*

Alex leaned forward. "Explain."

Logan looked away. "I know you're gonna hate me, but I think I might accept that scholarship to Peyton Institute—that industrial design school in Brooklyn, remember?"

Alex felt a surge of joy for his friend, but at the same time he was confused . . . and extremely jealous. "I thought that wasn't the school you wanted."

Logan shrugged. "Money-wise, it's my only option. I'd have to save up a lot more to go anywhere else that accepted me. And if I get there soon, I have more time to find a job."

"True."

Well, that was it. Alone. April was going to leave in the next few days, and then Logan would be leaving— to New York. He hadn't told Logan about the Marion Conservatory, but that was mostly because deep down he knew it wasn't going to happen. He hadn't even sent in his enrollment paperwork. He had one week left to do that.

"You hate me now, don't you?" Logan asked.

Alex waved his hand in the air. "No, I don't hate you. I'm just not ready for things to change."

Although, he had to admit not much was changing for him aside from losing a best friend. He'd still be at the warehouse, still dealing with everything he'd dealt with his whole life. He had a sudden urge to grab one of Logan's cigarettes, even though he'd never smoked a day in his life.

"If I'm being honest," Logan said solemnly, "I'm not ready, either. I'll miss you and Will most of all."

Alex leaned forward to kick Logan's shin. He had to laugh it all off so it wouldn't hurt so badly. "Don't get all sappy on me," he scoffed. "We can live it up until you leave."

Logan grinned and stood up. "I know it's lame, but Raven's probably got room in her car tonight. You wanna go?"

Alex rubbed the back of his neck. "What if we get caught?"

"Don't worry about that. You need this. I'll make sure we don't do anything stupid, okay? And if you wanna leave, we'll leave. I know how uncomfortable you get in crowds."

Alex looked up at the sky again, his heart pounding. Logan was the only person who understood that side of him—the anxious wreck-of-a-human side. "April and my parents will kill me when they find out," he said, searching for an excuse.

"So? Maybe it'll help them realize you're not a kid anymore."

Alex smirked. "Yeah, maybe."

# Four

From: Ina <ina.artgirl1979@hotmail.com>
To: Alex Winzelberg <winzwarehouse5@hotmail.com>
Date: June 12, 1999
Subject: Hi

Hey, are you still out there? Still living in that warehouse? I think about you sometimes, so I thought I'd email you to see if you're around. I keep wanting to travel, but things got complicated here and now it's hard to leave. It makes me wonder if you're still wanting to move to New York to get on Broadway. I live in the city. Maybe if you move here we can meet up. Let's make plans. I miss you.

—Not Katrina

P.S. I will finally answer your sunglasses question because I hope you'll email me back if I do. I asked if you sold sunglasses because that's how my email address got on that ten-dollar bill. I was 100% stupid and wrote down my email address on it for a guy on the street who wanted my phone number. He was selling those knock-off Oakley sunglasses and he was probably not much older than me, but I thought giving him an email address was smarter than giving him a phone number because, seriously, back then I was the only person I knew who even had an email address. He never emailed me. So, there you go. Curiosity satisfied. I just wanted to make sure you weren't the sunglasses dude.

From: Alex Winzelberg <winzwarehouse5@hotmail.com>
To: Ina <ina.artgirl1979@hotmail.com>
Date: June 13, 1999
Subject: Re: Hi

Hey, I thought I would never hear from you again! I had no idea how to find you, either. I mean, I don't even know your full name. Whose fault is that?

I'm glad the creepy sunglasses guy never emailed you. I'm a better pen pal than him. Right? I hope so ...

Here's the lame thing. I don't know if I'll ever get out to New York. I got accepted to a theater school there, but my parents really need me here at the warehouse. It's hard to explain. All I can say is I don't feel right leaving no matter how bad I want things to happen.

Of course, after last night, my parents might kick me out of here. Do you ever get hangovers? I'm an idiot and drank last night when I was out with some friends. Why did I do that? I've gotten drunk once before and it was the worst ever. My friends seem to handle it just fine. What is wrong with me?

P.S. I missed our emails. And I'm worried about you. What happened? Why did you stop emailing?


From: Ina <ina.artgirl1979@hotmail.com>
To: Alex Winzelberg <winzwarehouse5@hotmail.com>
Date: June 14, 1999
Subject: Re: Re: Hi

Okay, yeah, I guess it was weird I disappeared, huh? Well, since you're not giving me super-in-depth info about your life, I guess I can be vague too. Hint, hint. For now, until we're more comfortable sharing details, let's just say things got scary. I made some stupid decisions, but they ended up leading me to a good place. I mean, I have a great apartment. I have a job. I'm able to paint. Look at me being the adult I've always said I was.

P.S. I usually don't drink. I feel out of control when I drink, and the way my life is right now, I have to feel as in control as possible. I've had hangovers before, though. It sounds like you're one of those people who can't handle alcohol. It's not something to be ashamed of. It's less money you have to spend, right?

---

**From: Alex Winzelberg <winzwarehouse5@hotmail.com>**
**To: Ina <ina.artgirl1979@hotmail.com>**
**Date: June 15, 1999**
**Subject: Can't believe I'm doing this**

Yikes, details. More info. I think I can do that if it means getting more info about you.

Well, I graduated high school a few days ago, and I've got exactly four days to mail in my enrollment paperwork for that theater school. I don't think I can do it, though, because I know I can't go. You're wondering why, and I'll give you the straight-up facts just like you did when you told me about your family. My dad is sick. He has schizophrenia, a word I'm scared to type, and even more scared to say out loud because nobody really talks about it here. The truth is, nobody understands it. They're all scared of it, but my dad is not dangerous, and he's not a bad person. My mom needs me here, helping to run this place. She needs my support because I think she'd fall apart without someone she can 100% count on. My dad works hard, but we never know when something's going to happen.

My brother and sister have both moved out. Left me here. I try not to get mad about that.

So that's why I can't leave.

Wow. You have no idea how scary that was for me to write. It took me like an hour, and you're lucky I'm not deleting it all.

It's your turn, Ina. What's your full name? And why did you disappear? Spill it.

From: Ina <ina.artgirl1979@hotmail.com>
To: Alex Winzelberg <winzwarehouse5@hotmail.com>
Date: June 15, 1999
Subject: Fine, here goes

I want to kill you, Alex Winzelberg. I didn't expect you to give me the dirt so fast, and I'm not sure I'm ready to spill, as you say. But here goes.

I don't know how much I should say, but one thing I can tell you is right now I'm working as a freelance translator. It was a miracle I found a way to live on my own and support myself. But I've made it work. I speak four languages, and I'm learning a fifth. Don't ask how I know so many. It's too long of a story for now.

Anyway, I keep reminding myself why I started emailing you again in the first place. It's because I feel so alone right now. Remember that Jake guy I told you about? Well, I got caught in the middle of some bad stuff he was doing. Before that happened, I had nobody else I could count on after I left Harmony House, and I never graduated from high school (long story), so it was kind of impossible to get a job. Jake took care of me, but not in a way I can describe to someone like you. You're so . . . I don't know, Alex. You deserve better than what you're dealing with. You're kind and you listen. And you care. I don't know anybody else like you. Okay, I'll stop being sentimental now. This is all scary to write too, just like it was for you, so shut up.

I'm not going to explain it all, but I got in trouble, and that got Jake in trouble, and now he's gone. It took a while, but I'm in a good place now. I kind of have Jake to thank for it, too, which is weird and stupid and not fair because I hate him.

Now back to you for a minute. Why aren't you sending in those enrollment papers? DO. IT. NOW. It's what you want, isn't it? Figure something out with your parents. How much does your warehouse make? Is it enough to hire a caretaker to look after your dad so your mom can focus on the warehouse? There's got to be a solution. Figure it out. Man up. And then come out here so you can live the life you want.

If you come out here, I'll tell you my full name. Promise.

# Five

Alex stared down at the manila envelope in his hands. Three people were ahead of him in line at the post office, but unlike all of them, he wanted the wait to last forever so he'd never have to make another decision again. Ina's words kept flashing through his mind: DO. IT. NOW. He'd read her email yesterday morning. He still hadn't replied, but she had inspired him to fill out the enrollment paperwork. Now all he had to do was mail it off.

Ina was right. He needed to man up and figure out a solution to his problem. There had to be a better way than sacrificing his future. He knew the sooner he tried to get on Broadway, the better his chances, which meant he needed to train his voice, his dancing skills, his acting skills. He needed to start in small theater, get a survival job, look into agents. Everything. And the Marion Conservatory could help him do all of that.

The line inched forward until Alex was standing at the counter. He set down the envelope and leaned forward to address the clerk, a woman named Benita who happened to be Raven's mom. "I need to send this Certified."

Benita looked down at the envelope and smiled. "Oh, *Certified*, huh?" she drawled as she pulled two forms from a filing system and handed them to Alex. "Just fill those out and I'll get it sent off for you."

Alex let out a quiet sigh. He should have used the warehouse mailing system and sent the letter out himself, but he hadn't wanted anyone seeing it on its way out. Now he was stuck here with Benita, the worst gossip in town. He knew that even if he asked Benita to keep her mouth shut and she promised not to tell, she'd end up letting it slip to someone at some point. In less than two days his parents would know he'd sent off an envelope Certified Mail to a theater school in New York. His mom would call April, who would probably give in and spill that he'd been accepted. At that point, his dad would find out and be hurt that Alex hadn't told him right away. Not only that, but Benita would also let it slip to Raven, who would tell all her friends, including Logan, who would also be hurt that Alex hadn't told him right away.

This was all bad.

Too late now.

Grabbing a pen, Alex filled out the forms as fast as he could. If he didn't do it now, it would never happen.

"Here, I'll stick those on there for you," Benita said as he finished up. She snatched the forms and the envelope, placed everything where it needed to go, and then set the envelope on her scale.

"Three ounces!" she said loudly. "To The Marion Conservatory of Performing Arts in New York, New York! Is that in Manhattan?"

"It's not a big deal," Alex said, trying desperately to sound casual.

"Of course, dear. Your secret's safe with me."

He wasn't sure how much he believed her, but nodded in appreciation anyway as she rang up his total. He paid, suddenly sick to his stomach as he watched Benita set the envelope on top of a pile of other envelopes ready to be mailed. No going back now.

Once he had his change, Alex rushed out of the post office and hopped on his bike, taking off toward the west side of town. He really wanted to go home and email Ina to tell her he'd done it, but that would have to wait. Right now he had to force himself to do one more thing.

Ten minutes later, he rode up to River Meadows, Anniston's only assisted living center, and parked his bike at a rack near the entrance. His palms were sweating, and it wasn't from the summer sun beating down on his head. He stepped in front of the entrance and tried to gather up as much courage as he could. This was somewhere to start.

Inside, flower arrangements sat on clean, polished end tables. Pastel patterned carpeting led to a living-room area with a television set and a ping-pong table. Alex walked up to the front desk where two women in casual white uniforms were chatting. One looked familiar. She eyed him warily, as if waiting for him to start acting crazy. Sometimes people did that, as if they believed his dad's illness had rubbed off on him.

"Hi, Alex," she said. "Are you here to see someone?"

She was his sister's age, with curly red hair piled on top of her head. Alex looked at her for a moment, finally remembering that he'd met her several times at Dr. Huang's office. She'd been an intern there. He glanced at her name tag: *Leslie.*

"Hey," he said, smiling nervously as he wrapped his hands around the edge of the tall counter. "I called Dr. Huang this morning, and he said you might be able to help me."

Leslie smiled. "Oh, sure, what can we do?"

"He said you keep a list of certified caretakers in the area. I need to find someone to hire for my dad."

The other girl nodded. "You need someone full-time?"

He shook his head. "No. I don't know. Maybe? He doesn't need someone with him every second, but it'd be nice if there was someone there to make sure he's taking his meds and getting therapy and checkups and support— and someone who can help him if he starts hallucinating. Stuff like that . . . all the stuff my mom and I normally do."

Leslie put a finger to her chin. "It would definitely help you guys out. It'll be hard to find the right person for that job, though. Would you want them to live there? Like in-home care? That's super expensive."

Alex's heart sank a little. "I don't know. I don't even know where to start."

"I have some ideas," Leslie said, pulling out a filing cabinet drawer.

"I do too," the other girl chimed in. "Don't worry, Alex, we'll get you the info you need."

"Wow, thanks." Alex gave them an appreciative smile, but he knew the person he really needed to thank was Ina for nudging him in this direction.

---

**From: Alex Winzelberg <winzwarehouse5@hotmail.com>**
**To: Ina <ina.artgirl1979@hotmail.com>**
**Date: June 16, 1999**
**Subject: Thank You**

I would've emailed you sooner, but we had major drama here last night with my dad. He hallucinated again and it freaked my mom out. Actually, we're all freaked out because he's been hallucinating more than usual.

Thanks for telling me as much as you can about your past. (Um, five languages? I speak a total of one). It sounds like Jake is a dangerous guy, so I'm glad you got away from him, and I hope he never comes back into your life. Seriously, is there anything I can do to help? I'm kinda worried.

I hope I can see your artwork soon. Is there a way you could send me a picture?

Guess what I did, thanks to you? I sent that paperwork, and now I have to go. I will go. I'm going to make it happen. I also got a list of caretakers we might be able to hire for my dad. I haven't broken any of this to my parents yet. I'm kind of waiting until my dad is in a better headspace. Maybe tonight. I'll keep you posted. Thanks for all of your advice.

Do you want to meet in a chatroom? It might be fun. When would work for you? And where?

---

From: Ina <ina.artgirl1979@hotmail.com>
To: Alex Winzelberg <winzwarehouse5@hotmail.com>
Date: June 16, 1999
Subject: Re: Thank You

Would tonight in a few hours work for you? 9:00 your time, midnight my time. Are you on AOL? I just started paying for it, so if you want to meet in a room there, that could work. I'll send you an invite. Obviously, I'm artgirl1979. If I don't hear from you, I'll assume you're gonna be there.

# Seven

"This is not a good time," April groaned as she opened her bedroom door. She was already in her pajamas, hair pulled back, sleep mask pushed up onto her forehead. "I've got a five a.m. flight in the morning. *Five A.M., Alex.* Do you get how early I have to wake up to make it there on time?"

Alex gave his sister a pleading look. "I know, and I'm sorry, but this is important. I'm gonna tell Mom and Dad I'm moving to New York. They're gonna freak out, and I need you there."

April put a hand to her forehead. "Are you serious? Why didn't you do this earlier?"

"Because I was helping down in the warehouse and it took forever." He'd been in the middle of replying to Ina's email when his mother had come into the office and slapped a two-page to-do list on the desk. He looked at his watch and tapped his foot. He had to get this done in the next half hour so he could meet Ina online, and there was no way he was going to face his parents without April backing him up. "Please? It has to be now."

"*Fiiiine*," April sighed. She ripped off her sleep mask and stomped into the hallway. "Let's go."

"Thanks, Sis. Seriously."

"Oh, shut up. I'm proud of you. This is a huge step."

Their parents were sitting in the living room watching Jeopardy, a bowl of popcorn between them. Alex approached them, waiting for a commercial break before he stepped in front of the television set. "I gotta talk to you for a minute."

Alex's dad lifted the remote to mute the commercial. "Make it quick."

Alex prayed his news wouldn't trigger another episode like yesterday's hallucination. It had happened during dinner. Spaghetti had ended up on the walls. It had only lasted five minutes, but felt like an hour.

"This is important, Dad," April interrupted. "Alex needs to tell you guys something." She walked to the coffee table in front of their parents and sat down. "It's kinda like when I moved out."

"Thanks for giving it away," Alex muttered.

April motioned for him to come sit next to her. He did. It was too close to his parents. Less than a foot. His dad stared him down, confusion rippling across his face.

"You're moving out?" he asked incredulously. "I thought we agreed you were staying here for a while. What's the rush?"

Alex looked down at his lap and then up at his mother. She wasn't saying a word, just staring at him with widened eyes. She looked scared, and that made Alex want to shrink into a tiny ball.

He looked at both his parents. "I was accepted to a theater conservatory in New York. It was one of twelve applications I sent out with Mr. Barringer's help. I was lucky to be accepted to even one of them, and it's kind of a huge deal. I sent in my enrollment paperwork yesterday. Classes start in July."

"You *what*?" his father asked, his eyes widening. He leaned forward. "You can't leave. We aren't ready for you to leave." He glanced at his wife, who was staring straight ahead, silent. "Your mother isn't ready for you to leave."

Alex opened and closed his mouth, looking to April for support. She shrugged.

"Mom?" Alex said softly. "I'm not abandoning you, I swear. It's not like I haven't thought this through." He dug a folded piece of paper from his back pocket and carefully opened it up. He looked at his dad. "I have a list of people we can interview to help you while I'm not here. You should be able to afford it. I think it's something you should do even if I wasn't leaving."

His mother dropped her eyes to the paper.

"What about money?" His father sighed, leaning back into the sofa. "How do you expect to live in New York and pay for school?"

"They offered me a small scholarship, so that will help with the tuition. I plan on getting a job to cover the rest. I mean, I've worked here forever, so it's not like I don't have skills. I can do office work, a phone job, even find a warehouse position. I can wait tables if I need to. Plus, I have money saved up. I've been saving for a long time."

"How much have you saved?" his father asked, raising his eyebrows.

Alex looked down at his lap. "Last time I checked, my account was around $8,000."

"Wow," April said, her eyes lighting up. "I didn't know you had that much." She looked at her parents. "Do you guys pay him more than you paid me?"

"No," their father grunted. "He just doesn't spend it like you did. Neither did Aaron. How do you think he can afford to be wandering around Europe right now?"

A blush crept up April's cheeks. "You're right, I'm no good with money."

"You'll learn," their mother said, finally breaking her silent streak. She snatched the paper from Alex's hand and looked at it.

"So?" Alex asked a minute later. "Are you guys okay with this?"

His father kept his arms folded, a frightened look on his face. Alex couldn't blame him. Constantly feeling out of control was enough to scare anyone, then to find out one of the people you relied on was going to leave you . . . not a good feeling.

"I'm not sure you're ready," his mother finally said, lifting her eyes to Alex. "You're so young, and I think it would be better if we spent time doing everything the right way—finding you an apartment, a job, visiting the city together before you move out there. Let us be a part of it."

Alex slid his gaze to his father, who was nodding along in agreement. Great. His own parents didn't believe in him. He couldn't blame them, though. It was true he was young, and he didn't feel prepared, but what his mother was proposing meant putting everything off for a year or more.

"Logan is moving to New York," he said, pushing forward. "He was accepted to a school in Brooklyn. If he can do it, I can too. He's been to New York before. He knows stuff I don't. We could even live together and save on rent. He'll help me. I won't be alone."

His father's frightened expression hardened. "You can't live with Logan," he said sternly, meeting Alex's eyes. "There is something very wrong with him. I've tolerated your friendship with him, but you *cannot* live with someone like that. He'll steer you in all sorts of wrong directions, especially if you're living in a place like New York."

The room fell silent. Alex's heart pounded. Blood rushed to his head. Disappointment morphed into anger, and before he could stop himself, he stood up and glared at his father. "You're one to talk," he snapped. "You shouldn't judge Logan like that. It's like people judging you and calling you crazy." He folded his arms, still glaring at his father. "Maybe you *are* crazy."

April grabbed his arm and squeezed. "Alex, stop," she hissed.

He ripped away from her. "No, it's not fair." He kept his eyes on his father. "Logan's never hurt anybody. I've heard people say you're nothing but a ticking time bomb waiting to go off and hurt yourself or someone else. And you know what? The way you're acting right now, I agree with them."

He started stomping out of the room, pausing only a second when he saw tears running down his mother's face. But he couldn't stop now. He charged past her, his anger squeezing into pain. He was horrible. He'd made his mother cry. He'd said things to his father that he could never take back. Vindictive, awful things.

The worst thing was that he didn't have the courage to go back and fix it.

"Alex, stop right now," April called out behind him. He was almost to his room. He quickened his pace, but before he reached his door, April grabbed his arm again. She yanked him around. "How could you? You know you can't say those kinds of things to Dad."

Alex looked down at the floor. "I know," he whispered. "But it's not fair. They didn't act this way when *you* left."

April let go of his arm. "I was twenty-one. You're only eighteen."

"Almost nineteen," he muttered.

April sighed. "That's still not twenty-one. Big difference, but I don't expect you to understand that, being eighteen and all."

Alex rolled his eyes. "I didn't mean any of it," he said. "It's just not fair. They can't stop me from leaving. I have to go."

April folded her arms. "Do you really have to leave right now? I'm sure they could extend the acceptance another year. Lots of schools do that."

"Yeah, maybe, but . . ."

"Just think about it. You can always call and ask. It wouldn't hurt. That would give Mom and Dad enough time to get a caretaker and process the fact that you'll be gone. It would be a good transition."

"Yeah, I guess so."

That was when he realized it wasn't only the conservatory that was pulling him to New York. It was Logan too. And Ina. It was also the fear that if he stayed here for another year, something might happen to keep him here even longer.

He rubbed his forehead. "You should go back to bed," he muttered. "Have a safe flight home tomorrow, okay?"

April gathered him into a hug, squeezing him tight. "I love you, little brother. Call me and tell me what happens."

He nodded. "I will."

A moment later, he watched her round the corner toward her room. He looked at his watch. He had just enough time to make it downstairs to the office.

# Eight



**awinzberg**: Ina, are you here? My modem took forever to connect. Sorry.

**artgirl1979**: I'm here, yep. How are you?

**awinzberg**: Not so good. I told my parents I was leaving and it blew up in my face. I don't know what's going to happen now. My sister says I should wait a year. I might call the school tomorrow and see if that's possible.

. . .

**awinzberg**: Um, are you okay? You haven't typed anything for like five minutes.

**artgirl1979**: Yeah, I'm okay. I was eating, sorry. Are you near a phone? I was wondering if you could call me.

**awinzberg**: Oh, um … maybe not. I don't have a cell phone and if I use the landline here, it'll show up on our bill. My mom would flip if she saw I called New York. Maybe I can call you from my friend Logan's phone sometime. What are you eating?

**artgirl1979**: Curry. My neighbors make a lot of Indian food, like amazing Indian food. They're Guatemalan, but you'd think they were born and raised in India. Okay, and yes, I understand about the phone thing. I used to be 'policed' in a group home, remember? Is it okay for you to be here in a chatroom?

**awinzberg**: Yes, as long as I don't use up all our internet for the month. I don't think I've ever had curry. Any kind.

**artgirl1979**: NO CURRY? That's just sad. If you ever come here, there's all sorts of food you'll want to try. By the way, good job sending in that enrollment. Even if it doesn't turn out like you want, that's a step forward, right?

**awinzberg**: You're right, it is a step forward. What about you? Is there anything I can help you with? I feel like you've helped me a lot and I haven't done anything for you at all.

**artgirl1979**: Are you kidding? You're HERE. You listen to me. If you had any idea what I deal with sometimes, you'd understand. Knowing you're out there … I don't know. It's just nice.

**awinzberg**: What do you deal with?

**artgirl1979**: I don't think I can tell you. I'm sorry. Maybe in person, if you come here. When do you think that would be if it does happen this year?

**awinzberg**: Soon, probably. My best friend is moving out there too, and we'd probably want to go together so it's not so scary for me. I've grown up in a small town and New York freaks me out.

**artgirl1979**: It's not scary once you're here. Think of it like a lot of little towns smashed together.

**awinzberg**: What part are you in?

**artgirl1979**: Jackson Heights in Queens. I live right by the subway and bus station, so you can get here easy from anywhere. If you come, you should meet me at that station. What do you think?

**awinsberg**: Sure, you can show me around.

**artgirl1979:** What is it like there? Are there cows and stuff?

**awinzberg:** Cows? Yes, there are cows. A lot of farming here. A lot of fields and then some mountains and forest. We have one movie theater. One high school we share with a few other smaller towns. One post office. A half-dozen restaurants. One tiny library.

**artgirl1979:** And one shipping warehouse? How did that happen?

**awinzberg:** Oh, yeah, we're in a central location, like in the middle of a whole bunch of little towns. Stuff comes to WFS from bigger cities, and then we process it and ship it out to the smaller towns.

. . .

**awinzberg:** Are you still there? Did I bore you to death?

**artgirl1979:** Oh, yeah, sorry. I just got a phone call. It was Jake.

**awinzberg:** WHAT?! Ina, are you okay? I thought you said he was gone.

**artgirl1979:** He was gone. He still is. It's okay. I'm fine.

**awinzberg:** Seriously, what's your phone number? Can I call you? I'll explain to my mom later. Not a big deal.

**artgirl1979:** Please, don't worry. I can handle things now. It's not like it was before. I need to go. I'll email you soon, okay?

**awinzberg:** Okay. Please be safe. Don't make me worry again.

**artgirl1979:** I won't. Promise.

# Nine

## Ina

The smell of curry drifted into Ina's tiny apartment. Her stomach grumbling, she rolled over in bed to look at the clock. 7:30. The sun was beginning to set and she had forty minutes to get ready. It would probably only take her twenty.

"The Castellanos brought over more curry, but I'm eating out tonight," Ina's roommate, Emily, said as she opened the door and stepped over a pile of shirts. She and Ina shared the only bedroom, and the floor was constantly covered in Emily's clothes.

Ina rubbed her eyes. "Mmmm, what kind is it?"

Emily shuffled through a pile of clothes near her bed. "That nasty-looking green kind with the white cheese cubes. I love that one."

"Me too, but I'm probably eating out tonight too. My client's buying dinner because it's a restaurant meeting."

Emily looked up. "What language this time?"

"Italian." Ina suppressed a shudder. Italian was one language she would always hate, but nobody knew that. She sat up in bed, grabbing her laptop and settling it on her knees.

"Oh, man, I love Italian," Emily swooned. "It always sounds so romantic."

"Yeah, okay." Ina opened the laptop and pressed the power button to bring it to life.

"Is he hot, at least? Do you get to see pictures before you meet clients?"

"I have no idea if he's hot. Does it matter?"

"It would to me." Emily kept searching through her clothes. Her long brown hair brushed the floor as she bent over to pull out a skirt from beneath a pile of jeans. She was at least six feet tall, and rail-thin except for her large breasts. She belonged on a Victoria's Secret runway, and Ina thought it was a crime that Emily's modeling career had never taken off. She had to work as a law firm receptionist to pay the bills.

Ina focused on her computer as it started up. She plugged in the modem, tapping her fingers impatiently near the trackpad as she waited for the dial-up. She had promised Alex she would email him to let him know she was okay, and that was what she was going to do, even if it made her late for her appointment with Mr. Costa—or Conti or Cocci, she couldn't remember. She grabbed her planner from the end table and flipped to the correct page.

"Conti," she muttered. "Vincenzo Raffaele Conti. He's from Naples, here on business for some big stock trading thing."

"He could be hot," Emily said, smiling as she pulled on a black mini-skirt. "And rich. Do you raise your rates depending on how loaded they are?"

Ina snorted. "I wish."

"Still, you make a lot."

"I can make a decent amount if I've got a lot of jobs lined up, yeah."

Ina tensed as she realized, yet again, what a balancing act her life had been the last eight months. It had taken too much work to get here to let it fall apart now. That was why the phone call from Jake last night had sent her into panic mode. There was no way she was letting him back into her life. No. Way. She had made that very clear to him when she'd screamed a string of curses into the phone—several of them in different languages—and hung up before he could even say why he'd called. She knew why he'd called, and she hated him for it. She was going to have to change her number, which would be a pain because she'd probably have to pay the phone company for it.

Emily adjusted her tube top and stopped to look at herself in the full-length mirror hanging on the door. "I should do what you do," she sighed. "I mean, I hate the law firm. All those attorneys make so much money, and they pay me peanuts to sit there and look pretty at the front desk."

"You want to be a translator? What else do you speak besides English?"

"I took two years of French in high school, but I only remember basic grammar and stuff. *Où est-ce qu'on peut trouver des réstaurants, s'il vous plaît?*"

Ina laughed. "That's not gonna get you far. Your pronunciation is good, though."

Emily shrugged and glanced over at a corner of the room where Ina kept all her art supplies—easels, canvases, boxes of paint—all stacked on top of one another. "Well, how far is this translating job of yours going to get *you*? It's not even what you want to do."

Ina followed Emily's gaze and shifted uncomfortably. "I know. That's what I'm saving up for. There's a school in Brooklyn, but it's really expensive. If I can get in, I'll meet the right people. Doors will open."

"When are you going to do it?"

Ina rolled her eyes. "When are *you* going to quit your job and do exactly what you want? This stuff takes time. You're seven years older than me and you're not where you want to be yet."

"Yeah, yeah, I know."

Ina clicked on Alex's last email message and put her cursor in the blank message box. She looked up at Emily, who was still studying herself in the mirror. "I know it seems like I'm moving super slow on the art stuff, but this translating work is the fastest way. If I can keep up what I've been making in the past few months, it'll take six more months before I can afford that school. It's just . . . ugh . . . before I got this translating job, my life was a complete wreck. It's taking a long time to get where I want to be."

Emily's smile faded as she turned around to face Ina. "How was your life a complete wreck?"

The room fell silent. Ina hadn't told any of her old roommates about her past. Not all of it. Instead, she always told a sad, threadbare story about her dead father and her once-successful mother going to prison. They'd always accepted that as a good reason for why she'd never graduated high school, why she sometimes suffered panic attacks, why it was so emotionally difficult to get a steady job with a company instead of the inconsistent freelance work she was doing now. In reality, her childhood hadn't messed her up; it was Jake at the root of it all. But she'd never shared that with anyone except Alex, and she'd hardly told him anything.

She was tired of covering everything up, and Emily was nice—probably the nicest person Ina had ever lived with. She deserved to hear the whole truth. Deep down, Ina had wanted to tell her for a while now.

"Are you okay?" Emily asked.

Ina swallowed a lump in her throat. "Please don't think less of me," she said softly, "but I used to work for an escort service." She kept her eyes cast down. "And yes, that's exactly what you think it is. I mean, it was legal . . . well, the escort part was legal, but everybody did way more than that and got paid under the table, so yeah . . . yeah, you get the idea."

Emily put a hand on her hip. "Whoa, seriously? How old were you?"

Ina shrugged. "Eighteen when I started, so not that long ago. It was such good money. And it was my decision, not Jake's. I went with Francesca because when I found out what kind of money she was making, I thought it was my ticket out of there. It would be enough for me to leave and start a new life. It would be enough for art school."

Confusion crossed Emily's face, but her eyes were mostly filled with concern, like she wanted to rush across the room and give Ina a huge hug. It made Ina feel relieved. She should have known Emily wouldn't judge her.

"Tell me about Jake and Francesca," Emily said, stepping closer to the bed. "They got you into the escort thing?"

"Jake's the one who ran the escort service. I met him when I was living in a group home, and when I left there, I moved into his house. Francesca and a bunch of other escorts were already living there."

Emily's mouth dropped open, the confusion in her eyes morphing into shock. "You mean this guy recruited girls from group homes to be in his escort service? That's messed up."

"Well, no . . . no, not like that. He didn't *recruit* me." Ina let out a heavy sigh, realizing it was sounding like she was defending Jake. "It's just that I didn't have anywhere else to go when I had to leave the group home, so he let me live in his house for free. He didn't have me on his books as an escort. I didn't have to do what the other women were doing. Jake was helping me. He even hired someone to teach me Italian when I told him I wanted to learn it."

"So that's how you speak so many languages?"

Ina shook her head. "Only Italian. I already spoke English and Spanish and some Korean."

Emily was quiet for a long moment. Ina looked away, afraid of what her silence meant. Maybe she was going to judge her after all.

"Were you and Jake together, then?" Emily finally asked, her voice gentle. "I mean, did you think you owed him or something?"

Ina shook her head. "Me and Jake were never like that. I don't know why he let me stay there." She looked up, her skin growing cold. "Please don't look at me like that. It doesn't make me a bad person. It doesn't make me—"

"I didn't say that. I'm kinda shocked, that's all. I never would've guessed. Well, sometimes I've wondered if . . . I mean . . . oh, never mind."

"You're the only person I've ever told this to."

Emily crossed the room and sat on the edge of Ina's mattress. "It sounds like you think all of this is your fault," she said softly, concern filling her eyes again.

"It *was* my fault," Ina muttered. "Believe me, I know Jake was probably manipulating me. Yes, he's to blame for that, but the point is *I* decided to go live there. *I* decided to believe him when he told me I couldn't take care of myself." She took a deep breath and let it back out slowly. Her laptop screen went into sleep mode. "He was charming and nice. He was . . . Jake." She tapped the space bar to wake up the screen. "Jake made stupid decisions, but I have to own up to my own decisions too, right? That's why I'm doing what I can to be more independent now. Nobody else is going to do it for me."

Emily patted Ina's knee, and Ina could tell she wasn't going to think any less of her. She wanted to say thank you, but couldn't find the right words before Emily spoke. "You seem a lot older than you really are," she sighed. "And I mean that in a good way. Please let me know if I can help with anything, okay? *Anything.* Sometimes you seem so alone . . . and scared . . . and it makes me sad." She looked away, smiling nervously. "Like, I sometimes want to mother you."

Ina gave her a wry smile. "Please don't."

But as Emily stood up from the bed and started picking up some of her clothes (as if talking about being motherly had suddenly made her domestic), Ina wondered what it would feel like to have a mother figure in her life after her own mother had been absent for so long. The thought made her shift uncomfortably. She had taken care of herself for too long to let anyone take away her independence now.

# *Ten*

From: Ina <ina.artgirl1979@hotmail.com>
To: Alex Winzelberg <winzwarehouse5@hotmail.com>
Date: June 17, 1999
Subject: I am okay

I have a few minutes before I have to go to work, so I'm sending this email because you kinda freaked out in the chatroom yesterday. Jake can't hurt me, okay? Please don't worry. He found my phone number, but I'm going to get it changed. He can't get to me, so I'm not too worried. If any of that changes I'll let you know.

Tonight my roommate Emily got me thinking about whether or not I keep putting off what I really want because I'm scared. I don't think I'm afraid of trying. I think I'm afraid of succeeding. It's like I have so much confidence in my art that it's scaring me away from my art, from myself. I don't know how to process that. Do you feel that way about acting and theater?

The second thing I wanted to ask you is when do you think you'll be coming here for sure? I really want to meet you, and I think we should nail down a solid plan for you to fly out here and we'll meet at the subway station in Jackson Heights. Please, please, please?

Okay, so I just said all that to try to get you out here faster. I'm a selfish brat. Yep. I own that.

The last thing is I'm dying to see a picture of you, and I can send a picture of me to you too. Anyway, to give you an idea without a picture of me: I'm not super skinny, but I'm not heavy. I'm five foot eight with long, super-curly dark brown hair. Most of the time it's frizzy. Both my mom and dad have similar hair (Mom came to America from Spain and Dad's family came from Argentina). Anyway, I have his long fingers and toes and kinda big forehead. I also have a big nose, but I have no idea who I got that from. Wow, I just made myself sound super ugly. I'm not. I promise. Now spill it, Alex. What do you look like?

Now I really have to leave. Peace out.

# Eleven

Ina stepped out of the taxi and surveyed the restaurant in front of her. Manicured bushes and trees lined the front walkway, lit beneath a hanging roof of tiny white lights. The restaurant wasn't too far from Jackson Heights, settled in a small, upscale area Ina hadn't known existed. She'd dressed in a classic black dress and heels, and she'd twisted her unruly dark curls into a tight bun. It was a look she often chose for evening appointments.

She made her way up the walk and a uniformed doorman held the door open for her, smiling warmly as she breezed past him. Almost immediately, the maître d' approached her. She asked for Mr. Conti, and he led her to a table near the back of the restaurant.

"Have a lovely evening, Mademoiselle," he said, and left her standing in front of the table where a tall, olive-skinned man dressed in a dark three-piece suit stood up to greet her.

"Signorina Sanchez, *un piacere*," he said, reaching for her hand. "*Sono* Vincenzo Conti."

Ina smiled warmly and gave him her hand so he could kiss the top of it. He looked maybe ten years older than her, and he was far more a gentleman than some other clients she had translated for. "It's a pleasure to meet you too, Mr. Conti," she said to him in Italian. "Has the rest of your party arrived?"

Vincenzo let go of her hand and pulled a chair out for her. "Not yet, but they should be here shortly. We have much to discuss. You will help me immensely, as I speak very little English."

Ina nodded, following his Italian perfectly. He spoke with all the flair and manner of a refined gentleman—much more polished than her own forced dialect. "I'm happy to help," she responded politely, sitting in the chair and placing her small black handbag on her lap as Vincenzo moved to the chair next to her and sat down.

"Please," Vincenzo said, motioning to a leather-bound book on Ina's plate. "Choose a wine. You drink during dinner engagements?"

"Thank you, but I don't drink while I'm working," she explained.

Vincenzo cocked his head to the side, studying her with his chocolate brown eyes. He was clean-shaven, but Ina could see a fair amount of dark stubble beginning to show along his lower jaw. It was as dark as his carefully combed hair. He looked tired, as if he'd had a very long day. He kept his eyes on her, his expression softening with curiosity.

"Is there a reason you're looking at me like that?" Ina asked as lightly as she could.

"You look familiar to me. I am trying to remember where I might have seen you before."

Ina's stomach sank to the floor. She had worked for several Italian men in the past, but she was certain Vincenzo was not one of them. "Is this your first trip to America?" she asked.

"Yes, so I don't know how I could possibly have seen your face before. You seem very young to be a translator. You must be twenty-two? Twenty-three?"

Ina ran her fingers along the leather binding of the wine menu. "Yes, somewhere around there," she answered, keeping her eyes down. There was no way she was going to tell this man she was only nineteen. Many of her clients commented on her age when they first met her, but it had never posed a problem once she started translating. Her job was to disappear into the background, and that was exactly what she planned on doing this evening. She looked over her shoulder toward the entrance, wondering when everyone else was going to arrive. There were three other place settings at the table.

Whatever happened, she reassured herself, she would be fine. She was in a public place, and Vincenzo had already paid the fee for her services. That was handled by Philippe. Philippe handled a lot of things she didn't have to worry about: marketing, scheduling, payments, cancellations. In return, he made a commission on all of her bookings. She was one of many translators he represented.

Ina turned back to Vincenzo, shifting uncomfortably in her seat as she saw that he was still watching her. Something about him was beginning to rub her the wrong way. Maybe it was because he was Italian, and Italian men always reminded her of Jake's Italian clients. Or maybe it was because her past was weighing on her mind after talking to Emily earlier. Whatever it was, it made her want to stand up and run away. She didn't like Vincenzo simply because she could see he was attracted to her. She hadn't tried to look attractive—just professional—but sometimes it didn't matter.

"Ah," Vincenzo said, interrupting Ina's thoughts. "Here are the others."

Ina saw two men in suits and a tall, elegant woman in a purple floor-length gown approaching the table. The woman was Caucasian, the man on her left looked Latino, and the other man Asian. Ina wondered if she might get a chance to practice her Korean with him. She wasn't fluent yet, but she was working hard on it.

The three of them smiled at her and Vincenzo as they took their seats.

"This is Ms. Ina Sanchez," Vincenzo said in English. "She is our translator this evening."

The woman let out a polite laugh as she settled into her chair across from Ina. "Little need for a translator with your excellent English, Mr. Conti."

Vincenzo blushed as he looked questioningly at Ina. Ina smiled and immediately translated for him.

"Oh!" he laughed, pointing a finger at the woman. "No, you are mistaken. That was rehearsed!"

Ina translated his jovial answer to the woman and felt herself relax. This was what she had come here to do. In less than ten minutes, she felt more at home than she had all day. The only way she could feel more relaxed was if she was painting. Somehow, translating suited her. Philippe had once told her it was because it distanced her from others. She was there, but not there. Invisible.

And being invisible was exactly what she wanted.

"Ms. Sanchez?"

Ina finished the sentence she was translating before focusing her attention on the maître d' hovering near the table.

"Yes?"

The maître d' apologized for his interruption and then bent down to speak quietly in Ina's ear. "You have an urgent phone call," he said. "Would you like to take it?"

Ina's mouth went dry as she considered who might be on the phone. The only person who could know she was here would be Philippe. He wouldn't call her in the middle of a job unless he absolutely had to.

"Hang on," she said softly. With an apologetic look, she told Vincenzo in Italian that she had a phone call.

He waved his hand. "It is fine. Go, go."

"*Grazie.*"

After assuring the other guests that she would be back in a moment, she followed the maître d'. Everything about this felt wrong. Philippe would never call her here. Finally, she stopped at the front desk where a woman lifted the receiver from the cradle of a black phone and handed it over to Ina. She placed it to her ear. "This is Ina."

Nobody answered. The line was completely silent.

Ina looked up at the woman behind the desk. "Do I need to press a certain button?" she asked.

The woman leaned forward to look at the phone's display. "No, it looks like the line was disconnected. I'm sorry."

"That's all right." Ina handed her the receiver and turned to go back to her table, but something caught her eye.

*Jake.*

He was standing outside the glass French doors of the restaurant, his vicious blue eyes holding her in a death grip as he slipped a cell phone into his back pocket. Under the restaurant's outdoor lighting, his reddish-brown hair looked unusually bright. He had cut it since the last time Ina had seen him. She hated that he made her feel like a child in trouble.

She stood still for what felt like five full minutes. Her heart pounded. Her palms started to sweat. She was certain that if Jake walked through those doors, he'd get her to go with him without causing a scene.

She couldn't move. His eyes bored into hers, calmly saying, *If you run, I will find you.*

He took a step forward and Ina felt herself shrinking into nothingness. She couldn't fight or run away. For a moment, she almost found the courage to ask the woman at the front desk for help, but stopped as she reminded herself that Jake could talk his way out of anything. He would convince everyone Ina was the dangerous one, not him. He had done it before.

But as Jake stepped forward, the doorman who had ushered her in earlier held up his hand. Anger flashed across Jake's face as the doorman blocked his path.

Then Ina understood. The dress code. Jake was wearing jeans and a T-shirt. There was no way they would let him in. Ina knew this was her chance, but her feet wouldn't move.

Jake said something to the doorman, his expression calm now. Then he slid his eyes to Ina, who finally managed to take a step backward, wobbling in her heels. She was safe. For now. Jake watched her as she backed away, and with one triumphant look, she whirled around and left the lobby.

Her heart was still pounding when she reached her chair and sat down. Vincenzo smiled at her, his expression a little desperate as the others quietly conversed in English. It had only been a few minutes, but Vincenzo had probably not been able to communicate with the group the entire time she was away.

"I'm so sorry," she said in Italian, leaning closer to him as she set her napkin on her lap. Her plate was the only one left with food now. "Please resume your conversation."

Vincenzo nodded and picked up his glass of wine. A moment later, Ina was back into the swing of translating. Her food remained untouched, which was what always happened during dinner meetings. It seemed silly to order food at all, but she knew clients tended to feel more comfortable if she at least appeared to dine along with them.

The conversation went on for another hour, filled with business and banter. It was so draining, Ina almost forgot about Jake. He couldn't possibly still be out there waiting for her, could he? Then again, he was Jake. Of course he was still out there. The thought of him waiting for her made her stutter over a few of her translations, until finally Vincenzo gave her a sympathetic look and wrapped up the meeting. Ina said goodbye to the two men and the woman, and found herself sitting alone once again with Vincenzo.

"You seem distracted," he said, finishing off his wine. He glanced at her plate. "And you have hardly eaten. Please, finish now that you don't have to translate."

As much as Ina didn't feel like staying, she knew it was best. She truly was hungry, despite her anxiety over Jake. Plus, the longer she stayed in the restaurant, the more likely Jake was to leave.

"*Grazie*," she said quietly as she picked up her fork and stabbed a green bean. It was cold when she put it in her mouth.

"You are a talented translator," Vincenzo said as Ina continued to eat. "The other translator I have been using is not as invested as you. I suspect he skips much of what I say, and he seems to translate only my words instead of my meaning. Does that make sense?"

Ina swallowed a piece of her chicken. "I know exactly what you mean. Some translators seem more like robots than anything else. I think it's sad. You spend all this time learning a language, perfecting it, and getting a job to use it, and then you don't care? It doesn't make any sense."

"I agree," Vincenzo said, his face lighting up. "Robots. That is it. Do you think one day we will not need human translators anymore? With technology advancing as it is, I wonder if computers will take over the world." He laughed.

Ina set down her fork, intrigued by Vincenzo's insight. "You have a good point," she said. "I've thought the same thing before, but I hope it doesn't happen. I'd be out of a job."

"You are not a robot, and you will never be out of a job," Vincenzo laughed, resting his gaze on her face. "You are too talented."

"Well, thank you," she said, but wasn't sure she meant it. Translating wasn't the thing she wanted to be best at. Art was what she really lived for, and what she hoped she was really the best at. It felt more natural to her than translating, and that was saying something. It just didn't pay anything.

Concentrating on her plate, she tried not to look uncomfortable as Vincenzo started picking at the remnants of his meal. He was patiently waiting for her to finish, but Ina couldn't make herself rush. She didn't want to finish because that would mean she would have to leave the restaurant. If Jake was still out there, she didn't know what she'd do.

"May I ask you something?" Vincenzo asked as Ina finished up the last of her food and set her napkin on the table.

"Sure."

"Would you like to get a drink with me? I know you said you don't drink while you are working, but your job is finished now . . ."

Ina lifted her eyes to his, her heart beating fast at the thought that if she had a drink with Vincenzo, she would probably end up in his hotel room. That was most likely his intent. She hardly knew him, and she'd sworn to herself she would never sleep with anyone she didn't know ever again . . . but it was either leave with Vincenzo, or end up facing Jake alone. The answer was obvious: Vincenzo was her safest option out of here.

Cradling her chin in her hand, she tried to look as relaxed as possible. "I would love to," she said. "I'm ready to leave when you are."

Vincenzo's smile broadened into a grin. "I will call for a cab." He stood and offered her his hand. She took it and stood, not realizing that she was trembling until her knees began to wobble. Vincenzo tightened his hold on her. "Are you unwell?"

Steadying herself, Ina tried to laugh off her anxiety. "No, I'm fine," she said, her throat suddenly dry and tight. "I'm just wondering . . . could you . . . that phone call I received during dinner . . . it was a man who's waiting for me outside, and I don't want him to see me." Everything was starting to spin. She couldn't seem to catch her breath.

"Of course," Vincenzo said gently, pulling her closer to keep her steady. "What do you need me to do?"

Ina leaned against him, surprised at how good he smelled, like honey and vanilla. She took a deep breath to try to calm herself. "I don't know," she finally managed. Tears stung her eyes, but she blinked them back.

"Here, sit down," Vincenzo said, easing her into her chair. "I will have the maître d' call a cab to meet us at a back entrance. He speaks some Italian. You won't have to see this man who is waiting for you."

Ina nodded and sat down. She stared down at her hands, barely noticing as Vincenzo left. This was not the time to have a panic attack, but it wasn't like she could pick and choose when they came. She should have known seeing Jake would set her off.

A few tears managed to break free. She swiped them away, not caring if she smeared her makeup. She had to focus on steady, consistent breathing or she might pass out. Her vision was already going slightly dark. She saw a motel room, a man grabbing at her hands, his eyes angry. And then Jake was there, his fist slamming into her head. Ina fell back against the wall, helpless. Nothing could save her.

Then she heard Vincenzo's steady voice. "Ina?"

Surprisingly, Vincenzo's presence calmed her. She relaxed even more when he pressed his hand on hers and crouched down to look her in the eyes. "We can go out back. There is a cab waiting."

Nodding, Ina grabbed his hand to help pull herself up. She kept hold of him as they followed the maître d' through the dining area and into the back of the restaurant, past the kitchen, and out a set of doors leading to a parking area where a yellow cab sat idling.

"*Grazie,*" Vincenzo said to the maître d', who replied in broken Italian that he was happy to help and then returned to the restaurant.

Vincenzo opened the cab door and helped Ina inside. "Would you like to go home?" he asked. "You do not seem well."

Ina shook her head. "No, if he follows us, I don't want him to know where I live." She put her hands on her knees and held her breath for a moment. She was finally feeling like herself again. In control. She could outsmart Jake. He would not get the best of her. Not this time.

Vincenzo's brow furrowed. "Follow us? Who is this man?"

She glanced out the window. "He's nobody. Let's go get that drink."

Vincenzo nodded and leaned forward to speak to the driver. "This hotel, please," he said in his thickly accented English, and handed the driver a small card.

Ina looked at Vincenzo, raising an eyebrow. He caught her meaning and shook his head. "No, no, there is a bar on the ground floor. You do not have to come to my room." Leaning back in his seat, he gave Ina a quick smile.

She cleared her throat as the cab pulled out of the parking lot. "I guess we'll see how I feel," she said softly, reminding herself that Vincenzo could really be as much of a gentleman as he claimed. Unlike Jake.

*Jake.*

There he was, standing on the curb outside the restaurant, close enough to see inside the cab as it stopped at the intersection to turn left. His hair was tousled, like he'd been raking his hands through it. Ina ducked down with a gasp, but she already knew it was one second too late.

"That's him," she whispered as the cab swung around the corner, away from the restaurant. "He's there. He saw me."

Vincenzo touched her back, leaning down to try to look her in the eyes. "It's okay. We're away from the restaurant. He cannot follow us on foot. Who is that man, Ms. Sanchez? Do we need to call the police?"

"No, that would only make things worse." She was still doubled over, her face so close to the seat she could smell cigarette smoke and stale cologne. "How did he find me here?" she whispered to herself. "Maybe he knows where I live and he followed me here. I don't know what to do."

Vincenzo patted her back in long, smooth strokes. "Is there someone we can call? Do you have family?"

Ina sat up, her breathing rapid. "Family?" she laughed. Then she realized how stupid it was to let Vincenzo think she had no connections whatsoever. "Well, there's Alex."

"Who is Alex?"

"My brother."

Vincenzo kept his hand on her back. "Ah. We should take you to your brother, then. He can help you."

Ina put a hand to her forehead, her thoughts spinning. "Maybe when we get to a phone," she finally answered. "But it'll be okay. It's fine."

She started to relax. It felt strange to call Alex her brother, but she did wish he were here in New York. She imagined herself going to a play and seeing him on stage. That made her happy. She relaxed even more. Maybe he had answered the email she'd sent off earlier. She had asked him a lot of questions, and the thought of reading his answers made everything seem brighter. She didn't know why. Everything was erratic and disjointed in her head. She hated it when her brain did this, like the world was falling apart and she couldn't put the pieces back together unless she focused on one mundane thing—and that was Alex, apparently.

But was Alex mundane?

Far from it.

Alex was an adorably innocent small-town boy with a dream.

Alex was her friend.

Alex had never met her, yet he cared about her. Maybe Vincenzo did too. His hand was still on her back. It didn't bother her. If anything, it was helping her feel grounded. Slowly, she sat up and he lowered his hand. "I should be scared of you," she said as she regained control of her breathing.

Vincenzo gave her a curious look. The city lights slid across his face in streaks of yellows and blues. "Why is that?" he asked. "Because you don't know me? Because I asked you out for a drink and I'm older than you?"

"All of those things and other reasons I won't explain," she said, looking away.

"And yet you aren't scared of me," he said. "Why?"

Ina kept her eyes on the window. "Because that other man scares me more."

# Twelve

From: Alex Winzelberg <winzwarehouse5@hotmail.com>
To: Ina <ina.artgirl1979@hotmail.com>
Date: June 17, 1999
Subject: Re: I am okay

Hey, I was doing some work in the office and your email popped up. You're probably working right now, so I hope it goes okay for you. I've been dealing with family drama over me leaving. So far, we've all decided me staying for another year is probably the best thing. I called the school this morning and they said I can do that, but now your email has me second-guessing everything. Thanks a lot. Still, I think it might be best to stay. I'll just end up making everyone too upset if I leave now. Don't worry. A year will go by fast. I hope.

Now, to your questions.

You nailed it. I feel the same way about acting as you do about your art, and I know nobody will understand. My theater teacher says I shouldn't waste my gift, but if I talk about it like that people will think I'm full of myself and they'll hate me. I know I'm not God's gift to the stage, but I also know I have talent. Part of me wonders if it's been so hard to leave because I know I'll do great, just like you know you'll do great. So yeah, I'm already on that plane, in theory. One day I'll actually be on it. Soon. One year. It will happen.

You know what's funny? I never thought about what you look like. Not really. You sound pretty to me. Not sure what you'd think of me. I have no idea where any of my family is from. I do know a lot of my ancestors were Jewish, but that's all. Honestly, I just think of myself as average. I'm tall, but I'm kind of pale because I don't spend a lot of time outside. I'm not scrawny, but I don't have a six-pack or anything. Light brown hair, which is starting to get curly and it's freaking me out because I have no idea what to do with curly hair. I have big knuckles. Maybe that's a weird thing to tell you, but it's something people comment on all the time. Yeah, weird.

Do you think as soon as you get your phone number changed we should call each other? Since I'll be staying here, my mom is going to have to be okay with me making long-distance phone calls.

---

**From: Ina <ina.artgirl1979@hotmail.com>**
**To: Alex Winzelberg <winzwarehouse5@hotmail.com>**
**Date: June 17, 1999**
**Subject: Re: Re: I am okay**

I'm borrowing someone else's computer, so this might be short. I saw Jake tonight. He came to the restaurant where I was with a client. He couldn't get inside, though, so I left with my client out the back. Jake somehow followed us. I'm still with my client, so for now, I'm safe.

I just want you to know how much I think of you. The weirder things get right now, the more I think of you. I mean, why else would I be sneaking onto a stranger's computer to email you? Crazy huh?

I'll answer more of your email later. Your description makes you sound hot in the cutest way possible. Don't be mad at me for saying that. Gotta go.

# Thirteen

Ina closed Vincenzo's laptop and glanced at the bathroom door. It was still shut, but she could hear the squeak of the shower turning off. Vincenzo would come out any moment, expecting her to get down to business with him. This was his hotel room—a suite that probably cost more for one night's stay than she made in a week. It didn't matter. She was safe from Jake.

Ruthless, relentless Jake.

She'd stayed close to Vincenzo as they'd made their way to the hotel bar tucked into a dark, quiet corner of the building. It was far from the lobby, and after twenty minutes of waiting to see if Jake would show up, Ina had finally relaxed and let herself enjoy a few drinks.

The alcohol went straight to her head, and an hour later, she was on her way to the elevator with Vincenzo. Just as they rounded a corner, Ina caught a glimpse of Jake sitting on a sofa in the lobby, his eyes tired and droopy. He was looking in the other direction, so Ina stayed close to Vincenzo and hurried into the elevator before Jake caught sight of her.

Vincenzo had asked if she wanted to join him in the shower, but she'd said no, and now here she was, listening to Vincenzo finish up in the bathroom. The alcohol in her system was still making her feel tipsy and vulnerable, two things she did not want to be.

The bathroom door opened and Vincenzo stepped into the room, smiling. The only thing covering him was a white towel around his waist.

"It has been a very long day," he said, walking toward her. He had gorgeous skin, a defined chest, and perfect hair, even with it tousled and wet. Too bad Ina wasn't attracted to Italians. He watched her look him up and down, a smug expression on his face. "You like what you see?" he asked, sauntering closer. "I wish you had joined me in the shower."

Ina looked away, unsure of how to proceed. She was still seated at the desk, legs crossed, arms folded. She couldn't make herself any more closed off than she already was. And she knew she couldn't lead Vincenzo on any longer.

"I'm sorry," she finally said, looking up at him. "I thought I wanted this, but I'm not sure about it now. I feel like I've used you to get away from that man. I hope you're not upset with me."

Vincenzo's smug expression crumbled. He didn't look upset, but he certainly wasn't happy. He studied her for a moment, then snapped his fingers. "I remember where I've seen your face," he said excitedly. "It was a friend's photograph. He came here to New York for business, like me. He hired an escort one evening . . ."

His voice trailed off as he looked Ina up and down, a whole mess of emotions playing across his face. Disgust. Desire. Confusion.

Surprise overtook all of Ina's other emotions. "You've *got* to be kidding," she said, looking up at Vincenzo in shock. She knew Philippe had a lot of Italian customers, but what were the odds his clients would know Jake's?

She slowly stood up from her chair, stepping backward as Vincenzo watched her, frozen in place. "It could not have been you in that picture," he muttered. "Could it? You do not perform those services." His eyebrows shot up. "Or do you?"

Ina almost tripped on the carpet as she continued to back away. "I'm a different person now," she said shakily. "I don't do that anymore." She threw a nasty glare at Vincenzo, suddenly feeling confident. "And you shouldn't judge me. Your friend paid for that. He's no better than me."

Vincenzo lifted a hand to scratch his jaw. "No, you are right, of course." He caught her gaze, holding her in place with an apologetic look. "Please don't leave, Ms. Sanchez. You are welcome to sleep in the bed. I will sleep on the couch." He gestured to a couch in the suite's lounge area. "I will keep you safe from the man who is stalking you." He cocked an eyebrow. "Is he someone from this past life of yours?"

"Yes, he is."

"That is all the more reason to keep you safe from him." His voice was full of conviction.

Ina wasn't sure she should trust him. Jake had promised to keep her safe and then went back on that promise. Still, she didn't feel she had much of a choice at the moment. "Thank you," she replied.

Vincenzo nodded and looked down at his bare feet. "I will be honest, I am disappointed. You are very beautiful and I thought you wanted to be with me."

Ina's heart sank even further than before. "I'm sorry I'm so complicated," she said. "Maybe if I got to know you a little better. How long will you be here?"

Vincenzo frowned. "Only for tonight. My plane leaves in the morning."

"I understand."

He stepped closer to her, only a foot away now. "Did you call your brother?"

"My brother?" Oh yes, she had said Alex was her brother. She had to think fast. "I called him while you were in the bathroom to let him know where I am. He said to call him again if I need anything. He has a cell phone."

Vincenzo nodded. "A part of you must want to stay here then, no?"

She tried to hide a cringe, realizing the corner she'd backed herself into. "I guess so," she laughed nervously as she lowered her eyes to Vincenzo's bare chest and then back up to his face. "You *are* hot, Mr. Conti, and you have been really nice to me."

A smile teased the corners of his mouth as he stepped even closer. He didn't touch her, but he was close enough for her to feel his warmth and smell the soap he'd used in the shower. He looked into her eyes. "I will not force you into anything, Ms. Sanchez, but please know I'm here if you want me."

For the briefest moment, Ina wanted him again. It was a powerful sensation that raced like a bolt of lightning from her head to her toes. Then it was gone.

She looked down at the floor. "I can't," she said softly. "I'm sorry."

Vincenzo lightly touched her shoulder and she looked up at him. His brown eyes were filled with understanding. "I will get dressed, then, and perhaps I will call downstairs to get some extra toiletries for you. You should stay here tonight, and I will make sure to get you back home safely tomorrow."

Nodding, she took a step back. "Yes, that sounds good, thank you."

He headed back into the bathroom. As soon as the door closed, Ina sat back down at the desk and put her head in her hands. She could leave. Vincenzo was clearly not going to try to keep her here if she didn't want to stay. But Jake. Ugh. Jake.

"Don't let him control you," she whispered under her breath. He'd have to be gone by morning. A nice hotel like this certainly wouldn't let him camp out in the lobby. That thought made her a little more relaxed. Really, she didn't have that much to fear now. Vincenzo wasn't going to make her do anything, and she was safe. Everything would be fine. Still, there was one question she couldn't push out of her mind: How had Jake found her at the restaurant?

A moment later, she picked up the phone on the desk and dialed her apartment. She had no idea if Emily was home yet, but it was worth a shot.

"Hello?" Emily answered.

"Em, it's me. Sorry if I woke you up. How was your night out?"

"Obviously not that great since I'm home already. Yours?"

"Not good. Jake found me at the restaurant. That's why I'm calling. Did he happen to come by our place after I left?"

A sleepy pause. "Wait, who's Jake again?"

"The man I told you about earlier."

"Oh, that douchebag? I thought he wasn't in your life anymore."

"He's not supposed to be, but he was there at the restaurant. They wouldn't let him in, but I don't know how he found me there and I'm afraid he might know where I live. Like, maybe he followed me or something."

"Well, nobody buzzed the apartment before I left. Should I be worried about him dropping by? If he does show up, I can punch his lights out."

Ina almost laughed at the image of Emily decking Jake. Jake would not go down that easily. "No, Em, he's dangerous. If he manages to get in the building, don't answer the door, okay?"

"I was kidding, Ina. Of course I won't answer the door. Where are you? Are you coming home soon?"

"I'm staying in a hotel tonight. I'll be back in the morning."

"Why not just come home? We can call the cops if he comes by."

Ina let out a sigh. "I can't. It's a long story, but I feel better staying here. Everything's fine. I just wanted to be sure you knew about Jake."

"Okay, well, call me again if you need anything?"

"I will. Goodnight."

"Night."

Ina set the receiver back in its cradle. A quick, loud knock on the door made her jump right out of her chair.

Frozen in place, Ina stared at the door. It was deadbolted and chained.

Vincenzo came out of the bathroom holding a toothbrush, dressed in a pair of pajama bottoms. He was still shirtless. "Did you call the front desk?" he asked. "Who is knocking?"

Ina shook her head. "I–I don't know who it is. It could be him. I don't know how he found our room." Her voice was trembling. She hated how quickly the thought of Jake sent her into a full-blown panic. Vincenzo was a larger man than Jake; he could take him on if needed, so there was really nothing to be afraid of.

Except for Jake's manipulative words.

He could talk his way into or out of anything. That was probably how he'd managed to get out of prison so quickly. If he had ever been in prison. The police had never told Ina for sure if he'd been convicted of anything. She had just assumed he'd been serving time, but maybe he had never been in there at all.

Vincenzo headed for the door. "I will hurt him," he growled. "It is not right for a man to frighten you in this way."

Ina watched in horror as Vincenzo undid the locks on the door and cracked it open. There was a figure on the other side, but Ina couldn't see who it was. Vincenzo stood still for a moment, took a small piece of paper from the person, and then said, "*Grazie*," and shut the door.

He turned around, his eyes on the paper.

"What is it?" Ina asked.

"A telegram from my company in Italy," he said, still reading. He looked up and gave Ina a smile. "No need to worry."

Ina nodded. "No need to worry," she repeated in English. The next thing she knew, Vincenzo was right in front of her, holding her up as if she had started to fall.

"It's okay," Vincenzo said, guiding her toward the bed.

Something about his Italian . . . the way he was urging her toward the bed . . . his strong hands holding on to her . . .

Ina saw the man in the motel again, his eyes wide with excitement as her hands closed around his neck. She didn't want to do it. She couldn't. Then she was off the bed and the man was angry and Jake's fist was coming at her. She cried out, but she already knew nobody would save her.

# Fourteen

The room was dark and the air smelled like curry. That couldn't be right. The last thing Ina remembered was a hotel suite. Vincenzo. A telegram.

Wait.

*No.*

Had Vincenzo hurt her?

She sat up with a gasp. All she could see were a few faint outlines. Her pile of art supplies in the corner, the edge of her nightstand. The familiar sounds of traffic drifted up from the street below. The drapes were tightly closed over the window. How had she gotten home?

"Emily?" Ina yelled. "Em, are you there?"

A lamp flicked on. Emily sat up in bed, her hair askew. She blinked. "Not again, Ina. There's nobody in the apartment, I promise."

Ina shook her head, remembering the times she had woken Emily up because of an old recurring nightmare. "It's not that," she muttered. "It's . . . how did I get here?"

Emily squinted at her. "That hot Italian man brought you home in the middle of the night. I guess he was your client? He was super nice, but I couldn't understand him."

Ina closed her eyes, fighting to remember anything about Vincenzo bringing her home. How could she forget something like that? "He only speaks Italian," she muttered. "I didn't translate for you?"

"Well, no, you were really out of it. I think you were drunk."

Ina reached for her watch on the nightstand, but it wasn't there. She realized it was still on her wrist and she was also still wearing her black dress. "It's 5:30 in the morning," she exclaimed. "He brought me home in the middle of the night?"

"Yeah, it was super weird. He tried to tell me what was going on, but obviously I didn't understand. He handed me your keys and your purse and kept saying something that sounded like 'sleep,' so I took you to your bed. When I went back into the living room he was gone. The weirdest thing was it looked like he'd just been in a fight. His lip was bleeding."

"That *is* weird," Ina muttered. "I'm sorry, Emily. I don't know what happened. The last thing I remember was almost passing out in his hotel room."

Emily's mouth dropped open. "Did he drug you?"

Well, that was a definite possibility, but it didn't feel like the right answer. Ina narrowed her eyes. "I don't think so. I had a few drinks in the hotel bar, but at least two hours went by after that, and I felt fine. I doubt any drug would take that long to kick in. And why would he drug me and then bring me home? That doesn't make any sense."

"I guess not. He seemed really nice too—not like a man who would hurt you. At least, I hope he didn't hurt you."

Ina stared down at her quilt. She had to think. She had to figure out what had happened. The longer she stared at the quilt the more flashes of memory fell into place.

"I think I had a panic attack," she said as she looked up at Emily. "I have them sometimes when I think about what Jake did to me. It scares me so bad that my brain freaks out. Maybe I was freaking out so much that Vincenzo decided to bring me home. That has to be it. He must have found my address on my driver's license or something, and used my keys to get us up here."

"That doesn't explain why he looked like he'd been in a fight, or why you seemed drunk. Or were you the one who hit him?"

"I don't know. I feel bad for him, no matter what happened."

"He didn't seem upset with you. He seemed really concerned." Emily paused for a second. "Wait, what about Jake? Did anything else happen with him?"

"Not that I remember. He must have followed our cab because he was waiting for me down in the lobby. I doubt they would have let him hang around there all night, though."

"He followed you to the hotel?"

Ina nodded. "I didn't tell you that, did I?"

"Um, *no*."

"Sorry."

Emily swung her feet over the side of her bed. "Listen, you have to keep me posted about what's going on, okay? I'm going to worry about you even more now. Let me know if you feel like you're really in danger. I can always call the police for you."

"You cannot call the police," Ina insisted. "Remember when I told you about me and Jake getting in trouble? Well, the police were involved. I was in jail for a few days because of it. Jake told them really bad stuff about me. The whole thing was weird. I don't want to deal with any cops ever again. They can't stop Jake anyway. Nobody can."

"You don't know that."

"Then explain to me how he's been after me," Ina demanded, fear squeezing her tight. "I don't know if he was ever in prison to begin with. He should be there right now with everything I told the police about him, and he's not. How is that possible?"

"I don't know."

Ina realized how rude she was being, and clamped her mouth shut. She took a second to calm down and looked over at Emily. "I'm sorry," she said softly. "You're right. Let's wait and see what happens."

Emily nodded. "Maybe we both need more sleep."

Sleep sounded like a terrible idea. Ina pushed off her covers. "You go back to sleep. I'm gonna go take a shower."

"Good idea," Emily yawned, and rolled back into bed. "Wake me up in an hour, 'kay? I have to get to work. It's a good thing it's Friday, because I need a break."

"I'll wake you up."

Ina padded into the bathroom, her mind whirling with a million questions. Something was not sitting right about what had happened with Vincenzo. How could she have blanked out like that? She replayed the entire time in the hotel suite over and over as she started the shower and got ready for the day. She didn't even feel tired, which was stranger than anything else. She finished up in the shower, got dressed, and went into the kitchen for some breakfast.

* * *

Ina had just finished setting up a canvas and some painting supplies in the living room when Emily emerged from the bedroom, ready for work. "Have a good day," she said, opening the front door before throwing a worried look Ina's way. She paused with her hand still on the handle. "You sure you're okay?" she asked. "You want me to call in sick and stay here with you?"

Ina fiddled with some of her paintbrushes. "It's fine," she said, shrugging. "You can't miss work. Have a good day."

Emily opened the door the rest of the way. "Okay, see you tonight."

When she was gone, Ina stared at the door, her heart pounding in her throat. She *would* be okay, but something was still bothering her about last night. She just couldn't straighten it all out in her head.

After fiddling with her paintbrushes one last time, she took a deep breath and headed into the kitchen. She had to talk to someone who could give her some sort of answers. Philippe would be in his office by now. She picked up the cordless phone and dialed his number.

"*Salut*, Ina!" Philippe answered in his thick French accent. Ina imagined him leaning back in his office chair, dressed in one of his light wool sweaters and jeans, his peppery-brown hair styled to perfection. "How was your job at Le Bouchon last night?"

Ina started pacing the linoleum floor, a few crumbs crunching under her bare feet. "Someone found me," she said, her voice crackly. "Your bookings are private, right? Nobody can—"

"Ina, slow down," Philippe interrupted, worry in his voice. "Who found you? Did something bad happen?"

Ina stopped pacing. "A man named Jake Nichols," she said slowly. "I don't know how he could have found me last night. Nobody should have known I was at Le Bouchon except you and my client."

"Why wouldn't you want to see Jake?" Philippe asked. "You two are close friends, so why shouldn't I tell him where you—"

"Wait!" Ina interrupted. "You know Jake? I don't understand. How do you—"

"Of course I know Jake; he's the one who recommended you to me. How do you think I found you in the first place?"

Ina froze in the middle of the kitchen, her eyes squeezed shut as she took in this new information. Jake was how she had gotten her job?

"I thought my court-appointed counselor set up my interview with you," she said quietly, opening her eyes again. She focused on the sink full of dirty dishes. "She was helping me find a job when you contacted me, so I thought . . ."

Philippe laughed, as if this was all some big misunderstanding. "No, it was Jake. Funny we haven't had this conversation before."

"It's not funny," Ina snapped. She had to lean against something or she was going to fall over. She rested her hip against the counter. "Jake is not my friend. He's dangerous, and I don't want anything to do with him. Why would you tell him where I was?"

"Because I thought you were friends!" Philippe answered. "He always asks how you're doing, and last night he said he couldn't wait to see you now that he's back in town. I told him you were probably on your way to Le Bouchon, but not to bother you while you were working—maybe wait until you were finished. I thought seeing him would be a pleasant surprise for you. I'm sorry, Ina. I didn't know things were not okay between the two of you."

Ina rolled her eyes. "Jake is a liar. He manipulates people to get them on his side." She moved back to the sink, her breathing heavy as she ran a finger over the rim of a dirty bowl. Then a thought slammed into her. "Did you give him my phone number? Did you tell him where I live?" she growled.

"No, of course not. I would never give out that information."

"Good, and I don't want you talking to Jake about me ever again. Don't give him any information, do you understand?"

"Of course, Ina, of course. I had no idea Jake wasn't your friend. He made it sound like you've been close for years."

Ina sighed. "You were only doing what you thought was right."

"True. I'm still sorry."

Tucking the phone against her shoulder, Ina lifted the dirty bowl in the sink and turned on the tap to wash it. "It's over now. It's fine."

"It's over, yes. I have two bookings for you next week if you want to accept them."

"Sure, what are they?"

There was the sound of shuffling papers and the squeak of Philippe's chair rolling across the floor. "Two Spanish gentlemen for a conference in Manhattan on Monday, and a model flying in from Paris for an interview on Tuesday. That's in Manhattan as well."

Ina started scrubbing the bowl. "French? You know I'm not ready for—"

"*Tu es assez fluide*," Philippe interrupted. He kept speaking in French: "You certainly know enough to translate for a job interview."

It was true, Ina realized. She understood his French perfectly, and she already knew how she would translate his words into English for a client. It was second nature.

Philippe continued before she could respond. "That's your problem," he said gently, switching back into English. "You don't trust yourself. You barrel through things without looking at the entire picture. Yes, you're still learning French, but so is a French child! They can still communicate perfectly well with everyone around them, and so can you."

"Are you saying I only speak as well as a French child?" she blurted.

"You know you speak far above that. Stop twisting my words."

"Okay, but I'm getting *paid*," Ina emphasized. "My translations should be perfect."

"*Non, non*! Not perfect!" Philippe laughed. "Nobody expects perfection, Ina. They expect to understand and be understood, and that is all."

Setting down the bowl, Ina dried her hands on a towel. "*T'as raison*," she muttered. "I'll take both jobs. Let me know if any others pop up later?"

"Of course," Philippe answered. "I have several in the works, but for now I'll email you the details for those first two. I'm here if you need anything, agreed?"

"Yes, I know, thanks."

They both said goodbye and Ina set the phone back in its cradle. At least she knew how Jake had found her now. She still had no idea how he'd found her phone number, but at least he didn't know where she lived. Or she hoped he didn't. She glanced at the sink still full of dirty dishes and decided cleaning would be a good distraction for now.

* * *

Later, Ina stared at the canvas in front of her, confused. She was in the living room where she usually painted. The canvas was fairly small, but it didn't seem to matter what size she chose. Lately, every time she sat down to paint, all she could manage to create was an image of a little girl holding a teddy bear. The girl wasn't anyone she knew. She was random. So was the teddy bear. The scene was always black and white: a mostly empty room with a sofa, and a little girl about eight years old standing in the middle of the floor, wearing a pair of torn overalls. The teddy bear in her right hand had a red bow on top of its head. The bear was the only splash of color in the painting, and the red bow was brighter than anything else.

Ina stared.

And stared.

She scratched her head, realizing a second later that her fingers were covered in oil paint and she would now have to shampoo her hair five times to get it out. It didn't matter. All that mattered was figuring out why she kept painting this same thing over and over. A part of her hated it.

She stared some more.

And then, without thinking, she picked up a tube of black paint, squeezed a big blob of it onto her palette, and grabbed the biggest brush she owned. In ten strokes, the painting was covered in black.

If it was black, she wouldn't have to look at it anymore. The only problem was she was running out of black paint.

A knock on the door broke her out of her thoughts, and she set down her brush and wiped her hands on a rag. "I'm coming!" she yelled as the knocking continued. Ina knew it was her neighbor Mrs. Castellano. She always knocked with a *rap-rap-rap-RAP-RAP*.

"I'm so glad you're home!" Mrs. Castellano said urgently as soon as Ina had unlocked the deadbolts and opened the door. Ina had often asked if she could speak Spanish with her to stay fluent, but the woman was so insistent on "improving" her own perfectly good English that Ina finally gave up.

"Yep, I'm here," Ina said, and glanced down at the bowl of food in her neighbor's hands. "You're just in time. I'm starving."

Mrs. Castellano gave a hearty laugh. "I knew you would be!" She was a round, dark-skinned woman who always wore her long, thick hair in a braid. She eyed the paint in Ina's hair. "You've been painting," she stated, her voice almost reverent. "I interrupted your creativity."

Ina shook her head. "Seriously, I was finished. Don't worry about it."

"Well, then, you eat now." She pushed a bowl of hot tandoori chicken into Ina's hands. "We made too much. Please, take it." She peered up at Ina with her dark brown eyes. "Does Emily want some too? Oh, never mind, I'll get her a bowl anyway. I'll be right back."

Ina stayed in the open doorway, wondering how much money the Castellanos saved her and Emily in groceries. It was a lot, that was for sure, and Ina was eternally grateful.

Mrs. Castellano came back with three plastic containers stacked on top of one another. "Here. Take 'em all. One's rice, the other two are saag paneer and lamb korma." She rolled her eyes to the ceiling. "Mario insists I make all his favorite curries." She laughed. "It's a good thing for you!"

Ina's stomach growled as she took the containers. "Thanks, Mrs. C. We won't have to cook for a week."

Mrs. Castellano grinned. "Yes, yes! Now go eat." She waved and headed back to her apartment.

"See you later," Ina said, balancing the containers in one hand as she started to close the door.

"Oh!" Mrs. Castellano said, turning back to Ina. "I forgot to tell you—this morning a man was waiting for you downstairs."

Ina almost dropped her bowl and containers, but steadied herself at the last second. "Who?" she asked, her voice trembling. "Did he give you a name?"

"No, he said he knew you and asked if I'd let him in, but I told him if you don't buzz him in, he's out of luck."

"Did he have reddish brown hair and blue eyes?"

"He did. He also had a cut-up face, like he'd been in a fight. So you know him?"

The pieces came together. Emily had said Vincenzo had a cut lip, like he'd been in a fight. Could the two have run into each other last night? Had Vincenzo fought Jake, and then brought her back here to try to keep her safe? She knew he'd had a flight home in the morning, so he must not have known what else to do with her.

"Ina?"

Ina nodded slowly. "Yes, I do know him," she said, her eyes glazing over. Jake knew where she lived. He could get to her in her own home.

She had to leave.

She had to leave *now*.

"You don't like that man?" Mrs. Castellano asked, eyeing her carefully.

"You were right not to let him in," she said. "*Gracias.* I, uh, I gotta go now. Thank you for the food."

"*De nada.*"

Ina entered her apartment, set all of the food on the counter, and then closed the door, securing all three locks and sliding the chain in place. It didn't matter that the building had locked doors and someone could only get in if a tenant buzzed them in. It didn't matter that her door was heavy and solid and she had installed an extra lock on it when she'd moved in.

Jake would get in here. Somehow. And he would drag her back into his world.

There was no stopping him.

She had to run.

# Fifteen

From: Alex Winzelberg <winzwarehouse5@hotmail.com>
To: Ina <ina.artgirl1979@hotmail.com>
Date: June 17, 1999
Subject: Re: Re: Re: I am okay

I think a lot about you too. And now you have me all worried with this Jake stuff. I hope I hear back from you soon so I know everything's alright.

And how are you using a stranger's computer?

From: Ina <ina.artgirl1979@hotmail.com>
To: Alex Winzelberg <winzwarehouse5@hotmail.com>
Date: June 18, 1999
Subject: Bad, bad bad

I think the next few days are going to be crazy, so I don't know how much longer I'll be able to check my email. Right now, I've got to pack a bag. Jake is still trying to get to me. I don't know what I'm going to do to get him out of my life. I have to think of something. Can you send me your phone number? Mine is (917) 555-0199.

From: Alex Winzelberg <winzwarehouse5@hotmail.com>
To: Ina <ina.artgirl1979@hotmail.com>
Date: June 18, 1999
Subject: Re: Bad, bad, bad

I'm super worried now. I just tried to call that number and it went to your machine. I left you a message. Not sure if you have Caller ID, but here's my number in case you don't. (208) 555-0126.

You have a nice voice, by the way. Please stay safe.

From: Ina <ina.artgirl1979@hotmail.com>
To: Alex Winzelberg <winzwarehouse5@hotmail.com>
Date: June 19, 1999
Subject: Re: Re: Bad, bad bad

I just tried to call you from a pay phone, but a rude woman answered and said you weren't available. She hung up before I could say anything else. I'm not at my place anymore. I'm afraid Jake will find me there. Do you think you could come out here? Maybe just for a few days or something? We could meet at the subway like we talked about before. I would do almost anything to see you right now.

You feel safe to me.

From: Alex Winzelberg <winzwarehouse5@hotmail.com>
To: Ina <ina.artgirl1979@hotmail.com>
Date: June 19, 1999
Subject: Re: Re: Re: Bad, bad, bad

I'm really worried. I keep trying to call your number and it just goes to the machine. Please try to call here again. I've told my mom I'm expecting a call. That's a good idea about meeting. I don't think my parents could be too upset about that if they knew I was coming home in a few days. Well, maybe I won't tell them I'm leaving because I think they might freak out and stop me. Let's figure out the details because the more I think about it, the more I really want to come out there. It'll be a little vacation. That can't hurt.

Also, is everything okay? Maybe you should go to the police about Jake.

---

From: Ina <ina.artgirl1979@hotmail.com>
To: Alex Winzelberg <winzwarehouse5@hotmail.com>
Date: June 19, 1999
Subject: Please, please come visit me

Yes, details. And YAY about coming out here! Send me an email when you book your flight and what time you'll be flying in, then catch a bus to Jackson Heights and wait for me there at the station. Tell me what you'll be wearing so I can find you. Trust me, if you see me first, you'll know it's me, but just in case, I'll wear my acid wash denim jacket and red Vans sneakers.

Is all of that okay? I just don't know any other way to do this. I'll try to call you again when the phone is free so we can plan more details. I'm in an internet café and the one payphone that's not broken is being used by a lady who looks like she's gonna talk on it all day long.

---

From: Alex Winzelberg <winzwarehouse5@hotmail.com>
To: Ina <ina.artgirl1979@hotmail.com>
Date: June 19, 1999
Subject: Re: Please, please come visit me

All of that sounds good to me. I will have my friend Logan help me get a plane ticket. He's moving out there at the end of next week, so I'll probably come out with him if I can get a ticket on the same flight. I'd really like to talk to you over the phone, though, so I'll wait for your call.

# Sixteen

## Alex

"Well, that's it, then," Mr. Barringer sighed as he ended a call on his cell phone. "Peter can't do the part. He's officially been diagnosed with mono."

Alex looked up from the light board he'd been working on for the past two days. It was taking him forever to figure out what was wrong with it since he could only leave WFS for an hour each day. The musty smell of the auditorium was thick around him, and the air was cool and dank. Most people hated it in here, especially if it was nice outside, but Alex loved it. There weren't any beeping forklift trucks to interrupt his thoughts, no suffocating diesel fumes, no to-do lists, and no worrying about his dad erupting into a hallucination any second. Here, he could forget all of that.

They were backstage, right before rehearsal was supposed to start. Peter, who was only a few years older than Alex, had been cast as the lead, but had failed to show up for the last three rehearsals.

"Do you have a backup?" Alex asked, secretly hoping Mr. Barringer would say, "You, Alex!" But of course Mr. Barringer still thought he was leaving soon for New York.

Mr. Barringer looked over at Alex. "I hate to ask this of you, but can you fill in for today? Everybody's off book, but you can be on book. Here."

Alex caught the script Mr. Barringer tossed him, his heart pounding. He tried to wipe the stupid grin off his face. "Sure, I'll try."

"Great, thanks." Mr. Barringer put a hand to his forehead. "I can't believe this is happening. How the hell am I supposed to find *the lead* for my show this late in the game?"

Alex looked down at the light board and cleared his throat. "Mr. Barringer, I . . . I think I should tell you—"

"Oh!" Mr. Barringer interrupted. "Robbie Bell! Why didn't I think of him before? He'd be perfect if he's available. I'll give him a call." He gave Alex a grateful look. "Still, if you can fill in for today . . . ?"

Alex nodded. "No problem."

Mr. Barringer walked away, saying over his shoulder, "Be on stage in five minutes."

"Yeah, sure, but I should tell you . . ."

But he was already out of earshot, and Alex realized it wouldn't make any difference if he told Mr. Barringer he'd decided not to go to the Marion Conservatory for another year, anyway. The truth was that he wouldn't be able to take Peter's part, even if Mr. Barringer begged him to. His mother needed him at the warehouse, and that was that.

Five minutes later, he was reading lines opposite an elderly woman who had served him chocolate cake on his eighth birthday at the Two Spoons Café. He would never have guessed he'd one day be acting opposite her—or that she was such an amazing actress. Her heavy Italian accent was spot on. Alex got so into the scene that for several minutes he lost himself in the story that the woman was his grandmother, and that she was hilariously trying to emotionally blackmail him into a relationship with a beautiful woman.

An hour later, Alex said goodbye to Mr. Barringer and the cast and got on his bike to ride home, his heart pounding with post-performance high. Nothing compared to being on stage, even if it was just filling in for one rehearsal. But as WFS came into view down the road, his heart sank to the ground.

"You can't take two-hour breaks in the middle of the day anymore," his mother sighed as he walked into the office a few minutes later. "You promised me this wouldn't happen again."

"I know, Mom, but Mr. Barringer needed—"

"It's fine," his mother snapped, waving her hand as she stood up from the desk. "Just get your work done, okay?"

He nodded, eager to sit down at the desk so he could see if Ina had left any phone messages. She hadn't, and when he tried to check his email the modem wouldn't connect. He tapped his fingers on the desk, willing the phone to ring. It had been four days since his last email to Ina.

Four.

Days.

Was something wrong? Had Jake found her? If so, what could Alex do about it? He didn't even know her last name. He didn't even know her real *first* name!

He put his head in his hands. This was ridiculous. Ina was clear across the country. There was nothing he could do. A knock on the door made him lift his head. "What?" he sighed, dreading it was his mother there to give him another to-do list.

She cracked the door open and poked her head in. "Logan's here, but don't think you can run off and play right after you had a break. I've got a project for both of you."

"Oh, awesome."

His mother cocked an eyebrow. "Awesome that Logan is here, or awesome that I have a project for you?"

Alex rolled his eyes. "What do you think? Logan's leaving on Friday, so I'd like to spend *some* time with him before he's gone."

His mother nodded and then motioned for him to follow her out of the office. He stayed on her heels. "Well," she said, looking over her shoulder. "Since this project involves leaving the warehouse, I'm guessing you'll be overjoyed."

"Oh, yeah? Do I get to use the car?"

"Yes."

They rounded a corner to the packaging area. Logan was leaning against a table, a smile on his face as he chatted with a dark-haired guy named Everett, one of the new hires. Everett had pale skin and brown eyes. He was new in town, but the warm way he and Logan were talking to each other made it clear they'd already become good friends.

"Hey," Alex said, walking up. "What're you doing here?"

Logan smiled at Alex. "Oh, hey. I came by to see if you wanna hang out. You're off soon, right?"

Alex shook his head. "I took an extra-long break and just got back, so I'll be working way late. And if I'm lucky, you'll be helping me out. Right? Right."

Everett laughed. "Nice friend you got here."

Logan rolled his eyes. "As hard as it is to believe, Alex rarely gets free labor out of me, but I'll make an exception today. See ya around, Ev."

Everett waved goodbye as Logan followed Alex over to his mom.

"Okay, boys, listen. We'll be out of tape and packing material in the next day or two." She handed a set of keys and a credit card to Alex. "I need you to go down to the store and pick up enough to last until the end of the week. They might not have enough, but get what you can. Kent will kill me for cleaning out his stock, I'm sure."

Alex nodded, making a mental note to steer clear of Kent, the store manager. "Sure, we'll be back in a few."

"Make sure that's a few *minutes* and not a few *hours*!" she yelled as they headed for one of the exits.

"We're not gonna be just a few minutes, right?" Logan asked as Alex pushed open the door to the side parking lot.

"Unfortunately, we have to. I helped Mr. Barringer out today at rehearsal, and my mom's pissed I was gone so long." He went to the passenger side of his parents' chocolate brown Buick LeSabre. The thing was fifteen years old, but in perfect condition. If his dad did anything well, it was take care of the car. It was the only regular car they owned, and it probably wouldn't die until the year 2020.

"So," Logan said, settling into the passenger seat. "Where to first?"

"The store, you idiot. Then back here. I have to be responsible."

Logan sighed. "Fine, fine."

Alex drove in silence for a few minutes. "So," he finally said. "You've made friends with Everett?"

Logan kept his eyes out his window. "Yeah. He was in front of me at Subway and the line was really slow, so we started talking. The three of us should hang out before I leave town. He said he loves pizza."

"I'm all for pizza."

Logan smiled. "How's your dad doing? Your mom mentioned something about you guys hiring someone to help him?"

"He's been fine the past few days. Great, actually, but yeah, hiring someone was my idea. Well, it was someone else's idea. I just took her advice."

"Whose advice?"

Alex chewed on his bottom lip. He hadn't seen Logan since the night they'd gone clubbing in Boise. He'd been wondering since then if he should tell Logan what was going on. He wanted to. He was dying to, but he'd kept Ina a secret for so long, it almost felt wrong to tell anyone about her.

"Spill it," Logan demanded.

That was all the prodding Alex needed. He took a deep breath as he pulled into the general store parking lot. He found a spot for the car and killed the engine, keeping his hands on the steering wheel as he told his story about Ina. He started with the email address on the ten-dollar bill and finished with the email he'd sent four days ago. He didn't go too far into detail about his feelings for her. He wasn't even sure what they were at this point.

"So that's it," he said. "She hasn't called back, and I have no idea where she is or what to do. I mean, what *can* I do?"

Logan had been staring out the windshield the whole time, but now he was looking Alex in the eyes. "Are you seriously thinking about going to see her for a week?" he asked. "Because that would be epic. I mean, I might as well go with you, right?"

Alex nodded. "That's kind of what I was hoping, yeah. But I haven't heard back from her. We started making plans and agreed on everything except what day."

Logan tapped his fingers on the car door. "And you haven't heard from her in four days?"

Alex nodded. "What if she's in real trouble with this Jake guy?"

"I don't know, man. This is a weird situation."

"You're telling me." Alex pulled the keys from the ignition and opened his door. "Let's get my mom's stuff out of the way. Maybe we can stop by your house and I can check my email? I haven't checked since this morning. Our modem isn't working."

Logan smiled as he got out of the car. "Yeah, sure. I'm kind of dying to see if she's emailed you back."

# Seventeen

From: Ina <ina.artgirl1979@hotmail.com>
To: Alex Winzelberg <winzwarehouse5@hotmail.com>
Date: June 23, 1999
Subject: Can't wait to see you

I'm so excited to see you, Mr. Winzelberg! I want to tell you my real name so things are even between us when we meet in person. Here we go. Ina is short for Sabrina. Sabrina Mae Sanchez. Just don't ever call me Sabrina, okay?

Now do you believe how excited I am about meeting you? I'll see you tomorrow afternoon. Wait around for me, okay? You'd better be there. If not, let me know, but I hope, hope, hope you are.

Peace out.

P.S. I think this is the only way to get away from Jake. I'm counting on you.

# Eighteen

"Whoa," Logan said after he read Ina's email. "I'm confused. She's talking like you've booked a flight already."

"I haven't booked anything," Alex answered, leaning back in his chair. "I'm just as confused as you are."

They were in Logan's bedroom at his desk. Ina's email stared back at them from the desktop computer. Her message was weird, to say the least.

"Why does she think you're flying there tomorrow if you never picked a date?" Logan asked.

Alex shook his head. "I told her you were moving out there the end of this week and I could try to get on your flight, but I didn't say anything was definite. I was gonna come over tonight after work and have you help me, and then tell her when I was coming. But how can I not show up tomorrow? She says it'll help her get rid of Jake."

"How?" Logan asked. "This girl, she's kinda . . . I don't know."

"Wacky?" Alex offered. "You have no idea. I kind of like that about her, though."

"Do you want to try and call her again?"

Alex grabbed the cordless phone sitting on Logan's desk. "I guess it couldn't hurt, but I doubt she's there."

"Then leave her a message."

"Yeah, okay." He dialed Ina's number as fast as he could, realizing that he had it memorized. It rang three times.

"Hello?"

Alex almost dropped the phone. "Ina?" he gasped. "It's Alex."

"This is Ina's roommate."

"Oh, hi. Do you know when Ina will be back or how I can get a hold of her? This is really important."

The roommate let out a grunt. "Nice try, *Jake*. You're not gonna find her, okay? She's not here, so don't even think about buzzing the apartment again. Or calling. Or anything! I'll call the cops."

The line went dead and Alex pulled the receiver away from his ear and stared at it. "Her roommate thinks I'm Jake. I guess he's been trying to find her there."

Logan walked over to his bed and sat down. His room was still full of old Godzilla posters and Pokémon figurines, and Alex wondered if he was leaving them all behind.

"I know you want to help her," Logan said, giving Alex a worried look, "but tomorrow is like . . . *tomorrow*."

Alex realized what he was facing. He had to meet Ina, which meant he had to buy a plane ticket and actually get on the plane. Then he had to figure out how to get to Jackson Heights. Then he had to ride a subway. With people on it. A lot of people. And he had no idea how to navigate any of that. There were too many things he couldn't anticipate. He'd convinced himself he was ready, but he really wasn't.

"Dude, chill out! You look like you're about to implode." Logan sighed. "I'll help you figure this out. The question is can we get plane tickets that will get us there by tomorrow?"

Alex's mouth dropped open. "You're really going with me?"

Leaning back on his hands, Logan laughed. "There's no way you can do this on your own, man. Of course I'm going with you. It'll just mean I leave a day early. I'll call right now and change my flight and get you on the same one. Shouldn't be a problem."

"Really?" Alex's throat felt tight.

Logan shrugged. "Anything for you, man."

Alex swiveled in the desk chair and tossed the cordless phone to Logan. "Here you go, then."

Logan caught the phone. "How are you gonna pay for this?" he asked. "Do you have a debit card? I had to use Mom's credit card to buy my ticket, but there's no way she'd let you use it."

Alex drummed his fingers on the desk. "I have money, but I've never bothered getting a debit card. I always carry cash."

Logan looked down at Alex's pockets. "Didn't your mom give you a credit card? Use that and pay her back later."

"Oh, right." Alex dug the WFS credit card out of his wallet. His mom was going to murder him. Literally. She was going to see the charge on her account and she was going to shove a knife through his throat. Of course, he'd leave her the money in cash before he left. He'd write a note to go with it, because there was no way she or his dad could know he was leaving until after he was gone. They would probably tie him to a chair to keep him from going.

Logan was already dialing the airline. In a few minutes, he'd booked Alex's flight and changed his own. They were even going to be able to sit next to each other. Finally, Logan hung up the phone and handed Alex his mom's credit card. "They sent the tickets to my email," he said, motioning for Alex to move out of the desk chair. "I'll print 'em out. Hella cool, right?"

A few minutes later, he'd printed out the tickets and handed Alex his. It almost didn't look legitimate, but there was a barcode and official-looking numbers, so Alex hoped it was okay. He folded it up and shoved it into his wallet.

"How are we getting to the airport?" he asked. "We don't have a car."

Logan tapped his chin and then smiled. "Raven."

Alex nodded. "Sure, call her and ask. Make sure she doesn't tell her mom, though. Will your parents care you're leaving early?"

Logan laughed. "Hell no, they won't care. I'll tell Will, and he can tell them after I'm gone."

"My parents are gonna freak," Alex sighed. "Like, I hope this doesn't trigger my dad. I'd never forgive myself."

"He'll be fine," Logan said, clapping Alex on the back. "Leave them a note and make sure they know you're not leaving for good."

"I plan to."

Logan headed for his door. "I'm gonna go talk to Will. Be back in a sec."

"Okay."

Alex leaned back in his chair and closed his eyes. He was going to be in so much trouble, but maybe this was how he needed to do this—quick and sudden so he couldn't back out. Leave it to Ina to push him into it. Maybe that had been her plan all along.

* * *

"Where have you been?" Alex's mom snapped as soon as he entered the warehouse from the same door he and Logan had exited almost three hours earlier. "It shouldn't take all afternoon to get supplies. I told you to be fast."

Alex handed her the keys to the Buick and tried not to notice her wild hair and frantic eyes. If she found out what he had been doing, she would freak. "I told you, Mom, Logan and I needed to hang out before he leaves," he muttered. "He *is* my best friend. Plus, you haven't given me a day off in a week."

"A day off?" she growled, ripping the keys from his hand. "Your father is hallucinating right now as we speak, and you weren't here to help me! I had to call Dr. Huang, but he isn't here yet." She put both hands to her head, the keys still gripped in her fingers. "Why does this keep happening? The meds aren't working at all and I don't know . . . I don't know what to do. He's in his bedroom. Maria's up there with him because I had to handle things down here. We've got five trucks to get out, and the modem won't connect to the web, and I just read an article in the newspaper about this Y2K thing and how it might crash all of our computers, and I just . . . I can't deal with all of this." She glared at him, as if all of these things were his fault.

Alex tensed as a slew of emotions slammed into him. He felt guilty and frustrated, but he was also angry—angrier than he'd been in a long time. He was angry that his father was hallucinating *again,* and he was angry that his mother hadn't bothered calling any of the people on the list he'd given her, and he was angry at himself for planning to leave early in the morning without telling anyone. His mother was going to fall apart and it would all be his fault. She did not need one more thing on her plate to worry about. He calmed himself before opening his mouth, forcing his voice to remain steady.

"Listen, Mom, I'll try to get the modem working again, okay? Have Everett or someone else in packaging go out to the Buick to get all the supplies from the trunk. Dr. Huang will be here soon, and then Maria can come back down to keep things going. None of us can do anything about Y2K. Other than that, what else do you need?"

"I–I don't know. I'm sorry, Alex. It's your father, that's all. I'm worried."

"He'll be fine. I'll go check on him, okay?"

She nodded, her expression turning blank. "Okay, thank you."

Alex pulled her into a tight hug. His heart felt like it would tear into pieces. He couldn't leave her. She needed him too much. He would have to tell Logan he was staying. He would have to send Ina an email and tell her he wasn't going to meet her. But how could he disappoint her like that? She needed him too.

He had no idea what he was going to do.

"I'm sorry, Mom," he said as she held on to him. "I'm sorry I was gone so long. I'll fix things, okay?"

She nodded and pulled away. "I gotta go prep another truck, and Larriatte is expecting me to call them back."

Alex watched her walk away and then pulled out the thick bank envelop he'd shoved into his back pocket. It was filled with cash. He'd stopped by the bank and withdrawn enough for his ticket and a week in New York. Feeling the cash in his hand made his stomach churn. He'd already bought a ticket. Ina was counting on him.

Still, family mattered more.

Didn't it?

Steeling himself, he pushed the cash back into his pocket and walked upstairs to his parents' bedroom. The door was open. Maria was sitting on the floor with her back to the door, legs crossed, as Alex's father stood facing the window on the other side of the room.

"You are not a bad father," Maria said gently. "Stop blaming yourself for everything you think is wrong. Nothing is wrong."

"*I* am wrong," he muttered, clasping his hands behind his back. "I'm supposed to be the protector. I'm supposed to be the provider. I'm none of those things. I'm nothing but a burden to them."

Alex stood motionless as he realized his father was no longer hallucinating. That was a good thing, at least, but he didn't necessarily want to interrupt whatever serious conversation was going on between him and Maria.

"Everyone can be a burden in some way," Maria said after a long pause. "Treating yourself like a burden is the problem. You need to stop doing that. Let your family take care of you. Tell them how much you appreciate it. Tell them—"

"I do tell them that!" he shouted, spinning around to face Maria. "I tell Alex all the time how much I appreciate him, how much I need him! And now all he wants to do is—" He caught sight of Alex standing in the doorway. All the anger drained from his face. "How long have you been standing there?" he asked.

Maria twisted around to look at Alex. "Hello, Mr. Winzelberg," she said, sounding thoroughly unsurprised at his presence.

"Hi, Maria." He reached down to help her up. "Thanks for helping out. I'll finish up in here. My mom needs you downstairs."

"Of course. Have a good night, you two." She let Alex pull her up and left the room.

"Are you okay?" Alex asked when she was gone. "How bad was it this time?"

"It's a hazy mess in my head. I was helping your mother with an order and then she was crying and talking about a jar of pickles and I couldn't figure out why." He kept shaking his head, his eyes filling with tears. "I'm sorry, Alex. I'm sorry I'm ruining your life."

Alex crossed the room to his dad. "Dad, don't be sorry. It's not your fault your brain does weird stuff. And you're not ruining my life."

His dad stood stiff as a board. "But I am. I'm stopping you from going to New York."

Alex's breath caught in his throat. How did his dad know about his plans? Then he realized he meant going to New York for school, not Ina. His dad didn't even know Ina existed.

"It's okay. I'll go in a year. It's fine."

"No, it isn't. I want you to go now." He fixed his eyes on Alex. "I don't want to be a burden. You have a life to live. I've been thinking a lot about this. We talked about it in my therapy group. I want to do something for you. I want to be a good father."

Alex looked down at the carpet. "Well, Dad, if you really feel that way," he said, stepping closer, "I'm wondering . . ."

His voice faded as he realized what he was about to do. Maybe it would be okay if he left for a week. Hearing his father give him permission to leave opened up a door he hadn't even known existed.

"What are you wondering, son?"

"Can you keep a secret from Mom? Until tomorrow?"

His dad narrowed his eyes. "I suppose so. What is it?"

Alex knew how terribly this could backfire, but it felt like the right time to talk to his dad about it. "Would you be okay if I left just for a week? I won't move out for an entire year after that. I think Mom will be happier if I give her at least a year."

His dad blinked, clearly caught off guard. But he didn't look angry. "Where?" he asked, cocking his head. "To New York?"

"Yes, just to meet some of the people at the school. It'll help me keep my scholarship. You can tell Mom in the morning when she wakes up. I'll already be gone so she can't try to stop me. Raven will take me and Logan to the airport. I have money. I have everything figured out, and Logan's been there before and . . ."

His dad lifted a hand, cutting him off. "I understand. It's a small vacation, right? You deserve that."

Alex realized how fast his heart was beating. And loud! He almost hadn't heard his father's words. They sank into his brain one at a time. "It's only for a few days. And I'll call you every day."

"You'd better. You do realize your mother is going to kill you when you get back—if she doesn't die of worry before that."

Laughing, Alex rolled his eyes. "I'll write her a note and leave it on my desk."

"Okay."

Alex felt his heart slowing to a normal rhythm. He had taken a chance and it hadn't backfired. Maybe that meant everything was going to turn out okay with Ina, too. He could hope, anyway. He hadn't told his father the entire truth, but it was too complicated to get into now, and he figured it wouldn't matter in the long run. "We'd better both go down to help Mom, if you feel up to it," he said, nodding toward the door.

"Sometimes I think she's too uptight for her own good," his dad said, following Alex out of the room. "I'd blame myself, but you keep telling me not to do that, and now Maria's lecturing me about not acting like a burden. A man can't catch a break."

Alex laughed. "Everyone has issues. I guess some are just more obvious than others. You got unlucky with that."

His dad shook his head. "Maybe," he said, patting Alex on the back. "Maybe."

# Nineteen

Alex gripped the armrests of his seat as the airplane started moving down the tarmac. He knew the laws of physics would allow the plane to get in the air, but he couldn't quite wrap his head around it. The plane was huge. It weighed hundreds of thousands of pounds. How could it possibly get airborne? And once it was airborne, what would stop it from crashing?

"Dude," Logan said. "All we're doing is taxiing to the runway. You okay?"

Alex let out a little gasp and looked down at his hands. His knuckles were pure white. Slowly, he forced himself to let go of the armrests and put his hands on his knees. He'd had an extremely stressful morning: from sneaking out of his house, to Raven's speeding all the way to Boise to get them to the airport on time, to checking Logan's luggage and finding the right gate. He'd been half convinced his printed ticket was fake right up until the ticket agent had handed him a boarding pass. He was a complete wreck. No wonder he'd never flown before. Deep down, he'd known it would freak the hell out of him.

"I'm sorry," he whispered under his breath, keenly aware of the total stranger sitting in their row. She was by the window, Logan was in the middle, and Alex was next to the aisle.

"Lots of people are afraid to fly," Logan said way too loudly for Alex's liking. "Don't be sorry."

Alex shot him a death glare. "Shut up," he hissed. "I'm not afraid."

"You are too."

The plane jolted as it came to a stop at the runway, making Alex grip the armrests again. "Okay, fine," he gasped through shallow breaths. "I'm freaked out we're gonna die. I mean, I know the chances of us dying are next to nothing, but that doesn't matter. You know how it is when I get like this. Remember that rollercoaster at Silverwood when we were ten?"

Logan pulled a sour face. "The one where you threw up all over me?" He reached forward and grabbed a puke bag from the pocket of the seat in front of him. He tossed it into Alex's lap. "Seriously, do not do that again."

"I won't!"

"Is it flying or seeing Ina that's got you so freaked?"

Alex swallowed a lump in his throat. "I haven't even thought about Ina," he laughed dryly. "But thanks for the reminder. I hope she's read the email I sent her."

Logan shrugged and gave Alex a sympathetic look. "I'm sure she has, and I'll find a way to check your email when we get into Queens."

Alex nodded. "Okay, yeah." He could only hope Ina replied to the email he'd sent a few hours ago. He'd asked her to send him better instructions on where to meet and told her what he would be wearing so she could spot him. He at least knew she'd be in her denim jacket and red shoes.

"Chill," Logan said. "I'll make sure you survive to see her. Right now let's just get through takeoff."

A flight attendant at the front of the cabin started giving a safety presentation. As the man droned on about oxygen masks and flotation devices, Alex involuntarily started picturing worst-case scenarios. Finally, the plane started moving forward, and a few minutes after that Alex was squeezing his eyes shut as the force of the plane's take-off pressed him into the back of his seat.

"It's okay," Logan said over the loud whoosh and whine of the engines as the plane lifted into the air. "The worst is almost over."

Alex nodded. He hated the fear screaming inside of him. Logan was the only person in his life he didn't have to try to hide this part of himself from.

"See?" Logan said as the plane finally leveled out and the fasten-seatbelt sign turned off. "Just like we're on the ground."

Alex kept his seatbelt tightly fastened as the sound of buckles releasing echoed through the cabin. "It does *not* feel like we're on the ground," he whispered. He couldn't describe what he was feeling. It was almost a floating sensation, but maybe that was because he knew he was in the air.

"Well, we're safe, and we'll be there in six hours."

"Six hours feels like forever right now." Alex stared straight ahead and tried to ignore the clouds moving past the windows. "I don't know, Logan. I don't—"

"What are you gonna do?" Logan sighed. "Ask them to land the plane? You don't have a choice. I know you're freaked, but you've gotta get a grip. Here." He grabbed his headphones from around his neck and handed them to Alex. "Let me get my player and CDs. Just a sec."

Alex stared at the headphones in his hands. Logan was right. He needed to calm down, or as Ina would say, *man up*. Nobody else on the plane seemed to be freaking out, plus he was pretty sure a load of experiences scarier than flying were in his near future.

Logan got his CD player out of his bag and handed it to Alex, who took it and set it in his lap. He hadn't thought to bring his player.

"Listen to some Pantera," Logan said. "Or I've got Tool or Primus or Metallica or . . ." He unzipped his compact CD case. "Whatever you want."

Alex took the CD case and started flipping through the sleeves. He stopped on Radiohead's *The Bends*. He remembered Ina telling him she had that CD, way back when they had first started emailing each other. Listening to it now seemed appropriate. He slipped it out of the sleeve and popped it into the player. A few minutes later, he'd almost forgotten he was sitting on a plane, flying thousands of feet above the earth. The music definitely took the edge off.

Six hours was still going to be a long time.

* * *

Alex couldn't tell if the gray blanket covering New York was smog or low-hanging clouds. The water was gray. The sky was gray. The city was gray. But unlike Idaho in gloomy weather, it didn't feel depressing. From the tiny windows of the plane, it looked like a moody scene from an old noir film.

Taking a deep breath, Alex shouldered the only piece of luggage he'd brought—his backpack, and followed Logan through the airport. They waited at the baggage claim for Logan's luggage, stopped at a vending machine to purchase MetroCards, and then boarded a bus bound for the Jackson Heights station twenty minutes away.

"When were you here last?" Alex asked Logan as they pushed their way through the throng looking for a place to sit down with their suitcases and bags. Alex tried to keep his breathing normal. Being crammed into such a tight space always made him want to run. Feeling trapped on the plane for six hours had only made it worse.

"Maybe eight or nine years ago?" Logan answered, pointing to an empty bench seat at the back of the bus. "That was when my cousins lived here."

Alex warily eyed the empty seat as they approached. The blue plastic looked dirtier than anything he had ever sat on in his life. He sat down with a grimace and hefted one of Logan's big duffle bags onto his lap.

"Like, they didn't even have this MetroCard thingy back then," Logan said, holding up the blue and yellow card. "There were tokens. This is way easier."

Alex let out a long breath as the bus began to move forward. "I'm impressed," he said.

"With what?"

"With how chill you are. Like, you knew exactly where to go and what to do as soon as we got off the plane. I'd still be lost in the airport."

Logan laughed. "I just followed the signs, dude. And my mom told me about the MetroCard." He got a far-away look in his eyes. "I didn't tell you about that, did I?"

"About what?"

"Mom stopped me on my way out the door this morning. She gave me a hug and a bunch of cash and started spouting all this advice about living in New York." He laughed again. "It was hella weird. After all this time hating on me, *now* she wants to act like a mom? Maybe she's just happy to get rid of me."

"I'm sure she'll miss you," Alex sighed. "Your dad will too."

"Yeah, well, he wasn't there with Mom this morning, was he? Anyway, I'm not regretting leaving or anything. It was just weird."

Alex nodded. "I had my own weird experience last night." He recounted what had happened with his father, and Logan's eyes widened.

"Seriously? He didn't tell your mom?"

"Not as far as I know. They were still asleep when I left."

"Nice, well, we'll call them later today so your mom doesn't freak out too much. I want to get a cell phone once we're in Queens."

"Movin' up in the world," Alex laughed. "You're not wasting a second, are you?"

Logan stretched his arms behind his head and looked up at the ceiling. "Nope. I've been planning this for years."

Alex smiled and looked out the window at the passing city. It was still gray. Rain drizzled against the glass.

A few minutes later the bus exited the freeway and passengers started picking up their bags, looking eager to get off. It was still a few more minutes before the bus pulled into a terminal connected to the subway station. Alex looked around, noting the streets lined with red and brown brick buildings covered with colorful signs, the people on the sidewalks, the light traffic. It wasn't what Alex had pictured at all. To him, New York was tall Manhattan skyscrapers, bridges, graffiti, and taxicabs. This felt entirely different. It felt smaller, like a mini-city with a lot of stuff crammed inside it. Still, it was just as gritty and dirty as he had imagined.

The bus pulled into a cream-colored depot station built in an Art Deco style. Other buses were pulling in and out, the sound of their screeching brakes echoing off the walls. The bus lurched to a stop and most everyone exited, disbursing every which way onto the streets surrounding the station or into the area housing the subway lines. Small shops were tucked into every corner. Some looked like they had been permanently closed up.

Alex followed Logan off the bus and into the station. They descended some stairs and stopped as Logan looked around. Alex inched closer to him as people crisscrossed all around. An intimidating line of turnstiles and barred doors stood in front of them, granting access to the subway lines. Beyond that, Alex could see some stained concrete stairs leading up to the elevated lines and down to the underground lines.

"Should we go in or stay here?" Alex asked. "We can get in with our MetroCards, right?"

Logan nodded. "Yeah, but why would Ina wait for you in there? I'd think this is where she'd try to find you, or maybe up where all of the buses are."

They made their way back up to the bus terminal. The only benches they could see were occupied, and the rest of the space was full of shops, people, and dirty walls. Alex looked at his watch. It was 2:30 in the afternoon. All Ina had said in her email was that she would meet him later in the day, whatever that meant.

"I wish there was a way to check my email," Alex muttered. "She might have sent directions where to meet her."

Logan shrugged and started walking. Alex followed him to an empty stretch of wall, out of the way of the foot traffic. They dropped their bags, and then Alex moved away from the wall when his elbow hit a piece of old, hardened gum.

"Stay here and watch for her," Logan suggested. "Would you freak if I left for a while? I want to go buy a phone, and maybe I can find a way to check your email."

Alex's heart thumped at the thought of staying at the station alone. "I–I'll be fine as long as you're back in a few hours," he stuttered. "If Ina gets here, we'll wait for you to get back."

"Sounds good." Logan took off his backpack and pulled out a pen and some paper. "Write down your email stuff so I can check it if I find a computer."

Alex wrote down his login information and handed back the paper. "Thanks. Um, good luck?"

Logan flashed him a smile. "You too." He waved good-bye and walked away. He was dressed in ripped jeans, a fitted white T-shirt, and a denim jacket, average and plain, but he also looked confident. His blond hair was styled just so, and Alex realized his friend already belonged here.

"Not me," Alex sighed, and sat down on one of the duffle bags. He adjusted his baseball cap and started looking at every single person walking in and out of the area. The station was not one big open space. It went around several corners leading to places he couldn't see, so he had no idea how Ina was going to find him. Still, nobody else was wearing a red Anniston High School baseball cap. He had figured it was unique enough that Ina should be able to spot him. He hoped he'd be able to spot her. He'd already seen two women with curly hair and denim jackets, but neither was wearing red shoes.

His stomach growled, and he looked down at it, annoyed. He'd eaten on the plane, but that felt like hours ago. He couldn't leave to find something to eat now, and the smell of food drifting from a nearby café was starting to feel like torture.

He'd just have to wait.

# Twenty

From: Alex Winzelberg <winzwarehouse5@hotmail.com>
To: Ina <ina.artgirl1979@hotmail.com>
Date: June 24, 1999
Subject: I'm on my way

I'm excited to meet you too! I got a ticket and I'm leaving here in a few minutes to get to the airport. I've never flown anywhere in my life. I'm scared out of my mind. You and Logan are the only two people I'd ever admit that to. I've never told you this, but I get scared over the dumbest things. I've mostly learned how to hide it because it's embarrassing.

Anyway, do you think you can send me an email with details where to meet at the subway station? I'm confused because I don't remember deciding anything with you about meeting today, and you never told me where exactly to meet you at the station, either. If I don't hear from you, let's meet in whatever space is the largest, maybe? I'll be wearing a red Anniston High School baseball cap and a white T-shirt. If you can't find me at the station, can you send me your address? I tried to call you yesterday and your roommate hung up on me. She thought I was Jake.

I don't know how much I can help with Jake when I get there, but I promise I'll do what I can. Logan is coming with me and he can be a badass, so that could be helpful? I'm not sure what you meant when you said this is your only way to get away from Jake?

I have a lot of questions, obviously.

Stay safe, Ina. I can't wait to see you.

# Twenty-One



Ina stared at Alex's email, her stomach dropping to the floor. She was sitting in an airport café, amazed she'd found a place to connect to the internet. Boise was small and seemed behind on their technology.

Ina read the email again, not sure if she was seeing what was right in front of her. This couldn't be happening.

Alex was flying to New York. He was probably already there.

He was going to wait for her.

And she was in Idaho.

How had this happened? She had talked to him on the phone yesterday. She had told him about changing her mind and coming out there instead of making him fly to New York. It was the best way to escape Jake. It was perfect. He had told her okay. He had sounded excited.

She couldn't remember much of the conversation beyond that. Had she talked to someone else? Her heart pounded in her throat. Was Jake involved in this somehow? She closed her laptop and looked around, frantic.

The airport seemed empty compared to LaGuardia. Jake wasn't anywhere in sight. She had to calm down. Jake couldn't have followed her here. She had done everything she could to get him off her tail. She had gone from one hotel to another. She had paid for everything in cash. She hadn't called her apartment, or Philippe, or anyone aside from Alex. But wherever she went, somehow Jake always found her. She'd seen him out of the corner of her eye in hotel lobbies and crowded intersections, and it was a miracle she'd managed to get away each time. One morning, on her way out of a Starbucks café, she'd spotted him reading a newspaper across the street. If he had looked up in that moment, she would have been screwed. That was when she had decided leaving the state was the best idea.

She had thought it would all work out. She would meet Alex in Idaho and maybe he'd go back to New York with her. It was where he wanted to be, anyway. Or maybe she'd stay in Idaho. She didn't know yet.

But now everything had changed. She had to get back to New York. *Now.* She slipped her laptop into her backpack, grabbed her suitcase, and found an information desk where a tall woman with gray hair offered to look up the flight schedule for her.

"Nothing until tomorrow evening," she said in a nasally voice. "There's a 7:43 flight into JFK and a red-eye into LaGuardia. Do you want me to book one of those for you?"

Ina looked down at her suitcase and imagined Alex waiting in the subway station. There was no way he'd wait all day tomorrow and into the next day. She had to think of something else.

"No thanks," she said, and picked up her suitcase. She was making her way back to the café when she saw a row of pay phones along a wall. She rushed to a phone and dug some quarters out of her pocket. A minute later she was dialing her apartment number. Emily was most likely at work, but she usually checked the messages when she got home.

The machine picked up and Ina was surprised when Emily's voice started speaking instead of her own: *"Hey, this is Emily. Leave a message at the tone. Oh, and if you're looking for Ina, she's not here. Stop calling."*

Whoa. That made Ina sick to her stomach. Jake really wasn't giving up.

The machine beeped and Ina stuttered out her message, knowing she only had so much time before her quarters ran out. "Hey, Em, it's me. There's this guy, Alex, waiting for me at the subway station. He's wearing a red Anniston High baseball cap and a white shirt and it's super important you go down there and tell him I can't meet him. Tell him to call this payphone number. It's a phone in the Boise airport. I'll wait here, and if I don't answer, tell him to call again. Please don't tell anyone except him that I'm in Idaho. Alex is expecting me to meet him there and he's not gonna have a clue. Let him use our phone if he needs to. Thanks, Em. I miss you. Here's the number."

Ina recited the number listed on the payphone and hung up, realizing her heart was beating a million miles an hour. It was almost 3:00 in New York. Emily would be home in a few hours. Alex would wait at least until this evening. Right?

All she could do now was wait for Alex to call. First she'd send him an email just in case he was able to get online and check. She rolled her eyes. Things would be a lot easier if they both had cell phones. That was definitely on her list of things to buy in the near future.

# Twenty-Two

From: Ina <ina.artgirl1979@hotmail.com>
To: Alex Winzelberg <winzwarehouse5@hotmail.com>
Date: June 24, 1999
Subject: HUGE MIXUP!

If you somehow get to check your email, I'm in Idaho. I'm confused too. We talked to each other yesterday, don't you remember? I told you I was flying here to see you. Maybe I talked to someone else and they were pranking me? I have no idea. Is there anyone who would do that at your warehouse?

Anyway, I'm in the Boise airport right now. I'll wait by this payphone until you call. I keep thinking about you sitting there at the station waiting for me. Hopefully by the time you read this, my roommate Emily has found you and we've already talked to each other on the phone. She gets off work at 5:00, so it'll probably be around 6:00 by the time she makes it down there. I'm going to wait to book a flight back out there since I'm not sure what's going to happen from here. I'm mostly writing all of this to you to make myself feel better, but if Emily still hasn't found you, the number is (208) 555-0143. I feel awful. I'm so sorry. You've probably spent a lot of money to get out there and I'm not even there.

I still can't wait to meet you. I hope you call soon.

# Twenty-Three

## Alex

Alex read Ina's email for the third time. Logan had printed it out for him at an internet café down the street. He had then rushed into the station and pushed the paper into Alex's hands, apologizing for taking so long. He'd decided to open a bank account and then stopped for something to eat before buying a phone, and it had taken longer than he'd anticipated.

"She's in Idaho," Alex said flatly. He took a step back, bumping into the wall behind him, right into the gum again. He pulled away, disgusted. His back hurt. He was hungry and tired and thirsty, but he hadn't dared move from his spot. He'd been waiting there for three hours now.

"She says she talked to you on the phone," Logan said, looking just as confused as Alex. "So unless you're losing your mind—" He cleared his throat. "Sorry, but unless you're seriously losing it, someone obviously talked to her and pretended to be you."

Alex blinked. His stomach growled again for the hundredth time that afternoon as he crumpled Ina's email in his hand. "Who would do that?"

"Maybe your dad? You have similar voices."

Alex shook his head. "No, he wouldn't do that. He . . ."

Then Alex realized it was entirely possibly that his father could have answered the phone in the middle of one of his episodes. Not likely, but possible.

"Well, I have to call her," Alex said. "Her roommate hasn't shown up either, but it's only 5:30 and Ina said 6:00." He turned in a circle, his mind whirling. "Where's a phone? I gotta call her. I gotta—"

"Dude, chill out. You can use my cell phone!" With a flourish, Logan pulled a phone from his pocket. "They set it up for me at the store. The battery's even charged."

Alex's stomach growled again, this time loud enough that Logan could apparently hear it over all the noise of the station. Everything echoed here: squealing brakes, footsteps, conversations, crying children, honking horns, the *click-snick-clicks* of the turnstiles down the stairs. After listening to all of it for three hours, Alex wanted to cover his ears.

"C'mon," Logan said, motioning for Alex to follow him. "I'm gonna take you someplace quiet where you can eat something and call Ina. I'll come back here and wait for Emily." He swiped the hat off Alex's head and pushed it onto his own head.

Gathering up both duffle bags, Alex followed Logan out of the concourse, to a crosswalk, and down the road to a two-story building covered in signs. Apparently, it was a law office/barber shop/taco shop. Logan pushed open the door advertising tacos, and yanked Alex inside. He led him to a quiet table in a back corner and handed him his new phone. "Go ahead and call her. Don't talk too long, though, 'cause I only have five hundred minutes for the month. I'm gonna order you some tacos. Come find me at the station when you're done."

Alex nodded as he dumped the duffle bags onto an empty chair that looked just as dirty as the concrete at the bus terminal. He was too overwhelmed to respond verbally to Logan, and Logan knew it. In fact, Logan knew him so well that he was doing exactly what needed to be done so Alex didn't have a complete breakdown. He swore to himself that he'd repay Logan someday. Somehow.

As soon as Logan left, Alex examined the phone in his hand. It was a flip-phone. Nobody in the family had one. April and Aaron couldn't afford it, and his parents couldn't see the point of a cell phone when they practically never left the warehouse.

Alex opened the phone, unfolded the crumpled email still in his hand, and punched in the number Ina had given him.

It rang once.

"Hello?"

"Ina?"

"Alex! Is it you?"

"Yeah, hi! I'm so glad you answered!"

They sat in silence for a few seconds. Alex wasn't sure what to say. Ina's voice was light and airy. She sounded nice.

"I'm so sorry," she blurted. "So, so sorry. I don't know how this happened."

"I don't either. I'm guessing it was my dad you talked to on the phone."

"Oh, because he's . . . you mean he was maybe . . ."

"Yeah, maybe he was delusional at the time. I mean that in all seriousness."

There was a pause. "I'm sorry, Alex."

Alex dug his fingernail into a little hole on the Formica table. "Hey, it's fine. Logan found an internet café and printed out your email for me."

"Oh! So Emily hasn't shown up yet?"

"Not to my knowledge. I'm at a taco shop getting some food, but Logan's there wearing my hat so she'll be able to find him. At least, I hope she can find him. That place is kinda . . ."

"A dirty mess?" Ina laughed. "Yeah, I heard they're gonna tear it down and rebuild it in a few years. Where's Logan waiting?"

"By a café near where the buses come in."

"Maybe I should call her and tell her not to bother since you got the email," Ina said. "But maybe I should . . . maybe she could . . ."

She stopped and silence filled the line again.

"Are you okay?" Alex asked. "I'm sorry you had to wait there forever."

"Oh, I'm fine. I'm sorry you had to wait *there* forever!"

They both laughed, and it finally hit Alex that he was *talking to Ina*. After emailing her for so long, he knew her, and yet he didn't know her. It was a strange feeling.

"What're we gonna do?" Ina asked. "Did you already book a return flight?"

"Yeah, but it's not leaving until next Thursday."

"You're staying a whole week?"

"Well, yeah, I wanted to spend some time with you, like you said. Me and Logan got a hotel room for the week, and he's gonna try to find an apartment since he's moving here. He got into a school in Brooklyn."

"Oh, cool."

Another long pause.

"I don't know what to do," Alex said just as a waitress with a long blond ponytail came to his table and set down a basket filled with three tacos. Alex's stomach growled as he looked down at the food. Corn tortillas, fried strips of beef, and some sort of red pickled vegetable.

"Well," Ina drawled across the line, "I don't know . . . maybe I should just buy a—"

"Go to my place," Alex said quickly. He'd spoken without thinking. Did he want Ina meeting his father? What if she saw him having a hallucination? What would she think?

"Really?" Ina asked, breaking his train of thought.

"Y–yeah," he stuttered, thinking on his toes. It would be good, he realized. Ina would be safe there. Safer than here. "I'll call my parents and tell them what's going on. Stay with them and I'll find an earlier flight back. Maybe you can see some cows."

Ina laughed so loudly Alex had to pull the phone away from his ear. "You're hilarious, Alex Winzelberg. But seriously, won't your parents think this is weird?"

Alex cradled the phone against his shoulder and picked up a taco. "Of course they'll think it's weird," he said. "But who cares?" He took a huge bite. Some of the meat fell into the basket. He chewed as fast as he could. He wanted to say more, but Ina beat him.

"Um, I care. It was one thing when I thought you'd be there, but now you're not and—"

Alex swallowed. "They will love you, I promise. Listen, I'm gonna call them as soon as I'm off the phone with you. I'll have my mom pick you up from the airport. It'll be fine. I'll call you back at this number as soon as I know details. Can you wait there for a little bit longer?"

"Sure, I guess so."

Alex set down the taco. "You okay?"

"Yeah, yeah, I'm just nervous, that's all. It's so clean and quiet and empty here. I feel exposed."

Alex looked out a nearby window at the street. The city was pretty in its own way, but it was so unfamiliar. Two Indian women walked by, dressed in bright orange saris.

In Idaho, those would attract a lot of attention. Here, nobody even looked at them.

"It's strange here too," he said. "Like, if Logan wasn't here I'd still be stuck in the airport."

Ina laughed. "It's pretty safe. Just make sure you don't go out at night. Not sure you're ready for that."

"Um, yeah."

"Call me back after you talk to your parents?"

"Yep."

They said goodbye and Alex closed the phone. He felt better than he had all day. He quickly ate all three tacos and leaned back in his chair, ready to call his parents, but the taco shop was filling up with people. Some of them gave him dirty looks. He could only guess it was because Logan's two duffle bags were in an otherwise empty space. Soon, there was nowhere else to sit.

Feeling guilty, Alex stood, gathered up his and Logan's bags, and squeezed out of the shop and onto the street. He made his way to the crosswalk and back to the station. Logan was in his old spot, talking to a tall, skinny woman with long brown hair. She was laughing so hard she was doubled over. Finally, she straightened and put a hand on Logan's arm to steady herself.

"Hey," Alex said, approaching them. He tossed Logan's duffels to the ground and handed him his cell phone.

Logan grinned. "Emily, this is Alex. Alex, this is Emily. She literally showed up one minute ago."

Emily's face was bright from laughing. Of course Logan had her laughing within one minute of meeting her. Everybody loved Logan.

"Hi!" she squeaked, rushing forward and pulling Alex into a long, tight hug. She smelled warm, like spices, and since she was wearing heels, she was at least three inches taller than himself. "Ina said I had to come down here to tell you to call her."

"Oh, I already did," Alex said as she pulled away. He got a better look at her now, and she was absolutely gorgeous with her tiny waist, big breasts, and flashing brown eyes. Not to mention her legs that went on for days below her short denim skirt. She looked like a model. Maybe she *was* a model. Alex tried not to stare.

"She emailed me the number and . . . long story. She told me she might call you again so you wouldn't have to come down here, but too late now."

"Oh, this is fine. I tried to call her when I got her message, but the line was busy. Is she okay? Why is she in Idaho?"

"It was a huge mix-up," Alex explained, unsure of how else to put it. He was still confused about the whole thing.

Emily huffed. "She left almost a week ago. Didn't even tell me where she was going. All she did was leave a note that said . . . well, I guess all I can say is she felt like she had to get away from someone. I've been worrying like crazy."

"Are you talking about Jake?" Alex asked.

Emily's eyes widened. "You know about him, then?"

"Not much, but yeah."

Emily leaned in close, like she was suddenly afraid someone was going to hear her. "Do you want to come up to my apartment?" She glanced at Logan. "Both of you? I think we need to talk."

"That's a good idea," Alex said. "And can I use your phone? I need to call my parents. I'll call Collect so it doesn't run up your phone bill. I've already used a bunch of Logan's cell minutes." He looked apologetically at Logan. "Sorry, dude."

"You have a cell phone?" Emily asked, jealousy sparkling in her eyes as she looked down at the phone in
Logan's hands. "I want one so bad."

"Yeah, just bought it," Logan said proudly. "I'm afraid
to go over my minutes, though."

"You can use my landline as much as you want." She
motioned for them to follow her. "Come on."

* * *

Ina's apartment building was only two blocks away, but
as Alex passed all the varied food vendors and restaurants,
he felt like he'd seen half the world in a few minutes.

"Is there any food you can't get around here?" he
asked.

Emily laughed. "You name it, we got it. And if you
want Indian curry, I've got a whole bunch in the fridge we
can heat up. It's way more than I'll ever eat."

"Your Guatemalan neighbors make it, right?"

Emily smiled at him over her shoulder. "Ina must've
told you that." She motioned for them to follow her under
a brick archway leading into a well-kept cemented courtyard filled with planter boxes and squared-off mini gar-
dens. Trees towered over them, shading and cooling the
area. The air was perfumed with flowers.

"I wouldn't mind living here," Logan said, looking
around as they walked up to a glass door. Emily pulled a
set of keys from her bag and twisted one in the lock. She
pushed the door open and they walked into a small, clean
lobby, past an unmanned front desk, and into an elevator.
Emily let out a sigh as she pushed a button for the fifth
floor.

"Can I ask how much your rent is?" Logan asked.

Emily leaned against the wall and wiped a sheen of sweat off her brow. Even hot and tired, she looked flawless. "With a roommate it's $700 a month," she explained. "Double that if Ina decides not to come back. I'll have to find a cheaper place or another roommate." She gave Alex a curious look. "Do you know if she's coming back?"

Alex shrugged. "No idea. I can ask her when I call her. I gotta set up everything with my parents first, though. She's gonna stay at my place in Idaho."

The elevator dinged and the doors slid open. They exited and walked down a carpeted hallway to the last door. Emily pulled out her keyring again, using two separate keys to unlock two deadbolts and the door handle. The other apartments they'd passed only had one deadbolt.

"Come on in," Emily said, opening the door for them.

Logan went in first, then Alex. The apartment was fairly clean. There was one leather couch in the small living room, an old television set that looked like it had been around since 1970, and a wall full of paintings.

"Are those Ina's?" Alex asked, rushing over to check out the artwork.

"Oh, yeah. She loves to paint, but you probably already knew that. I really want to call her, but you can call your parents first." She grabbed a cordless phone from its cradle on the kitchen counter and tossed it to Alex, who caught it. "You guys hungry?" she asked, heading to the refrigerator. "I'm starving. I've got some butter chicken, if you want some."

"Nah, I just ate," Alex said. The air smelled like spices, the same smell he had noticed on Emily when she had hugged him. It was a good smell, and even though he was still full from the tacos, he was tempted to tell Emily he'd changed his mind.

"I'll try some," Logan said, staying with Emily in the kitchen. "We don't have any Indian places in Anniston, and the one I tried in Boise sucked. I mean, maybe I just don't like it, but I'd like to try it more than once."

"Oh, just wait," Emily said excitedly. "Sit down at the counter there."

Emily continued talking about curry and the neighbors who made it, but Alex tuned her out as he studied Ina's artwork. Most of the pieces were oil on canvas. Some watercolor. Most were small, about the size of a sheet of paper, but others were larger. Some were cityscapes and others were interpretations of city objects, like a fire hydrant surrounded by a web of weeds, or a wet city painted upside down as it reflected the city lights right side up. It was Ina's use of color that stood out the most. Many of the paintings were done in drab browns and grays with one shock of color drawing the eye. The fire hydrant wasn't red. Instead, everything was done in shades of brown, leaving a perfect space for Ina to paint one neon purple flower on an otherwise ugly weed.

Alex studied each painting, inching across the room until he was at the far end where he looked down to see two stacks of canvases leaning against the wall. One stack was blank canvases, but the other stack looked to be completed paintings that hadn't been hung up yet. Curious, Alex bent over to look through them, studying each one until he got to the back where six or seven of the paintings looked as if they'd been painted over in pure black. Images peeked out from the edges, but other than a few random shapes, Alex couldn't tell what was underneath the black. Maybe Ina had been experimenting.

"Hey, Alex!" Logan called out.

Letting go of the canvases, Alex stood up straight, feeling like he'd been caught looking at something he shouldn't. "Sorry, what?" he asked.

"You gotta try this. It's amazing." Logan held up a bowl of steaming curry. "And don't you need to call your parents?"

Alex shook his head. "Yeah, I was just . . ." He looked back at Ina's artwork, surprised at how it had sucked him in, especially the strange black ones. "I was just looking."

"You can use the bedroom if you want some privacy," Emily said as she nodded toward a door. "You don't need to call Collect."

"You sure? I might be on for a bit."

Emily waved her hand. "It's fine, seriously. Ignore the clothes on the floor. I have issues with laundry."

Alex nodded and headed into the bedroom.

# Twenty-Four

## Ina

Ina answered the pay phone on the first ring. "Alex Winzelberg, what took you so long?"

"Sorry. Emily was at the subway station, and then we came up here to your apartment and I had to call my mom. It took forever."

Ina leaned against the edge of the pay phone, relieved Alex was okay, but sick to her stomach about what was going to happen from here on out. "How ticked is your mom?" she asked. "She's not gonna let me stay there, is she?"

"What? Of course she is. You're gonna sleep in April's bedroom."

"Who's April?"

"My sister, but she's in California right now."

"Okay." Ina rubbed the back of her neck and turned around to face the phone booth. Someone had scratched swear words all over the plastic sides. Some things were the same no matter where you went. "Staying at your place without you here is weird, Alex. I don't know how cool I am with it."

"My mom's already on her way to pick you up. It'll be fine, I promise. She's excited to meet you. I think she's got it in her head we're a thing."

"*What*? We are not!"

There was a pause. Was Alex hurt that she didn't think of him that way? Not that a relationship with him hadn't crossed her mind, but it seemed like a lot of things would have to happen first. Like actually meeting in person.

"It's fine," Alex said, breaking the silence. "If that's what's going to make her happy right now, what can it hurt?"

There was another long pause. Ina opened her mouth to say something, but couldn't find any words.

"Are you mad at me?" Alex asked. "I'm sorry. It's just when I told her about you, she sounded so happy, and my mom is almost never happy. I couldn't tell her we aren't really—"

"It's fine. So what's the plan now?"

"Well, she should be there in about an hour. She'll be in an old Buick LeSabre. Chocolate brown. Looks nicer than it sounds. I'm gonna try to change my flight, but until I get back, she said you can hang out around the warehouse. I told her she's not allowed to make you work, though. Seriously, she would do that."

Ina shook her head. "That's fine. I mostly want to know what the plan is for you? You have a hotel, right?"

"Yeah."

"You're in my apartment right now?"

"Yeah, I'm using your landline. Emily said it was okay. She wants to know if you're coming back. She's worried about rent. Well, she's worried about you too."

Ina's grip on the phone tightened at the thought of returning home. "I don't know. It depends on Jake. I don't think I can go back there as long as I know he's trying to find me."

"Yeah, about Jake. I think I might try to find him for you. I want to find out what he wants and let him know you have people to protect you. I want to help."

Ina's heart hammered in her chest. Alex couldn't do that. It was too dangerous. But hadn't that been what she'd secretly wanted all along? He was the only person she completely trusted to help her. She certainly couldn't face Jake on her own.

"I–I don't know," she said, her voice trembling. "Jake's a strong guy. He could hurt you, and I don't think I could handle that. I can't lose you. I've never even met you!"

"You're not gonna lose me. I've got Logan with me, and he can take care of himself. We'll be fine, trust me. If things get out of hand, we'll go to the police. I just need you to give me more information about Jake. Like, what's his last name?"

"It's Nichols." She spelled it out, trying not to shudder. Thinking about Jake was making her cold inside. Goosebumps were popping up on her skin. "But there are some things you should know if you're going to find him, and I don't want you going to the police if you don't have to. He's lied to them before, and he'll just do it again. He gets away with all sorts of stuff."

"Okay, forget about the police, I guess. But what should I know about him?"

She had never thought she would have to tell Alex about her past. But she cared about Alex, and she had never lied to him, not once. She might have skimmed over the truth, but she had never deceived him. If he was going to help her, she had to give him more information.

"I'm here," Alex said over the line. "It's okay."

"I know it is. I just . . ."

Deep shame welled up inside of her at the thought of those months she had lived in Jake's house—and all of the things she had done to make money.

"Jake is . . . he . . . is . . . I can't say it, Alex. I can't say it because you'll see me differently. If your mom found out, she'd never let me near you."

"He's what? I don't understand."

Ina hung her head, not sure if she loved or hated Alex's innocence. "Ask Emily," she sighed. "She'll tell you. She can give you Jake's phone number too. It should be on the caller ID. Maybe if he calls again, you can answer. Ask him what he wants. Tell him he'll never find me. Maybe you can tell him I'm dead."

"That's not a bad idea," Alex said after a moment. "Do you think he'd buy it?"

"Probably not. I think the only way he'll leave me alone is if he knows I have people on my side, looking out for me. I've always been a loner, so he must think it'll be easy to get me under his control again."

"Okay, that makes sense. Is there anyone else who might be able to help? Someone who would side with you against Jake?"

Ina started rubbing her arm with her free hand. "Maybe my boss?" she said, feeling the goosebumps still forming on her skin. "Jake used him to find me. If you call him, he could maybe help. His number's on the speed-dial, under Philippe."

There was a long pause. "So your boss knows Jake is after you?"

"He knows Jake is trying to find me, but he doesn't know everything. I trust Philippe, but he's super busy and I don't want you to bug him if you don't have to."

"Okay." There was shuffling. Ina wondered where Alex was. Maybe he was in her bedroom. She wondered if he had looked at her paintings in the living room and what he thought of them.

"Thank you," she said. "For everything. You have no idea what it means to me."

"I'll do anything I can to help you." His voice was firm and resolved. "I know we're not a thing like my mom wants us to be, but I care about you. I don't know how else to say that." He cleared his throat and there was some more shuffling. "It's not fair you have to be afraid right now."

All the coldness Ina had been feeling slipped away. "I care about you too," she said softly.

There was a pause over the line, but it didn't feel empty. Ina held on to it, like she was holding on to a hand. She didn't want to let go.

"So, uh, Emily wants to talk to you," Alex finally said.

"Oh, okay."

"One sec."

There was some more shuffling, the squeak of a door opening. Ina knew that squeak. It was her bedroom door.

"Ina?" Emily's voice boomed over the line. "I've been so worried. Jake's been calling here so much that I blocked his number, but sometimes he tries calling from other numbers. I can't believe you just left like that. I've—"

"I've missed you too," Ina interrupted, a laugh in her voice. "I'll answer all your questions, but first let's talk about the boys. They're going to need a better place to stay than a hotel room."

"Oh, I already thought of that. They can stay here as long as they need."

"You're okay with that?"

"Sure. You trust them, and after meeting them I'm pretty sure they're not gonna slit my throat and rob the apartment. They're from *Idaho*, Ina. Logan's fine, but

Alex is a wreck. You should've seen how scared he looked down at the subway station."

Ina held back a laugh. "You want to mother him, don't you?"

"Kinda, yeah."

"Well, I won't stop you. Please keep an eye on them. They're going to try to get a hold of Jake and find out what he wants."

"Is that a good idea?"

Ina started chewing on a fingernail. "It's the only idea I have. I can't hide in Idaho forever, and I'm too scared to face him alone. I just . . . I can't. I—"

"Hey, hey, it's gonna be okay. You don't have to face him. Me and the boys will take care of this, okay? Even if it means involving the police."

Ina let out a heavy breath. "That should be a last resort. The police think I'm . . . It's just not a good idea. I understand if you have to, though. Thank you, Emily. Thank you so much."

"Anytime."

Ina went over a few mundane things with Emily—bills and rent and such—thanked her a dozen times, and then hung up. It was time to go meet Alex's mother.

* * *

Outside on the curb, Ina anxiously scanned the passing cars for a brown Buick. It was an hour past the time Alex had said his mother would show up. Maybe she wouldn't come at all.

Then Ina saw a brown car with a frazzled-looking woman behind the wheel. The Buick pulled up to the curb and stopped. The woman stepped out and shut the door.

She was average height, fairly thin, with dark blond hair pulled into a ponytail. Ina tried to imagine what Alex might look like based on her features, but had a hard time envisioning it.

The woman walked around the front of the car, smiling warmly. "You must be Ina!" she said. "Alex gave me a description, but I didn't think I would recognize you. I was wrong!"

Ina relaxed at Mrs. Winzelberg's friendly greeting, even if she was only being friendly because she thought Ina and Alex were a thing. "How did he describe me?" she laughed.

Mrs. Winzelberg scratched her chin. "Dark curly hair, *maybe* darker complexion, he wasn't sure . . . and I hate to say this, but he said you might have a big forehead."

Without thinking, Ina reached up to touch her forehead. "Of course he'd mention that," she chuckled. "I made a big deal out of it when I described myself to him. It *is* big."

"But it's not a bad trait," Mrs. Winzelberg said as she reached down and grabbed Ina's suitcase. She headed for the back of the car, chatting the whole time. "I think you're very pretty. Oh, and call me Marsha. Alex hardly told me a thing about how you two met. He said you're from Queens? I've never been there. I can't believe Alex is there right now. I yelled at him for five minutes over the phone. I mean, leaving like he did? I got his note this morning and almost had a heart attack!" She opened the trunk and tossed Ina's suitcase inside. "But apparently he's fine—he's with your roommate? I hope she can take care of him and Logan." She closed the trunk. "Well, you ready?"

Ina was too stunned to reply. She wasn't sure she had absorbed everything Marsha had said. She was still stuck on the fact that the woman was welcoming her into her life as if she was another one of her children.

Marsha walked to the driver's side. "Hop in. I've got a lot to do at the warehouse. We have a night shift coming in, and I don't like to leave Daniel for too long."

"Oh," Ina said, nodding. Daniel was probably Alex's father. She opened the passenger door, set her backpack on the floor, and slid into her seat. The interior smelled like peppermint candies. It was an older car, but looked well taken care of. The leather seats weren't even worn out or cracked.

"So?" Marsha said as she pulled away from the curb. "Tell me how you and Alex met! We've got an hour drive ahead of us, so don't skip details."

"Oh, uh . . . well, it was through emails. Since '97. Alex found my address on a ten-dollar bill." She relayed the story in a nutshell.

"That's precious," Marsha chuckled, and put a hand to her heart.

Ina shifted in her seat. The leather creaked. "Um, I need to tell you something," she said, wondering if Alex would kill her if he found out what she was about to say. Or maybe he wouldn't get the chance because Marsha would stop the car and dump her out once she knew her son didn't actually have a girlfriend.

"What is it?" Marsha asked.

"Me and Alex aren't together. I mean, how could we be? We've never even seen each other. He said you might think we are, and if that's the only reason you're letting me stay at your place, maybe this isn't a good idea. I'm not comfortable with—"

"Oh!" Marsha gasped with a laugh. "That's not what I thought at all! I was just happy Alex has friends outside of his little group from school."

Ina let out a sigh of relief. "Oh, good."

Marsha pressed the gas as she merged onto the freeway. She was quiet for a few minutes, tapping her index finger on the top of the steering wheel as she kept her eyes glued to the road. Ina stayed quiet too, unsure if she was supposed to say anything else.

"I have to be honest," Marsha finally said in a tone she hadn't used before. She sounded sad. And very, very serious. She had definitely been putting on a happy face until now. "There are a few reasons I want to help you," she said. "First, I like to think of myself as a nice person, and second, Alex told me Daniel might have been the one you talked to on the phone when you thought it was Alex and arranged this whole thing. I don't know how that happened, but I apologize. I'm sure Alex has told you about my husband's mental illness, and that phone call must have been during one of his delusions. So I feel like all of this is partly our fault.

"The third reason is because I'm scared to death Alex will get hurt over there in New York. I'm worried sick. But when he told me how much you mean to him, I knew I had to take you in until he gets back. I need to take care of you just like I'd take care of him." She let out a nervous laugh. "I need Alex back as fast as he can get here. I know he needs to grow up and move away at some point, but I'm just not ready."

Ina noticed Marsha's anxiety, the way her breaths were coming faster, the shiny film of sweat on her forehead. The woman was clearly terrified of losing her son, or at least that was how Ina was reading it. If Marsha knew about Jake and everything Alex was planning to do, Ina was sure she would be even more terrified. The poor woman might keel over dead.

Gripping the sides of her seat, Ina stared at the road ahead. It was straight and flat, a long black line cutting through an expanse of hills covered in sagebrush and weeds. There were some hazy mountains off in the distance in the direction they were headed. Ina felt the landscape's emptiness expanding inside of her. She was scared for Alex's safety, and she hated that it was her fault he might be in danger. But she had no choice. He was the only one she could count on.

# Twenty-Five

## Alex

"I just canceled the hotel room," Logan said as he slipped his cell phone into his pocket. "They charged me fifty bucks, but that's better than what we were going to have to pay for the whole week." He turned to Alex. "Any luck with the airline?"

Alex kept the cordless phone to his ear. "I'm still on hold." He looked over at Emily unrolling a deflated air mattress in the middle of the living room. "Your phone bill is gonna suck, I'm sorry."

Emily stared down at the mattress. Apparently, she had no idea how to use the air pump sitting next to it. "Ina said she'd help out if I can't afford it," she said nonchalantly as she picked up the instruction manual for the pump. "Stop worrying about it."

Alex shifted the cordless phone against his ear just as the hold music cut off and someone finally got back to him about changing his flight. A few minutes later he hung up the phone.

"I'm flying out Saturday afternoon," he announced, walking into the living room where Logan was now hooking up the air pump to the mattress.

Emily sat down on the couch to watch. Alex sat next to her. They were all quiet while Logan ran the pump. It was so loud there was no use in talking. When he was finished, Logan closed off the valve and flopped onto the mattress.

"This is comfy," he sighed, and rolled onto his side to face Emily and Alex.

Emily looked at each of them, her eyes worried. "You guys are serious about helping Ina, right?" she asked.

Alex nodded. "Yeah."

"You realize what kind of people you're dealing with, then? What Jake does and everything?"

Alex shook his head, remembering the fear in Ina's voice when she'd been unable to tell him about Jake. "No, but she said you could tell me."

Emily sat up straight, looking from Logan to Alex. Every time she looked at Alex, she looked more and more worried. She took a deep breath.

"Jake is a pimp," she announced. "He runs some sort of escort service that sounds more like a brothel, and I'm pretty sure he recruits young girls out of group homes to work for him. Ina was one of them, and she managed to break away from that. Now he's trying to get to her again. I don't know what he wants, but it's gotta be something bad." She rubbed her arms as if the room had just gone cold. "Ina swore to me everything she did while she was with him was her choice, but a part of me doesn't believe that. If he gets to Ina now, we might never see her again."

Alex shuddered. He hadn't guessed Jake was a pimp, exactly, but it made perfect sense. No wonder Ina hadn't wanted to tell him.

Logan sat up straight. "Well, I'm not scared of an asshole like that. I say we find him. Any ideas where to start?"

Alex smiled over at his friend, grateful for the fact that he wasn't backing down. "Ina said we can try and call him," he offered. "His number should be on the Caller ID."

Emily stood up. "Yeah, it is. I guess now's as good a time as any." She walked into the kitchen and pushed a few buttons on the answering machine before writing something down on a piece of paper. She walked back into the kitchen and handed the phone and paper to Alex.

Alex looked at the paper and tried to force down a lump in his throat. What was he supposed to say to this guy if he actually answered his phone? *Hey, douchebag, keep away from our girls or we'll beat the shit out of you!*

Yeah, right.

"You should get him to meet us somewhere public," Logan suggested. "I want to see this pimp in person."

"Where should we meet him?" Alex asked.

"Blend Café," Emily answered as she sat on the air mattress next to Logan. "It's a cop hangout around the corner. Good coffee too."

"Okay," Alex said. "And what if he won't meet with us?"

Emily shrugged. "Then we'll have to think of something else. I'll call in sick tomorrow so I can help you guys."

Alex tossed the phone onto the couch cushion next to him and put his head in his hands. He was so nervous he was starting to sweat. "I think we should just call the police."

Emily shook her head. "Ina doesn't want us to do that. We should try talking to Jake first. If the police get involved, they won't keep us informed. The whole point is to find out what Jake wants. He's been trying to get to Ina for a week now. He'll go for it, trust me. He sounded desperate when I talked to him. I hung up on him, anyway. I should have let him talk."

Alex grabbed the phone and stood, squeezing the paper in his hand. "Okay," he said. "Okay, I'll do it."

"You got this," Logan said.

Alex walked into the bedroom and shut the door.

# Twenty-Six

## Ina

Ina had never seen anything like the Winzelberg warehouse. It was surrounded by dry, brown fields and a sky
so big and blue it made her feel like she had to take deeper
breaths to get it all in. The road looked like it had been
paved back in 1955. The car bounced up and down over
countless potholes.

"There's cows everywhere," Ina said as they pulled into
a parking lot.

Marsha gave her an amused look. "Farming is the
major source of income around here."

Ina shook her head. "I've never been in a place like
this."

"You haven't? Doesn't New York have a countryside?"

"Yeah, but I've never been out there. The only time
I've been outside the city was when we went on our group
home retreats to a ski lodge. But there were a lot more
trees and—"

Realizing her mistake, Ina shut up immediately. What
had made her spout out that information? That was the
last thing she wanted to think or talk about.

"Oh, you went skiing? That sounds fun." Marsha got
out of the car, her mind clearly not on the conversation
anymore. She was looking at her watch.

Ina unbuckled her seatbelt and got out of the car. "I can get my stuff," she said as Marsha unlocked the trunk. "You go do what you need to do. Maybe just show me where I'm staying? I won't get in your way."

Marsha smiled and opened the trunk. "You're a guest here. We'll have one of the boys haul your bag up to your room." She hefted Ina's suitcase out of the trunk and extended the handle to wheel it along. Ina followed her to a side door, waiting patiently as Marsha punched in a code and pulled the door open. "Come on in," she said.

Ina followed Marsha through a maze of pallets and boxes and past a line of a dozen employees who didn't even glance up from their tasks. Most of them were wearing headphones and had a Walkman hooked to their hip. The place smelled like cardboard and dust.

"Marsha!" a man wearing an orange hardhat yelled as he hopped off a forklift a few yards away. "We've got a problem!"

"I'll be there in a sec," Marsha yelled backed at him. She came to a halt, and Ina stopped behind her just as a guy dressed in ripped black jeans and a baggy T-shirt walked by. He was carrying a stack of heavy-looking boxes.

"You there . . . Everett, right?" Marsha asked.

He stopped in his tracks, looking around the boxes. "Yes, ma'am?"

"Take Ina up to the house, will you? Show her to April's room. I've got fires to put out."

The guy shifted the boxes in his arms. He had black hair and fair skin. He looked about nineteen. "Where is April's room, exactly?"

"At the end of the main hallway, past the living room."

He nodded. "Sure, ma'am."

Marsha gave Ina an apologetic look and handed over her suitcase before jogging over to the man in the orange hardhat.

"I'm Everett," the guy said. "I'd shake your hand or whatever, but yeah."

"Let me help you," Ina said. She reached out and pulled two of the boxes off his stack. They were as heavy as they looked. She shifted them in her arms. "Where do these need to go?"

"Just over there." He nodded to an open area filled with pallets. "And hey, thanks."

"No problem. I'm Ina."

"Are you family or a friend?"

Ina left her suitcase in the middle of the floor as they headed over to the pallets. "I'm Alex's friend, but we've never actually met."

Everett's eyebrows shot up. "Oh? Alex isn't even here. He and Logan left this morning for New York." He set his boxes on a pallet and Ina followed suit. "You must be that friend Logan mentioned. I thought they were supposed to be meeting you in New York?"

"It's a long story. Is Logan a friend of yours?"

Avoiding Ina's eyes, Everett shrugged. "He was, but he's gone now. Come on, I'll take you upstairs."

They retrieved Ina's suitcase and Everett led the way up a set of stairs to a balcony and a door. It was nicer than what Ina had envisioned. The door opened into a living room area. It looked just like any home. Well-worn furniture. An old television set. Outdated family picture on the wall.

"Hold on," Ina said as Everett walked past the living room toward a hallway. He stopped and turned around. Ina stepped up to the picture. "Which one is Alex?" she asked. "I've never seen him."

Everett's mouth dropped open. "Not even a picture?"

"We never sent pictures."

"Oh." Everett looked at the portrait for a moment and then pointed to a boy who looked about fifteen. "I think that's him. I've only known him for a week. Or maybe that's him. They kinda look alike, don't they?" He pointed to another boy a few inches taller.

"No, it's the first one," Ina said. "It's gotta be. I feel like I'd know him anywhere." Ina held her breath. Alex wore a black polo shirt and jeans, his light brown hair freshly cut and styled. He was gangly, with a goofy smile. He was adorable in the hottest way possible, just as she'd told him. He probably looked amazing now. At least, she imagined he did.

Wait, was she crushing on him?

Maybe.

She stepped away from the picture. "We can go," she said. "Sorry."

"No problem."

Everett led her down the hallway and around a corner, both of them nearly smacking into a tall, broad-shouldered man walking toward them.

"Whoa there!" the man said, throwing them a startled look. "What are you two doing in here? You lost?"

"Oh, hi, Mr. Winzelberg," Everett said warily. He took a step back and Ina did too. So this was Alex's father. He was intimidatingly large in the small hallway, blocking their path. Dark scruff on his jaw. Bright blue eyes. He reminded Ina of Jake.

Jake.

Jake.

Ina took another step back, nearly tripping over her own feet.

He wasn't Jake. It was okay. He wasn't Jake.

"—then get her to April's room and get back downstairs!" Mr. Winzelberg was barking when Ina tuned back in.

He was not Jake.

She needed to get a grip.

She forced herself to look at him. He was glaring at Everett, his nostrils flaring.

"I don't want people like you in my home, you understand? It's bad enough I have to deal with you down in the warehouse. I'll have a word with Marsha about this."

Everett nodded quickly. "I'm sorry, sir. You'll never see me up here again." He skirted awkwardly around Mr. Winzelberg with Ina's suitcase, Ina right behind him. She met Mr. Winzelberg's eyes as she passed him.

Mr. Winzelberg smiled at her. "It's nice to meet you, Ina," he said warmly. "I'm Daniel. Marsha filled me in on what happened. We're glad you're staying. Hopefully Alex can get back soon so you two can meet."

Ina's eyes widened in surprise. He had gone from malicious to sweet in a matter of seconds. "Thanks," she answered.

"You're welcome. If you're hungry, help yourself to anything in the kitchen."

He disappeared around the corner and Ina followed Everett to a bedroom door. He stood in front of it, staring down at the floor.

"Are you okay?" Ina asked. "Why was he so mean to you?"

Everett shrugged as he opened the door. "He doesn't like me. I'll put your suitcase by the bed."

"Thanks." Ina followed him into the room. A fuchsia quilt covered the white iron-framed bed. It was a good thing the pink floral wallpaper was mostly covered with posters of *Friends* and *Buffy the Vampire Slayer*. She hated pink.

"Well, I better go," Everett said.

"Wait." Ina reached out to stop him from leaving. "Seriously, why doesn't he like you? Is he mean to all the employees? Is he mean to Alex?"

"No, just guys like me." He looked down at the floor. "I'm gay, and he hates anyone who's gay . . . or who acts gay . . . or who even *might* be gay."

Ina gave him a sad look. "Wow, that sucks. It's not that big of a deal in New York."

Everett grunted. "Yeah, can you imagine a guy like Mr. Winzelberg in New York with lots of gay people around? He'd be even more psycho than he is now."

Ina looked away, realizing why Alex had avoided talking about his dad's problems. Alex had said nobody around here used the word schizophrenia, but it just seemed rude to call Mr. Winzelberg a psycho.

"Hopefully he can get better," she said gently. "I'm sorry he's such a jerk to you."

"I'm used to it." He met her gaze, a smile lifting his lips. "You're nice, though. I'll bet Alex really likes you."

She laughed. "Thanks." She motioned to her suitcase. "And thanks for your help. See you around?"

"Yeah, sure, see ya."

Once he had closed the door, Ina slipped off her backpack and sat on the edge of the bed. Warehouse sounds drifted through the walls: a forklift beeping as it backed up, engines running, echoing voices. She liked the extra noise. It felt more like home.

Falling back onto the bed, she stared up at the ceiling. There was so much to take in. She still couldn't believe what Alex was doing for her. It felt like she was taking advantage of his kindness, but she didn't know what else to do. All she knew was how desperate she felt, how scared she was that Jake was still going to show up any second and drag her back to his house. He would tell her she was safe. He would tell her she didn't have to do anything to repay him for taking care of her. And then . . . then he would turn on her, call her crazy, make other people believe she was a liar. She would wait in a jail cell with a cut lip and a black eye. She would keep asking where Jake had gone, if he was in trouble, and an officer would promise to let her out of jail if she told him everything Jake had done. She would confess everything. She would tell the truth, but for some reason they wouldn't believe her. They would send a doctor to talk to her. A counselor. And then they would let her go . . .

Ina sat up, her breaths coming fast and hard. She had to talk to someone. She looked around the room, spotting a telephone on a desk by the window. Sliding off the bed, she walked over to see that it was an older phone with no ID screen. She picked up the receiver. There was only one person she could think of to talk to right now.

She sat down at the desk, waited for the call to connect, and asked to be put through to her mother.

"Ina?" Reina Sanchez's smooth voice reached into the depths of Ina's heart. "You haven't called in so long. What's the matter?"

Ina choked on her words for a moment before she was able to speak. "Mom, I . . . I miss you. I need you. I'm in trouble, and I don't know what to do."

Her mother was quiet for a moment. "Oh, sweetheart," she said gently. "Talk fast and I'll try to help."

"He's after me," she whispered. "Jake, the man I told you about before. He's after me and I don't know what to do."

There was a long pause. "You're stronger than you think," her mother finally said. "Remember how strong I was when you were little? I did everything for you and your daddy. I know you can be strong like me."

Ina sniffed. "Okay, but Mom . . . what about that day Dad died?"

"I gotta go. I love you."

The line went dead, and Ina pulled the receiver away from her ear and stared at it. Finally, she put it to her ear again. There was one more call to make, one more person she could talk to.

"Hello?"

Ina breathed a sigh of relief. "Philippe!" she gasped. "*C'est moi!*"

"Ina, *c'est toi?*"

"*Oui, je suis si heureux que t'aies répondu.*"

Philippe switched to English. "I've been worried. You didn't go to either of the appointments I booked for you. What's going on?"

Ina started rolling a ballpoint pen back and forth on the desk. "I'm so sorry. So much has happened."

"You poor thing. Tell me about it? *S'il te plaît?*"

Ina took a deep breath. "I'll tell you everything."

# Twenty-Seven

## Alex

Blend Café was definitely a cop hangout. Two officers had already come and gone in the five minutes Alex had been sitting at a quiet table near the back. Logan was in line waiting to order. He kept looking over at Alex, and then at the door. Jake could walk in any minute.

Last night, the phone call with Jake had been quick. He had immediately agreed to meet the next morning and insisted he meant no harm to Ina. "There's a lot you need to know," he'd said in a low voice. "But you're right, we should meet in person."

Alex had tossed and turned all night. What if Jake didn't show up? What if he somehow found a way to hurt them, even in a public place with cops around? What if he demanded something they couldn't give?

"You Alex?" a gruff voice asked.

Alex scrambled out of his chair, realizing he'd been staring down at the table instead of watching the door. In front of him stood a tall, muscular man in his thirties. His reddish-brown hair made his blue eyes look freakishly bright. It was unnerving.

Composing himself, Alex motioned to an empty chair at the table. "Yeah, you're Mr. Nichols?"

"Call me Jake." He looked around as he smoothed a hand down his unwrinkled gray T-shirt. "Where's this friend of yours you said would be here?"

"He's in line. The blond guy. Do you want me to have him get you a coffee? Something to eat?" Alex scolded himself for being so nice, but he figured it might not hurt. Pissing the guy off wouldn't get them anywhere.

"No thanks." Jake sat down.

Alex sat across from him, shifting uncomfortably in his chair as he noticed a faint, fist-sized bruise on Jake's cheek, right below his left eye. It had begun to heal, but it didn't help make him look any less threatening.

"How do you know Ina?" Jake asked, intertwining his fingers as he rested his elbows on the table. "I didn't think she had any friends."

Alex narrowed his eyes. "How would you know if she has friends or not? She said you were out of her life."

Jake looked down at the table. "You're right, I've only tried to get a hold of her in the past week. Before that, I left her alone." He looked back up, his eyes hard again. "I don't want to hurt her, and I don't want her involved in prostitution again. Is that what you think all of this is about? Is that what *she* thinks?"

Alex blinked. He wasn't sure what to make of this guy. "Well, yeah," he said. "You've been stalking her. She's scared out of her mind."

Shaking his head, Jake leaned back in his chair. "Damn it," he hissed. "I should've known." He looked at Alex again, his eyes pleading. "All I want to do is talk to her. I've been worried about her. I didn't mean to ..." He looked down at the table and cursed under his breath. "I didn't mean to frighten her. Does she still think I hit her on purpose? Is she upset about what I told the police?"

Alex furrowed his brow. "I don't know what you're talking about. She never mentioned any of that. All I know is you're running some sort of . . ." Lowering his voice, he looked around and leaned in. "You're running some sort of escort service, and you made Ina a part of it."

Jake let out a heavy sigh. "I spent time in prison for that, okay? I got out two months ago and I've put my life in order. But Ina still needs help, and that's what I'm here for. I'm the only person who can give her the help she needs."

Alex was surprised at the man's sincerity. He was intimidating, sitting there with his big biceps and chilling eyes, but his concern for Ina was absolutely unfeigned.

"And why are you the only person who can help her?" Alex challenged him.

Just then, Logan came up to the table with two disposable coffee cups. "Oh, hi," he said. "You must be Jake."

Jake sized up Logan with an irritated expression. "Have a seat," he muttered.

"You haven't missed much," Alex explained as Logan sat next to him. "Jake was telling me all he wants to do is help Ina, and he's the only one who can."

"Oh?" Logan set one of the cups in front of Alex. "Why you?"

Jake eyed Logan warily and then spoke to Alex. "I know her better than anyone, and I know things she . . ." He looked away. "It's complicated, okay? I'm going to help her figure out what's wrong. She hears things that aren't there, sees things, makes things up in her head. I thought I was protecting her, but it wasn't in the way she needed, and I see that now." He paused, leveling his gaze at both Alex and Logan. "I think I've finally figured out how to help her the way she needs to be helped."

*She heard and saw things that weren't there?* Alex couldn't respond. All he could think about was everything his father had gone through. Ina couldn't be sick. She couldn't. He would have spotted it. But then, he didn't know Ina *that* well . . .

Logan looked worriedly at Alex and then glared at Jake. "What kinds of things does she hear and see?"

"She'll talk to herself like she's having a conversation with someone, and sometimes she'll have panic attacks so intense she's difficult to control. Half the time, she doesn't remember what happens during those attacks."

"We're pretty convinced anything wrong with her is from trauma *you* inflicted on her," Logan snapped. "Her roommate told us what you are."

Jake sat back in his chair and folded his arms. "No, it's not *me*. Ina kept saying I hit her on purpose, but it was an accident. I was trying to stop someone else from hurting her." He leaned forward, gripping the edge of the table so hard his knuckles turned white. "I took care of all my escorts," he insisted. "They wanted to work for me. They chose that life, and I made it as safe and comfortable for them as possible. All I ever did for Ina was try to protect her. I didn't know why her brain was doing strange things, but I cared about her. I still do. I think it *is* trauma, just like you said. But it's not any trauma I inflicted, that's for damn sure."

"Trauma from what, then?" Alex asked. His mouth had gone dry as he'd listened to Jake. He felt lightheaded. There was too much to process. "Why is she convinced you're going to hurt her?"

Jake leaned back in his chair again, his eyes going distant. "Something happened when she was a kid, and she's not remembering it. I mean, I'm sure she remembers it deep down, but she's repressed most of it. Maybe she didn't understand what happened at the time, and now her subconscious is finally working it out."

Anger roiled inside of Alex. He leaned forward, his upper lip curling as he spat out, "Ina doesn't want your help. She hates you. She's scared to death of you."

"I'm telling you, it's not really me she's scared of," Jake growled.

"Yeah, right!" Logan grunted. "You don't think what she was doing totally messed her up?"

Jake's eyes looked like they might shoot fire. The muscles in his forearms flexed. "You have no idea what I've done for Ina," he said. "I never made her do anything she didn't choose to do on her own. She's just angry with me for telling the police about her mental issues. I told them about the times she snapped, how I've caught her on the phone having a conversation with someone who wasn't there. Maybe I shouldn't have said anything, but I couldn't possibly cover it up after what she did in that hotel room, and I was trying to keep us both out of jail—"

"Wait," Alex interrupted, his voice shaking more than ever. "Back up a sec. She talked to an imaginary person on the phone?"

Jake nodded. "I heard her talking to her mother on the phone, as if she was calling her in prison, but . . . well, obviously that wasn't possible. When I checked my phone records later to see if she'd really been talking to someone else, there was no record of that phone call at all."

Leaning back in his chair, Alex stared down at the table. His thoughts were spinning out of control. He felt sick to his stomach. If what Jake said was true . . .

"*That's* what happened," Logan breathed. "She didn't talk to your dad, Alex. She was talking to herself."

"It's not true," Alex muttered, his eyes still on the table. The room was starting to tilt. He couldn't accept this. He couldn't. "Ina's not mentally ill. Lots of people talk to themselves."

Logan grabbed Alex's wrist and leaned over to look him in the eyes. "I don't wanna trust this guy any more than you do, but think about what he's saying. Don't you think it explains a lot?"

Alex stared at his knees. "I don't know," he whispered, his eyes glazing over. "I don't know anything right now. He could be lying. He could have set all this up so we'd believe him and let him get to her. He could be—"

"I'm not lying," Jake snapped. "Ina needs help. She needs someone to protect her while she's so vulnerable. She's already had one man take advantage of her, don't you understand?"

Alex looked up. "Who? When?"

Jake started rubbing at a spot between his eyes. "It was a little over a week ago. Ina wasn't taking my calls, so I talked her boss into telling me where she'd be working that night so I could check up on her. When I stopped by the restaurant she was at, I tried to call her to tell her I was outside, but my cell phone died before she got to the phone. Then she saw me, and she had such a strange look on her face that I knew something was wrong. The doorman wouldn't let me in because I didn't meet the stupid dress code, and Ina ended up leaving with some man. He took her out the back like he didn't want anyone to see them leave, and I followed them to a hotel. I couldn't get anyone at the front desk to help me find out which room they were in, and I'm afraid he might have . . . well, let's just say she didn't look very good when he brought her back out. Seemed like she was drugged or drunk, I don't know. I got a few good swings at the bastard when he was trying to get into a cab with her, but then he hit me so hard I fell. When I got back up they were gone."

"Why didn't you call the police?" Logan asked, incredulous.

Jake threw up his hands. "And tell them what? Ina's got a record. You know what the cops would think if I told them she was stumbling out of a hotel with some guy in the middle of the night?"

The whole room was spinning now. Ina had been in more danger than Alex had realized. Every part of him was desperate to help her, protect her, fix whatever was wrong, but he had no idea how to do that. Jake's story seemed too bizarre to be true, but Logan was right that the pieces seemed to fit.

"I need more evidence," Alex said. "We need to call Ina and ask her—"

"No, no, no, you can't do that," Jake said, reaching across the table and grabbing Alex's wrist. He squeezed hard. "You can't talk to her about this on the phone. It needs to be in the right setting, with the right people. She doesn't know anything's wrong, and I'm the best person to get her through it. She thinks I'm the bad guy, don't you see? I need to show her I'm not the bad guy. I'm *not*."

"Well, you're not the *good* guy," Alex snapped, ripping his arm away from Jake's hold. He hated this man who had brought Ina so much pain. For all Alex knew, Jake was covering up a million lies to hide what he'd really done. "I don't care what you say. What you've done isn't okay. How did you get out of prison so soon, anyway? The police must've nailed you for all sorts of things. Ina's roommate said you were recruiting young girls from group homes."

"Those women were over eighteen, and I was running a legal escort business," Jake retorted. "Yeah, there was some shady stuff under the table, but I was careful, so there wasn't much they could actually charge me with. But

I'm still on parole, so it's not like I'm a completely free man."

"Good," Logan muttered. He took a sip of his coffee and glared at Jake over the rim of the cup. "That'll keep you from leaving the state."

Jake's eyes widened. "Why would I want to leave the state?" He looked at Alex, his brow furrowing. "Did Ina leave New York? Is that why I can't find her?"

"You'll never find her," Alex said. "I'll be the one to help her now." His hands were shaking so hard he had to slide them under the table and grab his knees. All he could think about was Ina in the warehouse. With his dad. With his *mom*. If Ina somehow snapped while she was staying there, his mom could not handle it. He had to do something. He had to get back home.

That was, if anything Jake said was true.

Logan gave Alex a worried look. "Um, thanks for the information," he said to Jake, setting his cup down. He stood up and motioned for Alex to get up too. "We're gonna split."

Alex stood, but didn't step away from the table. He was waiting for Jake to protest them leaving, but the man just stared up at them with a sad look on his face. He seemed broken, like he'd given up. He kept his eyes on Alex as he said, "Promise me you'll get a doctor to help her. If you knew anything about what she's going through, you'd—"

"Alex understands more than you think," Logan interrupted. "There's nobody better to help Ina."

Jake looked at Alex, his eyebrows raised in question.

Alex leaned over and grabbed the coffee cup he had left untouched until now. He wasn't sure if he was ready to leave yet, but Logan seemed eager to go, and they did have the information they had come for.

"I'll take care of her," Alex promised. "She'll be okay. Thanks again."

"Call me if you have questions," Jake said. "I can guarantee you, at some point you're gonna want to talk to me. Or Ina will."

"We have your number," Logan said. He nudged Alex out of the coffee shop, and when they were out on the sidewalk, they headed back to Ina's apartment.

Alex took a sip of his coffee. It was lukewarm.

"Are you all right?" Logan asked, giving him a sidelong glance. "Because that was intense. Like, I'm kinda expecting you to freak."

"I'm fine."

"Yeah, okay."

Alex shot him a glare. "I'm *fine*." He took another sip of coffee as everything inside of him started hurting. He was confused and angry and worried. It was all churning together. Squeezing. "I just don't know if I believe any of it."

"Yeah, I know, but it makes sense. Sure, he's a creep, but he didn't seem like he wants to hurt Ina. I think he really cares about her."

Rounding a corner, they walked under the brick archway leading into the courtyard of Ina's apartment building. Alex took a deep breath of the flower-scented air. It was hard for him to imagine Ina walking through here every day, living in a world fractured by mental illness. *If that was true . . .*

"I need more evidence than what Jake's told us," he said as he and Logan stepped up to the glass door. "There's gotta be something else we can do before I leave on Saturday. I need to know the truth before I see her."

Logan pressed the buzzer to Ina's apartment. "Well, let's talk to Emily. I don't think you should call your parents or Ina yet."

Emily's voice sounded over the intercom. "Alex? Logan? That you?"

"Yeah, let us up," Logan answered. "We've got some news."

"Okay, but take your time. I just got out of the shower and I'm kinda naked."

"Oh, for the love," Alex muttered as the buzzer sounded and the door clicked open.

"What?" Logan laughed as they walked inside. "I know you think she's hot."

"She's totally bangin'," Alex admitted as they headed for the elevator. His thoughts were jumbled. His emotions were even worse. "Like, she's the hottest girl I've ever seen. But that doesn't mean I want her." He jammed his thumb against the elevator button.

"You want Ina, then? What if you meet her and she's a dog?"

"I don't think I'd care," Alex answered as the elevator doors slid open. "And she's not a dog. She described herself. She sounded pretty."

Logan nudged Alex into the elevator. "Okay, so maybe she's super hot. But what if she really is mentally ill? What then? Like, how much are you willing to put into your relationship with her? That's a lot on your plate. You know, with your dad and everything. I mean, face it, man . . . you're not the best at handling a bunch of crap all at once."

Leave it to Logan to point out the obvious truths and ask the hard questions. Alex glared at him. "I don't know," he muttered. He thought about how difficult it would be to deal with his father as well as another person who might need just as much care. "I honestly don't know."

# Twenty-Eight

"He thinks Ina is crazy?" Emily asked as soon as Alex and Logan shared what Jake had told them. "Like, legitimate lost-it crazy?"

Alex winced. "Please don't use that word," he said softly. "He didn't actually say she was mentally ill—just that she's acted really weird sometimes."

Emily nodded, her eyes going distant for a moment.

They were back in the apartment. Emily hadn't bothered getting dressed. Instead, she'd wrapped a towel around herself and was now standing in the middle of the kitchen with a puddle forming around her bare feet.

"Do you think Jake is right?" Alex asked, determinedly keeping his eyes on Emily's face.

She blinked. Her hair was pulled up into a towel, but a few wet strands were stuck to her forehead. "I don't know," she said. "Maybe? I mean, he's right about her doing weird things sometimes. Like, I've caught her talking to herself, but everyone does that, right? And sometimes she wakes up in the middle of the night from nightmares, thinking someone's after her." She waved her hand in the air, as if to dismiss everything she'd said. "Everybody has nightmares. Right?"

"I guess so," Logan said as he pulled off his denim jacket and set it on one of the bar stools. "I've never met Ina, but everything I've heard makes me think Jake might be right." He threw a sad look at Alex. "As much as you don't want to believe it, man, you have to admit . . ."

Alex looked away. "I know, I know."

Emily started pacing the floor. "I wonder if I should call him," she muttered.

"Call who?" Alex asked, leaning against the counter. "Don't call Jake. He's creepy and I don't think—"

"No, not Jake." Emily stopped and faced Alex and Logan. "Ina's boss, Philippe. I don't know if it has anything to do with all of this, but Ina came home with one of her clients the other night. She—"

"Jake told us about that!" Alex cut in. He quickly relayed Jake's version of the story, and Emily followed by filling in her side of it.

"Philippe can help us find out what happened," she said excitedly. She reached across the counter to grab the phone. "I mean, who better to help us than a translator, right?"

* * *

The elevator dinged and the doors slid open. Alex stepped out first, surprised at how sophisticated the fifth floor looked compared to the drab first floor. They were in the building that housed Philippe's office. It had been a twelve-block walk, and Alex's feet were tired. He had no idea how Emily had managed the walk in heels.

The lobby was decorated in thick European rugs, floor plants, and dark leather furniture. There was no front desk, just the open lobby and a hallway leading to a few doors. One of them was open.

"Is that you, Ms. Murphy?" a man's accented voice called out from the direction of the open door. He pronounced Murphy like "Maire-fee."

They hurried down the hallway and stepped into the office to see a small room lined with bookshelves. A large desk sat near the window, and behind the desk was a petite, dark-haired man dressed in a lime green sweater and jeans. He was leaning back in his chair, a cigarette in hand as he blew out a puff of smoke.

Alex smiled. *This* felt like New York to him. It was exactly how he had imagined what an agent sitting in his office might look like. An agent *he* might have one day. If he ever got to the point where he could move here.

"Welcome!" the man bellowed in a voice that seemed far too loud for such a small person. "Have a seat." He motioned them to a sofa crammed into a corner of the room. It blocked a whole set of shelves filled with books. "I'm Philippe." He watched as Emily sat down in the middle of the sofa and Alex and Logan sat on either side of her. "You're Emily," he said, pointing his cigarette at her, "but you didn't tell me the names of your two friends."

"This is Alex and Logan," Emily said. "They're friends of Ina's."

"Ina is staying at my place right now," Alex explained as Philippe dragged on his cigarette. "She's safe there. She was afraid of Jake, so she—"

"Ah, yes, she disappeared soon after her last call to me, and I haven't heard from her since. She missed two appointments with clients, which is unlike her. I left messages on her machine, but she did not call back. That's when I started to worry." He lowered his cigarette and trained his eyes on Alex. "So, where is she?"

Squirming a little, Alex glanced at Logan for direction. It didn't seem like a great idea to tell anyone else where Ina was. They needed to protect her as much as possible.

"Ah, you don't trust me," Philippe laughed.

"We trust you," Alex said. "We just want to keep Ina safe. We're worried about her . . . mental health."

Philippe cocked his head and raised an eyebrow. "Mental health? Is that why she has disappeared? Is she not well?"

"That's the problem," Alex answered, frustration overwhelming all his other emotions. "We aren't sure." He felt like he was going to explode any second. This was too much. He had to know if Ina was truly sick. How could he help her otherwise? In a sudden burst of courage, he stood up from the sofa and walked across the room to Philippe's desk. Pressing his palms against the edge, he leaned forward to look directly into Philippe's eyes. "You've worked with Ina for a while now, right? Does she seem healthy to you? Mentally stable?"

Philippe blinked as he lowered his cigarette. The smoke curled up toward the ceiling. "Ina has always seemed mentally stable to me," he said gently. "She's a charming, talented woman." He tipped his cigarette toward Emily. "How about we do what you came here to do and call Mr. Conti? Perhaps he can tell us what he thinks happened that night." He looked at his watch. "It is almost 7:00 p.m. in Naples. Let's hope he answers his telephone."

Alex relaxed a little as Philippe stubbed out his cigarette in a metal ashtray and lifted the receiver. He did everything with a dramatic flourish, as if he was putting on a show.

"You okay?" Logan asked as Alex returned to the sofa.

"Yeah, I'm fine. I'm just worried what this guy is gonna tell us."

Emily started biting one of her perfectly manicured fingernails. "Me too," she whispered.

"*Buonasera*!" Philippe said jovially into the phone. "*Avete riposte*!" He started speaking rapidly in what Alex assumed was Italian. It sounded especially muddled with his heavy French accent. "*Sì, sì,*" he finally said. He covered the receiver with his hand. "I'm assuming none of you speak Italian?" he asked.

Logan's hand shot up into the air as if he was in a classroom. "I speak a tiny bit."

Alex raised his eyebrows at him. "Since when?"

Logan shrugged. "Since three years ago when I decided I was going to travel the world someday and bought all those language CDs, remember?"

Alex laughed. "You mean you've actually used them? Who does that?"

"Um, me? Just Italian and German, though, and I don't know *that* much."

Alex shook his head. "Overachiever."

Philippe sighed. "Ah, well, it's not enough for you to speak to Mr. Conti yourself," he said, looking disappointed.

"What's the matter?" Emily asked, leaning forward. "Why is it important we speak Italian?"

Philippe waved his free hand in the air. "I want to make sure you know Mr. Conti is speaking the truth, and how can you know that for sure if I'm the one translating?" He nodded at Alex. "You seem very reluctant to trust anyone."

Alex looked away, but he wasn't about to apologize.

"Does Mr. Conti have a translator on his end?" Emily suggested.

Philippe smiled. "Ah, that is an idea. Thank you, Ms. Murphy." He uncovered the phone and started speaking again.

"Can you understand anything he's saying?" Alex asked Logan.

"Not a lot. His accent is pretty thick."

A few minutes later, Philippe put the phone on speaker and leaned back. "Go ahead, Mr. Conti."

A string of Italian flowed from the speaker, making Logan sit up straight. "Now *that* I understand," he said, smiling. "Well, some of it. He's introducing himself. He—"

Mr. Conti stopped speaking and a woman's voice took over in English. Her Italian accent was strong, but easy to understand. "Hello, I am Vincenzo Raffaele Conti. I recently traveled to your country for some business and engaged the services of several translators. One of those translators was Ms. Ina Sanchez. May I ask who I am speaking with?"

Philippe motioned for the three of them to introduce themselves. They did, and the translator relayed the information to Vincenzo, who began speaking again. The translator came back a moment later: "It is nice to meet all of you, and it is nice to speak to you again, Emily. I am sorry I couldn't properly speak to you the evening we met. I was in a great hurry. However, I am particularly interested in the gentleman named Alex. Are you Ina's brother? She told me about you."

Alex furrowed his brow. "No, I'm not her brother."

"Then why would she tell me so? I am confused. You are her boyfriend, then?"

Alex frowned. "No, I'm not her boyfriend either. We're just friends, but I care about her a lot and I want to know what happened to her that night you took her home."

"I understand. It may seem that I hurt her, you think?"

"Well, no . . ." Alex looked nervously at Emily, who shrugged.

Vincenzo started speaking again. It went on for a full minute, and Alex wondered how the translator could keep track of it all.

She finally spoke: "I did not hurt her. When my meeting was finished, Ina . . . she . . . how do I say? She flirted with me, yes? I invited her to my hotel for a drink and she accepted. Then she told me she was frightened of a man waiting for her outside the restaurant. I arranged to take her out the back way. We went to my hotel. I thought she wanted . . . how do I say . . . she told me flirting was a mistake. She did not want sex. She wanted to feel safe. I told her I would keep her safe. I had no intention of harming her in any way."

"Why did she seem drunk when you brought her home?" Emily asked.

As Vincenzo started speaking, Philippe sat up in his chair, his eyebrows raised.

"What?" Alex looked to Logan. "What is he saying?"

Logan shook his head. "He's talking too fast. I can't catch all of it. Something about crying."

Finally, the translator came back on the line: "What happened next was very, very strange. Ms. Sanchez began to faint. I caught her and took her to the bed to set her down, but before I could get her there, she attacked me. She screamed and cried and kicked. I thought she was scared that I was going to rape her. I tried to explain to her that I was not doing that. She called me Jake. She thought I was Jake. She kept telling me she had to talk to someone on the phone, but when I took her to the phone she got even more upset. It was all very, very odd."

Vincenzo began speaking again. Alex waited on the edge of his seat for the translation. This was all too bizarre for anyone to make up. It had to be the truth. The next thing he had to do was call Ina. He couldn't put it off anymore.

The translator began speaking again: "This went on for one full hour. I do not exaggerate. She would not believe anything I said. She begged me not to take her back. I felt so bad for her. I knew I had to take her home, but how?"

Vincenzo started speaking again, and then the translator came back: "I had sleeping pills in my bag for the long flights. I thought they would calm her down enough for me to take her home. My flight was departing the next morning. I could not just leave her in the hotel. That seemed wrong."

"She wasn't drunk," Emily said quietly. "She was drugged."

"Yeah, but he was helping her," Logan said. "I mean, can you blame the guy?"

The translator started speaking again, Vincenzo interjecting every now and then: "I gave her some pills. Not enough to harm her. I was frightened she would act out again. I wanted to get her to a safe place where she would be comfortable. When she calmed down, I found her identification and her address in her purse and I took her downstairs to a taxicab. That is when the man I assume was Jake attacked me. He told me to stay away from Ms. Sanchez and he hit me. I was angry with him and hit him back. I got in the taxicab and took Ms. Sanchez home."

There was a long pause. Vincenzo finally spoke again, his voice worried. The translator put the same worry into her own voice: "I hope I did the right thing? Please do not be angry with me. I never meant any harm. I hope Ms. Sanchez is okay?"

"She was fine the last time I talked to her," Alex answered quickly. "That was yesterday. I'm going to call her again today. Thank you for telling us your side of the story, Mr. Conti."

Vincenzo answered, quickly followed by his translator: "You are welcome, Mr. Alex. Please tell Ms. Sanchez I am sorry that I frightened her."

"I will."

Philippe said a few things to Vincenzo and then hung up. He leaned back in his chair and lit another cigarette. "Looks like Ina might have some problems after all," he said sadly.

# Twenty-Nine

## Ina

Ina reached into her bag of popcorn, finding nothing but a few hard kernels. She should have bought a larger bag. Or a pretzel. She was still hungry.

Shifting in her seat, she looked around the theater. It was mostly empty, probably because it was 11:30 on a Friday morning in the smallest town in the United States of America. Well, she knew Anniston wasn't the *smallest* town in America, but it was insanely small. There was only one theater, a handful of restaurants, and a completely non-existent transportation system. Ina had been forced to borrow Alex's bicycle to get here. She couldn't even remember the last time she'd ridden a bicycle. She was lucky she hadn't wiped out on any potholes.

She'd been too nervous to eat breakfast at Alex's house, so she'd waited until the Winzelbergs went to work in the warehouse before she emerged from April's room. She'd tracked down Marsha in the office to tell her she was riding Alex's bike into town, but the woman had been so busy that she'd hardly seemed to notice Ina at all. It made Ina feel sad for Alex. Between his dad's issues and his mom's intense work ethic, he'd probably grown up a little neglected.

Ina tried to focus on the movie. The theater only had two screens, and her matinee choices had been *Notting Hill* or *Tarzan*. She'd figured *Notting Hill* was her safest bet. It was a chick-flick, but it was entertaining so far. If only her stomach would stop growling. She was used to eating a big bowl of curry for breakfast or an early lunch, and she'd hardly eaten anything yesterday. She had to go out and get something else to eat.

A minute later, she was in the lobby staring down through a pane of glass at the candy selection. None of them looked great.

"Of course I'm not gonna work here forever!" a cheery voice laughed. "I'm not a total loser!"

Ina looked up to see a pretty black girl standing at the register. She was talking to a middle-aged man holding an empty tub of popcorn. He wore glasses and a brown cardigan.

"I never implied you were a loser, Raven," he said, handing her the empty tub. "I'm just saying you have talent and you shouldn't waste it here in this town. It's the same thing I've told Alex for the past year and a half. Now look at him! Accepted to Marion!" He raised his hands in the air, as if he was announcing the news to the world.

Ina's eyes widened. It was Alex's drama teacher, Mr. Barringer. It had to be. She should have known she might run into people Alex had mentioned in his emails.

Raven set the popcorn tub on the counter and leaned forward. "Well, don't tell anyone, but I just gave Alex a ride to the airport yesterday morning. Him and Logan Caldwell. Alex will be back, though. He told me he's planning on staying here for another year because of his dad. Marion said they'll still take him next year. Did he tell you any of that?"

Mr. Barringer straightened his shoulders, looking a little upset. "No, he didn't. He's been helping me out with the play, and he hasn't breathed a word. If I'd known that, I would have cast him as my lead. He would've been brilliant." He cocked his head and raised an eyebrow. "Where would Alex and Logan be flying off to?"

"New York. Logan's moving there, and Alex went to meet a friend and check out the school. His mom didn't know he was going. If she finds out *I* was the one who drove them there, she'll probably kill me. She's hella scary."

Mr. Barringer cleared his throat. "She's a very busy woman," he corrected her gently. "Why don't you get to work on refilling that popcorn so I don't miss any more of the movie?" He glanced over at Ina, who quickly turned back to the candy selection as she tucked a strand of hair behind her ear. Small-town gossip really was a thing. If she wasn't careful, this Raven girl would be gossiping about *her* in no time. The last thing she wanted was for people to know who she was and where she was staying.

"Hello, there. Are you new in town?" Mr. Barringer asked.

Ina shook her head. "Just visiting."

"Ah, I thought you looked unfamiliar. Welcome."

Ina gave him a genuine smile. "Thanks."

Raven looked over at Ina as she shoveled popcorn into Mr. Barringer's tub. "Where ya stayin'?" she asked, clearly not as concerned about politeness as Mr. Barringer. "'Cause the Motel 6 sucks. You can cancel your room and move over to the Two Spoons Bed & Breakfast at the end of town. My grandparents run it. Mention me and they'll give you a discount."

Ina forced a smile. "Thanks for the suggestion."

"No problem!" Raven finished filling up the popcorn tub. "Why are you visiting here, anyway?" she asked. "There's, like, nothing here. You got family in town?"

Mr. Barringer took his popcorn from Raven and gave Ina a sympathetic smile before leaving. Ina sighed inwardly. "Just visiting a friend," she said politely. She pointed to the display. "Can I get the peanut M&Ms, please? And do you have pretzels? The soft ones? I'm starving. You don't have hot dogs, do you?"

Raven shook her head and jerked her thumb over her shoulder. "If you want real food, you should go to the Two Spoons. It's a regular restaurant too."

Ina nodded. "How would I get there?"

"It's fastest to cut through the fields behind the theater. Then go north through town until you reach a dirt road. That leads to the Two Spoons." She raised an eyebrow. "But don't you want to finish the movie?"

Ina's stomach growled, and she hid an embarrassed grimace. "Um, not really. Can I ride a bike through the fields? Or should I go around?"

Raven squinted past Ina through the glass front doors. "Is that the bike you rode? The lime green one with the purple seat?"

Ina nodded. "Yeah."

"That's Alex's bike. Wait, is Alex the friend you're visiting? I thought he went to New York to find—oh wait, *wait*!" Her squinted eyes popped wide open. "Are you *Ina*?" she gasped.

Ina cringed. "Alex told you about me?"

Raven nodded enthusiastically. "Yeah, you're his email friend! He tried keeping you a secret, but he ended up spilling the whole story on our way to the airport. He gave me fifty bucks to keep my mouth shut about it too, but hey, you're Ina, so I can talk to *you* about it, right?" Her hand fluttered up to her mouth as she bounced up and down on the balls of her feet. "I can't believe this," she squealed softly. "Does he know you're here? Is he coming back? What happened?"

Ina stepped back. "I don't feel comfortable talking about it," she said as gently as she could. "I'm sure Alex will fill you in when all of this is over. Right now I need to—" She gestured toward the door. "I gotta go. Thanks for the advice. I really appreciate it. Please don't tell anyone you met me, 'kay?"

Raven nodded, but looked sorely disappointed. "See ya around," she said, giving a little wave goodbye.

Ina waved back and left the theater. She hopped on Alex's bike and pedaled around to the back of the building. Raven was right. There were fields behind the theater, stretching for miles. The north field, however, seemed to cut across to another section of town. Ina pedaled in that direction, weeds brushing against her jeans as she found a thin bike trail and rode over packed dirt and dead leaves. There were piles of old tires here and there, a tree stump, and a million grasshoppers. Several of them jumped high enough to get caught in Ina's hair. She batted at them with one hand, suppressing the urge to freak out. She'd never been assaulted by so many bugs before. She was used to the occasional cockroach or spider scuttling across the floor in her apartment, but that was about it.

A few minutes later, she emerged onto a sidewalk lining a quiet road. It was paved, but looked as cracked and worn as the road leading to the warehouse. She still couldn't wrap her head around this place. Everything about it felt foreign. Too open. Too exposed.

Riding as fast as she could, she kept heading north until she reached Main Street and then passed through a small cluster of houses, keeping north until she finally hit a dirt road. Dust swirled up around her. It smelled like oil. Finally, she spotted a wooden sign that read Two Spoons Bed & Breakfast in bright red. The picturesque building was two stories, and looked like it probably passed for a mansion in this town. In stark contrast, the other buildings nearby were squat and ugly, one of them advertising Joe's Tack & Feed. Classy.

There were no bike racks anywhere, so Ina dismounted and left the bike leaning against a large pine tree on the lawn. She felt strange not locking it up, just as she had at the theater, and she hoped nobody would steal it. The only people she could see were two men in cowboy boots coming out of the Tack & Feed store. They didn't look like they would want to steal a bike.

Taking a deep breath, she walked up the steps into the bed and breakfast. Immediately to her right was a glass door advertising the Two Spoons Café. A bell dinged as she entered. The interior reminded Ina of a charming little café back in Queens—one that tried very hard to capture a "country" feel.

But this was the real deal, from the hardwood floors and checkered curtains, right down to the smell of freshly baked apple pie drifting from the kitchen.

"Welcome to Two Spoons!" a black woman who looked to be in her seventies called out from the front counter. She was sitting on a barstool behind a register, a tattered paperback novel in her hands. Next to the counter was a large glass display showing off homemade pies and pastries. "What brings you here, dear?"

Ina stayed close to the doorway. There were several people seated in the café. None of them had looked over at her. "Just here for some lunch," she answered, noting the woman's stark white hair and weathered skin. She didn't look old, though—just grandmotherly. Since Ina had never known her grandparents, and had always wanted to, she found herself drawn to the woman, and smiled.

"You came to the right place," the woman declared, grinning back at Ina as she set down her novel and slid off the barstool. She was short, probably under five feet tall. "Did someone recommend us to you?"

Ina decided not to mention Raven. "Not really."

The woman motioned for Ina to follow her into the dining area to a booth next to a window overlooking a stretch of the pine forest Ina had seen as she'd ridden up the dirt road. "My name's Caroline. I'll be your server today. Menu's right there at the end of the table. I'll be back in a jiffy with some water."

Before Ina could reply, Caroline left. Ina settled onto the bench seat and grabbed the menu, smiling at the listed items. Country-fried steak. Pot roast sandwich. Biscuits and gravy. Definitely no curry here.

When Caroline came back with a glass of water, Ina ordered a turkey club sandwich and a slice of apple pie. "Excellent choices," Caroline approved. "Should be out in fifteen minutes."

Ina nodded and leaned back in the booth as Caroline left. She kept her eyes out the window, focusing on the line of trees and the dark forest and mountains beyond. She'd never seen mountains like that. They were so big this close.

She wondered where Alex was now. Marsha had said his flight wasn't coming in until tomorrow evening, so he was either sightseeing or hiding in the apartment. From what Ina knew of him, she guessed he was hiding in the apartment. He'd seemed terrified when she had talked to him on the phone. Then again, he had flown out to New York just to meet with her. That took courage, especially for someone born and raised in a place like this.

Sipping at her water, Ina tried to imagine what it would be like when Alex came back. She'd never had a boyfriend before. She'd slept with a handful men, of course, but none of them counted. That was just business. The closest she'd come to having a boyfriend was that boy Raphe at the retreat. He was from an all-boys group home, and a bit of a loner, but Ina had taken a liking to him. She had hung out with him a few times. They had even made out, but before anything deeper than that could happen between them, she'd panicked.

And she had no idea why.

Squeezing her eyes shut, she remembered the night Raphe had snuggled up with her on one of the benches by the frozen lake. The air was bitterly cold, but the blanket they'd brought with them kept them warm enough. They had decided to brave the frigid temperature so they could make out in private, and it had been wonderful for a few minutes at least . . . until Raphe had pulled away, gasping.

"Kissing you is amazing," he said with a laugh, "but I can't breathe. My nose is all stuffed up from this stupid cold. Now you're probably gonna catch it."

Ina had laughed, reaching out with her mittened hand to touch Raphe's reddened nose. "It's okay. We can go back inside if you want."

He shook his head. "Nah, I'll risk suffocation to make out with you." He leaned in to kiss her again, his lips brushing against hers.

The next thing Ina knew, Jake was holding her and telling her to calm down. Dirty snow was clumped in her hair and clothes, and Raphe never spoke to her again. Jake told her she'd had a panic attack, and promised he would take care of her and that nothing bad would ever happen to her again.

"But he broke that promise," Ina hissed under her breath as she opened her eyes and looked out the window at the forest. "He lied."

Caroline approached the table with a plate of food, and Ina unclenched her fists. She'd managed to get herself so tense she was trembling. She needed to eat, that was all.

"Here's your sandwich, dear," Caroline said cheerily as she set the plate in front of Ina. "I'll bring your apple pie in a bit." She paused for a moment, her gaze lingering on Ina's face. "Are you all right?"

Ina didn't answer right away. She'd just realized that her back was facing the doorway, which meant she wouldn't be able to see who was coming and going out of the restaurant. It was a small thing, but it suddenly seemed super important. "I'm fine," she said, forcing herself to smile up at Caroline. "Thanks."

Caroline smiled a little uncertainly and left the table. As soon as she was gone, Ina slid from her seat and sat down on the opposite side of the booth, pulling her plate of food across the table. She stared down at the sandwich, her appetite completely gone, and then lifted her eyes to the door. It was glass, so she could see through to the main entrance. Nobody was out there. She didn't know why she was so shaky and nervous. Jake wasn't here. He couldn't get her here. Nobody could get her here.

Picking at her sandwich, she managed to eat half of it before Caroline brought her the apple pie. "Oh, you've hardly touched your food!" the woman exclaimed.

Ina forced another smile. "I'm not as hungry as I thought. Could you bring me a box, though? And one for the pie too? I have to get going."

Caroline nodded. "Sure thing."

Five minutes later, Ina had her food boxed up and secured in a plastic bag. She said goodbye to Caroline and hurried out to Alex's bike. She didn't know why she had felt compelled to ride all the way out here for lunch. It seemed like a mistake now. It was so far away from everything. She should have stayed at the warehouse.

Once she'd mounted Alex's bike, she hung her bag of food on the handlebars and looked over at the bed and breakfast. Caroline was watching her from the plate glass window near the cash register, a worried look on her face. Behind her, standing near the counter, was a man. He was tall with broad shoulders. He looked angry. He was saying something, and Caroline moved away from the window to talk to him.

Ina's breath stuck in her throat. It couldn't be Jake. But it *was* him. Even through the glass, several yards away, she could see that it was him. How was that possible?

Scrambling to turn the bike in the right direction, Ina took off down the dirt road, her tires kicking up clouds of dust behind her.

# *Thirty*

Alex

"Your mom's calling you *again*," Logan said as he looked down at his cell phone. He had put it on silent, and it was vibrating as the call came through.

Alex lowered his hamburger and reached for the phone. He flipped it open and said hello.

"I'm so glad you answered," his mother said frantically. "I need to talk to you about Ina. She's . . . she's not okay. I don't know what to do."

Alex sat up straight in his chair. "What happened?"

"She went into town this morning, and when she came home this afternoon I could see she'd been crying. When I asked her what the matter was, she excused herself and went up to April's room. She hasn't come out since. I knocked on the door, but she won't talk to me. I don't want to just barge in on her, but I need to make sure she's all right. I thought I'd call you first to see if there's anything you think I should do."

Alex stared down at his half-eaten food. His appetite was completely gone now. "Go knock on her door again," he said quickly. "Tell her I'm on the phone."

"Okay."

There was a shuffling sound, a quick knock, his mother's soft murmur, and two seconds later a sob echoed over the line. "A–Alex?"

"Ina, it's me. Tell me what's wrong."

"H–he's here," Ina sobbed. "I don't know what to do. He found me."

"Who found you?" He looked up at Logan, who appeared as concerned and frightened as Alex felt.

"Jake!" Ina cried. "I rode your bike out to that bed and breakfast at the end of town. I ate lunch there and I saw him as I was leaving. How did he get here? How did he know I was here?"

Alex shook his head, his eyes still on Logan. "It couldn't have been him. I think you've made a mistake. It was just someone who looked like him."

"It *was* him! I know it was!"

Alex opened his mouth to tell her he and Logan had just seen Jake that morning and that it was impossible he could have flown across the country and found her so quickly, but he couldn't make himself say it. If this was anything like when his father hallucinated, she wouldn't believe him anyway, not while she was so upset.

Right now, all he could do was comfort her.

"Listen, Ina," he said calmly. "I know you're scared, but the warehouse is safe. Every door is locked with a keypad or a deadbolt. People can't just walk in."

"That's true. I had to ring the buzzer when I got back. You're right." Her voice sounded a little steadier now.

"Right. See? We have plenty of security there, and all the employees will help keep you safe. Stay in April's room and you'll be fine. I'll be coming back tomorrow, just like I told you. Will you be okay until then?"

Ina took a long, shuddering breath. "I–I think so. You promise he can't get to me in here?"

"I promise. I'll tell my mom what's going on so she can make sure you stay safe too. Is that okay?"

"I–I think so . . . yeah . . . I think so."

"Okay, good. I'm sorry you're scared, but it'll be okay." Alex looked down at this food again, realizing he was using the same tone of voice he used with his father whenever he was hallucinating. This was the last thing he had ever imagined happening between him and Ina.

"You're right," Ina said, sounding calmer now. "I feel better talking to you. Maybe it wasn't him. Maybe . . . no, no, it was him. I'm sure of it. Anyway, I'm okay. I really am." She paused for a moment. "I was thinking about you today. I was wondering if you were out sightseeing."

Alex felt a soft smile lifting his lips. He started playing with the edge of his napkin. "Yeah, me and Logan went to see the Statue of Liberty after we talked to . . . after we ate breakfast. It was a lot smaller than it looks in pictures. I'm not sure why."

"After you talked to who?" Ina asked, her voice on edge again.

"We, uh, we . . ." How could he tell her this without implying that she had imagined seeing Jake? Maybe it was for the best. "We met with Jake early this morning," he said calmly. "He told us he wants to protect you, but we're not sure we believe him. The conversation wasn't very long."

"And then he caught a plane out here," Ina said firmly. "Did you tell him where I was? How did he know where to find me?"

"We might've said you were out of state, but—"

"That's how!" Ina interrupted. "It has to be."

Alex gave Logan a concerned look and then started rubbing his hand against the edge of the table until it hurt. He didn't stop. "Ina, think about it. We didn't tell him you're in Idaho. How could he have tracked you down and flown out there so quickly? The fastest flight is still six hours. You must have seen someone who looks like him, that's all."

Silence.

"Ina, are you there?"

"What? Yeah, yeah, I'm here. You might be right. Maybe."

Alex didn't like that she was brushing off firm logic, but it was something he'd grown used to with his father.

No.

No.

Ina was not like his father!

"What did you think of Jake?" Ina asked.

Alex kept rubbing his hand against the table. "Honestly?" he said, his voice cracking. "He kinda scared me. I can see why you want to stay away from him."

"Exactly," Ina said. "I'm so glad you're okay. I was worried he'd try to hurt you. He must've thought you aren't a threat, which is . . . well, that's not good because he'll keep trying to come after me."

Alex finally stopped rubbing the table. His skin felt raw. "Well, you're safe where you are," he said. "And I'll be there soon. We'll figure all of this out."

Ina let out a long sigh. "Thank you, Alex. When does your flight leave tomorrow?"

"Around 1:00."

"Oh, good. That means you'll have time to visit your theater school, right? Oh, guess what? I saw your teacher this morning!"

Alex sat up straight. It was strange to think of Ina and Mr. Barringer in the same room. His worlds were colliding in the weirdest way. "Really? Where?"

"At the movie theater. That's where Raven told me about the bed and breakfast."

His stomach dropped. "You met Raven?"

"Yeah, and she was gossiping about you with Mr. Barringer. This town is a minefield. Can anyone keep a secret here?"

Alex rolled his eyes. "Nope."

"I figured. That's why I'm so nervous about Jake finding me."

"He won't find you."

"Okay, okay. He won't. I believe you." She cleared her throat. "So are you going to visit your theater school before you fly out? I know how important that is to you."

Alex furrowed his brow at the thought of visiting the Marion Conservatory. Logan had mentioned it earlier when they'd ridden the subway into Manhattan, but Alex had shrugged it off, insisting he'd come back later when he had more time. Why would he visit a school he wasn't going to attend for another year? It would only upset him that he wasn't able to attend right away. It seemed stupid to put himself through unnecessary emotional trauma.

"Yeah," he finally answered. "I guess I should."

"Yes, you should. Are you actually going to?"

Alex felt Logan's eyes on him. Could he hear Ina over the phone? If he could, Alex was sure he'd be on her side about this. "Yes," he said, lowering his voice. "Of course I am."

"Why don't I believe you, Alex Winzelberg?"

"I don't know."

"What's stopping you from going?"

He lowered his voice even more. "I don't know. I guess I don't want to see what I'm missing out on right now."

There was a long pause. "Okay . . . I guess."

"You *guess*? That's the truth!"

"Okay."

Alex huffed. "You don't believe me?"

"I don't know."

"Now you're the one being vague."

Ina laughed, and the sound of it seemed to brighten the room. "I guess so. Your mom just knocked on the door and says she wants to talk to you."

Logan tapped on the table. "Getting short on minutes," he whispered, pulling a pleading look.

Alex nodded. "I need to go soon anyway. Are you sure you're okay?"

"I'm sure. Thank you, Alex."

"Anytime. Bye, Ina."

"Bye."

A moment later there was the sound of a door shutting and his mother came on the line. "Is she okay?" she asked, her voice strained. "What happened?"

"She's fine. Listen, Mom, there's something I've got to tell you and I don't have a lot of time because I'm using all of Logan's cell phone minutes."

"Okay." She still sounded worried.

"Ina's really paranoid that someone is after her, but I'm not sure that's really what's going on, and I'm worried she's . . . she might need some help, that's all. Like, maybe we can call Dr. Huang for her when I get back."

"Dr. Huang? What are you saying?"

He put a hand to his forehead. "I don't know. I don't know anything right now. Just keep an eye on Ina, okay? Don't let her leave the warehouse if you can help it. She thinks she's in danger right now, and she needs to feel safe. I don't think she'd try to leave, but anything can happen."

His mother took a moment to respond. He imagined her pacing back and forth with the phone. "This isn't good. I've got enough—"

"—on your plate, I know, Mom. I know. I'm so sorry. I'm trying to get home as fast as I can, okay? I can take care of everything when I'm back. You, the warehouse, Dad, Ina. It'll all be fine once I'm back, okay?"

She let out a heavy breath. "Okay. I'll stay up tonight to make sure Ina stays here. Maybe I'll ask one of the boys from the warehouse to help me out."

"That'd be good, Mom, thanks. I'll sleep better knowing she's safe."

"Anything for you, Alex. Stay safe, okay? And tell Logan thank you for letting us use his phone. I'll pay his bill if he goes over on minutes."

Alex smiled. "I'll let him know. Night, Mom."

"Good night."

Alex hung up and handed the phone back to Logan, repeating what his mother had said.

"She's way too nice," he laughed. "I'm pretty sure I caught most of the conversation between you and Ina. If she thinks she saw Jake in Idaho, even after you told her we just met with him this morning, she's seriously got a screw loose."

"I know."

"Do you think Dr. Huang can help?"

"He's a great doctor. I don't see why not." Alex slumped in his chair. "I still don't want to decide anything until I actually meet Ina, though."

"Yeah, I get that. I guess we're visiting your school tomorrow before you fly out?"

Alex picked up a fry and squeezed it between his fingers, focusing on trying to get the soft potato out of the crunchy shell. "Nope," he muttered. "I don't wanna go, not even with your help."

Logan rolled his eyes. "Why the hell not?"

Alex dropped the fry. "Because I just don't! Back off, okay? It will all happen when it's supposed to happen. I have other things I need to do. People need me."

It was true. If he let himself get distracted, bad things would happen, he just knew it.

Logan tucked his phone into his back pocket and took a sip of his drink. "Whatever, man. You say back off, I'll back off. For now." He stretched his arms behind his head and looked up at the ceiling. "Guess that means we can sleep in tomorrow. I'm so tired. Emily said she wants to take me out to some clubs tonight, but I don't know if I wanna go." He slid his eyes to Alex. "I know *you* won't want to."

Alex put a finger to his chin. "Alex Winzelberg and New York City clubs. I don't see those two things mixing."

Logan sighed. "Neither do I, man."

# Thirty-One

## Ina

Ina sat up in bed with a gasp, her skin cold and clammy. She clawed at the air in front of her, terrified someone was trying to put a pillow over her face. She was in danger. She needed to hide. Now. She swung her legs over the side of the bed, stopping just as her feet touched the carpet and reality hit her.

The carpet was not familiar, and she was not in danger. She was in April's room. Alex's house. She didn't need to hide. It was that stupid nightmare that someone was after her, that was all—the same one she'd had over and over since she was a child. She had never figured out why that nightmare kept haunting her.

Slowing her breathing, she slid under the covers and tried to go back to sleep, but it was no use. She sat up again, staring at the phone on April's desk. She wanted to call Alex, or maybe Philippe, but it was 3:30 in the morning.

Then she remembered Jake in the Two Spoons window.

Maybe it wasn't the nightmare that had woken her up. She trusted Alex when he said she was safe here, but Jake was still out there. Somewhere.

Sitting up in bed, she looked over at the plate of food Marsha had brought her at dinner time. Roast beef, potatoes, and broccoli. It was sitting on the desk near the phone, untouched. The thought of Jake had erased her appetite completely. She was sure it had been him at the Two Spoons, no matter what Alex said. It was possible, especially if Alex and Logan had met him early enough that he'd have time to get to LaGuardia and catch a non-stop flight. There was still an hour's drive from Boise to Anniston, but there was also the two-hour time difference. It was definitely possible.

*Wasn't it?*

Ina took a deep breath, realizing for the first time that the smell of the roast beef and broccoli in her room was making her stomach turn. Throwing off the pink bed covers, she walked to the desk and grabbed the plate. As quietly as possible, she slipped into the hallway and headed for the kitchen.

The house was completely silent. A window off to her left let in a few bars of light from the warehouse security lights, but the blinds and curtains kept most of it out. A nightlight in the kitchen guided her to the sink where she set the plate of food. On her way back to April's room, a sudden thought made her stop in the middle of the kitchen, her bare feet cold against the smooth linoleum. The only sound was the soft hum of the refrigerator. She squeezed her eyes shut.

Jake.

Jake.

Jake.

Alex's words played through her mind: *You must have seen someone who looks like him, that's all.*

Maybe Alex was right. Maybe it wasn't Jake she'd seen at the Two Spoons, or in New York reading a newspaper outside Starbucks, or even outside the restaurant or the hotel lobby. Maybe every time she had seen him it had been someone else who looked like him.

Was she that paranoid?

She couldn't be . . . could she?

The floor creaked as she shifted her weight from one foot to the other. It was the middle of the night. She needed more sleep, that was all. Everything would be clearer in the morning. She was safe here, just as Alex promised.

She had just started heading back to April's room when a soft *thump* made her jump half a foot in the air. She covered her mouth to keep any sound from coming out. The thump had come from the next room.

She crept toward the living room, peeking around the corner until she caught sight of Marsha fast asleep on one of the sofas, her chest gently rising and falling. A lamp was on in the corner, and on the floor near the sofa was an open hardback book with some of its pages bent back. It must have fallen from Marsha's lap and made the *thump*.

Letting out a sigh of relief, Ina relaxed for half a second before something else caught her eye. The front door at the other end of the room was slightly open, allowing a thin bar of warehouse light to fall across the darkened entryway.

Ina took a step back, fear crawling across her skin.

Then something moved, a slight change of light through the crack in the door.

*Someone was out there.*

Ina froze.

Thirty seconds passed. Then a minute.

She hurried to the door, intending to shut it and twist the deadbolt. Then she noticed a figure sitting on the balcony, facing the warehouse. It looked like a boy. Dark hair. Thin frame. He didn't look threatening at all.

"W–who's there?" Ina whispered through the crack in the door.

The figure spun around, and Ina stepped back, glancing over at Marsha. She was still fast asleep, but Ina was ready to wake her up if the person on the balcony made any sort of threatening move.

"Ina?" the figure asked.

Ina scrunched her brow. She recognized that voice. The dark hair. The thin frame.

"Everett?" she gasped, opening the door wider. "What are you doing here?"

He looked down at the floor of the balcony, stuttering for a moment. "Um, I . . . um . . . I don't know what to say," he managed to get out. Finally, he looked up, his face backlit by the security lights shining in the warehouse behind him. He craned his neck to try to see into the house. "Is Mrs. Winzelberg still up?"

Ina glanced at the living room again. "She's out like a light. Do you need to talk to her?"

Shrugging, Everett looked back down at the floor. "She asked me stay out here in case you—I mean, in case . . ." He looked back up, cursing under his breath. "I'm sorry. I didn't think you'd come out here. She was supposed to stay awake. I was just a backup plan."

"Backup plan for what?"

"For you. Mrs. Winzelberg said you think someone is looking for you and you might get scared and try to leave."

Ina remembered Alex saying he was going to tell his mother what was going on. This was the result. And that was okay. Looking over her shoulder one last time, Ina opened the door wide enough to slip through, and gently closed it behind her. Everett stayed in front of her, blocking the stairs leading down to the warehouse.

"Are you trying to leave?" he asked, a tinge of panic in his voice.

Ina shook her head. "I was just taking my dinner plate to the kitchen. Then I saw this door was open and it scared me."

"Oh, sorry." Everett sat down on the top step. "Guess I can chill if you're not gonna try to leave, then." He leaned against the stair railing and let out a long, wide yawn.

Ina stared down at him, surprised. "You've stayed up all night in case I came out here?"

"Well, yeah."

"Just because Marsha asked you to?"

"I'm still on the clock, but sure. She said Alex was worried about you, and I'd be helping him out bigtime. I don't mind helping Logan's friends." He looked down at his knees. "I really like Logan, and I think he liked me too. It sucks he had to leave."

Ina moved forward, exhaustion suddenly hitting her as the adrenaline in her system started to wear off. "I'm sorry he moved so far away," she said, sitting next to Everett. "How long did you know Logan before he left?"

Everett's laugh was sarcastic. "Less than a week. Isn't that stupid? We barely knew each other. I mean, how well can you get to know someone in less than a week?"

Ina thought of all the emails she and Alex had exchanged. "Well, you're not the only one. I'm staying in Alex's house, and I barely know him. Then there's Jake; he's the opposite." Her body tensed as she said his name. "I'd been around him for years. I thought I knew him, and then one day he hit me and told the police I was mental. He called me *crazy* over and over and over again. He said the meanest things about me, and it made me realize he's always thought those things about me. Things I . . . I . . ."

Her voice shuddered to a stop as tears welled up in her eyes.

Everett looked over at her, apprehension crossing his face. "He told the police you were crazy? What kind of crazy?"

Everett sounded worried, and that put Ina on edge. She narrowed her eyes. "What does that matter?" she snapped. "You don't go around calling people crazy. You did it yesterday when you were talking about Daniel. Sure, he's got mental problems, but would you ever say that to his face?"

Everett raised an eyebrow. "Well, no, but he knows he has mental problems. Everybody knows. I just wanna know what you meant by that man saying you were crazy."

"I meant exactly what I said. He told the police I was insane and they believed him. They sent counselors and psychiatrists to talk to me. I mean, how could he do that to me? He took care of me for so long. He protected me. And then to turn on me like he did, just to save his own ass? It sucked, and now he's after me again."

"Mrs. Winzelberg didn't tell me that much. All she said was you might be a danger to yourself, just like Mr. Winzel—"

He stopped short, and Ina looked him square in the face. "She told you *what*?"

"N–nothing," he stammered. "She told me Alex said you were scared and we should make sure you don't leave the house until he gets back."

"*And* she implied I'm a danger to myself?" She couldn't believe it. Marsha thought she was crazy too! And Everett believed her, apparently. She stood up, her chest heaving. "I have to get out of here," she gasped. "I have to leave."

Everett popped up so fast Ina stumbled back toward the door. "You can't," he said frantically, blocking the stairway. "Please, Ina? Please, let's talk, okay? You seem so nice. You aren't crazy. There's nothing wrong with you. You're just scared."

He had his hands out, like he was afraid she was going to charge him. After a moment, he lowered his hands. "I know what it's like for people to think there's something wrong with you—to want to fix you. It's a shitty feeling."

Ina stared at him, her anger and frustration dulling to a faint buzz inside her head as she considered Everett's words. "You really do understand," she whispered.

Everett nodded.

Ina stood still for a full minute before moving forward. "Sit down," she said softly. "Let's talk some more. I'm not gonna leave."

Everett hesitated, but finally sat back down on the stairs. Ina sat next to him, her heart pounding.

"What happened?" Everett asked. "Who is this Jake guy? Why does he think you're crazy?"

Resting her elbows on her knees, Ina stared out into the warehouse. Only the security lights were on, so it was still fairly dark, the big shelves and rows of stacked pallets full of shadows. It reminded her of sitting in the café earlier and staring out at the mountains and the trees. The forest had reminded her of the retreat and the way Jake had held her after her panic attack with Raphe. He'd stroked her head, promising her nothing bad would ever happen to her again. Months later, at another retreat, he had kept his distance from her, but was still constantly in sight, a reassuring presence.

Now, sitting next to Everett, Ina clenched her jaw and buried her face in her hands. "I am not crazy like he said," she muttered. "I'm not."

"Of course you aren't," Everett assured her. "What made him say that in the first place?"

"I don't know. My panic attacks, maybe? Sometimes they're super intense. They're triggered by the dumbest things. And he said I talk to myself. But that doesn't make me crazy, right?" She lifted her head from her hands. Everett was watching her with worry in his eyes. "Nothing is wrong with me," she whispered.

"Of course not. Lots of people have panic attacks. And everyone talks to themselves."

"Yeah, they do," Ina said, nodding her head vigorously. "They really do. I have conversations with myself all the time. It's usually to make myself feel better when I'm under a lot of stress. Th–that's normal. I'm fine. I'm . . . *fine.*"

Everett looked over at her, an eyebrow raised. "Then why do you sound like you're not fine?"

Ina reached up to swipe away some tears rolling down her cheeks. Everything was coming at her now. All the memories. There were so many of them, and so fast that she couldn't separate them all. It was more like a jumbled mess of emotions wrapping around her, squeezing, making it hard to breathe. Her face felt cold, tingly, and numb. She leaned forward and pressed her forehead against her knees.

She knew it now.

She'd known it all along.

The phone calls.

Nothing else could explain those. They proved the truth.

"It wasn't real," she whimpered against her knees. "I pretended to call Alex and made myself believe he invited me here. I knew what I was doing, but it's like my brain wouldn't admit it, like I was watching myself and couldn't stop it. In that moment, it was so real. So, so *real.* I never called Mom either. She never wanted to talk to me, so I had to make myself believe she did. See? I'm not crazy. I *know* I did those things. I can see it now. I just . . . I still don't know if I really saw Jake. Why did he say those things about me? Why did he hit me? I don't know what to do if he finds me. What does he want? Why do I keep painting the same thing over and over? Why do I freak out? I don't—"

"Ina!" Everett's voice cut through her panic. "Ina, stop!" He grabbed her face and forced her to look at him. "*Stop*," he said firmly. "Get a grip. Breathe, okay? Breathe in and out."

Ina took in a deep breath, watching Everett do the same thing. He had pretty eyes, she realized. They were a deep, fervent brown. They drew her in, coaxing her to breathe in and out until the tingling in her face faded to a soft, fuzzy sensation. Tears kept rolling down her cheeks.

"It's all my fault," she finally managed to say. "What's wrong with me? I can't trust what my brain is telling me."

Everett kept his eyes on hers. "Nothing is wrong with you. Do you seriously think you're losing your mind?"

She shook her head and sniffed. "No, I don't think so. But there are things that scare me—things I don't understand. I don't know why I feel the way I feel. I don't know why I can't get rid of certain thoughts in my head. It's driving me . . . It's driving me crazy," she whispered. "So crazy I haven't been able to admit any of it to myself until now."

Everett lowered his hands from her face. "I know how you feel. I hid some of my deepest, darkest secrets for so long I thought I was gonna end up in a mental hospital. I was so scared to talk about any of it that I started lying to myself until I finally met someone who helped me face the truth."

Ina looked up. "Who helped you?"

"A friend at school. She helped me see if I kept hiding from myself instead of facing what I was going through, I wasn't going to survive. I'm pretty sure she saved my life."

Ina took a long, deep breath. "Well," she said softly. "I need to figure this out. I'm scared of so many things and I don't know why. It's like there's this dark space in my mind. I've tried to paint it. I know I've dreamed about it. I've even tried talking to myself about it, but every time I get close to figuring it out, I panic."

Everett squeezed her hand again. "Maybe you need someone to help you, someone who knows about this kind of thing. Like a doctor."

Ina looked up, her eyes widening. "Maybe," she said, almost breathlessly. "Maybe that's the answer."

# Thirty-Two

## Alex

"I didn't come all this way for nothing," Logan grumbled as the subway train slowed to a stop and the doors slid open. "Get out."

Alex stayed rooted to his seat. The subway alone had been enough to put him on edge—all the people, the grunge, the noise, the smells. He just wanted to get back to LaGuardia Airport where he could catch his plane and fly home.

Unfortunately, that flight wasn't taking off for four hours, which left plenty of time for Logan to drag him into Manhattan so they could visit the Marion Conservatory.

So here they were, in the heart of Greenwich Village, and Alex was frozen to his seat. "I don't want to," he said as people in their car stood up and filed out of the doors. An entirely new group of people was already boarding the car and filling up the seats.

Logan bent down and grabbed Alex's arm, pulling him out of his seat. "I don't care if you don't want to," he growled, as if Alex was five years old. A few seconds later they were out on the platform, the doors closing behind them.

"Dude," Alex sighed as Logan nudged him toward the stairs leading up to street level. "I really don't wanna go.

I'm not ready to see all of that yet. It'll just make me sad I'm not going this year."

Rolling his eyes, Logan grabbed Alex's wrist and started pulling him up the stairs. Alex finally relented and walked willingly behind Logan up to the street. It felt and looked the same as yesterday morning when they had come into Manhattan to see the Statue of Liberty. Only this time there was a sinking feeling in Alex's gut that made him want to hurl all over the sidewalk. He didn't understand why he was so anxious about visiting Marion. He just was. He couldn't envision himself here every single day, walking these streets, seeing so many people everywhere all the time. It was so different from Anniston. It didn't feel safe, and it certainly didn't feel like something he wanted to do now. What had made him think it was a good idea to be an actor?

They walked a few blocks and crossed several streets, finally entering a quieter street than the others. It was lined with maples, their leaves rustling softly in the morning breeze. Many of the tan-brick buildings were apartments. There was laundry hanging on some of the fire escapes, the sound of a baby crying from an open window a few floors up. People were getting in and out of cars parked along the street.

"See?" Logan said as they walked past a fire hydrant covered in graffiti. "There are quieter places in the city. I think the conservatory is a few blocks down from here." He pulled a folded piece of paper from his back pocket and studied it. "Yep, two blocks."

Alex stayed by Logan's side, his heart beating faster as he kept walking. His mouth had gone dry. He'd barely said three words to Logan since leaving the subway station. Finally, Logan stopped to look at a building across the street. Sandwiched between two modern business complexes several stories tall, it looked old and worn down, but the sign out front was new. It proudly proclaimed THE MARION CONSERVATORY OF PERFORMING ARTS in red, white, and gold above the front entrance. A woman dressed all in black was walking inside.

"You ready?" Logan asked Alex, a grin on his face.

Alex took a step back. "No," he said, his voice cracking. "No, I can't. I know where it is and how to get here. That's enough for now."

Logan's grin slid off his face. "I thought I understood you, but sometimes you pull crap like this and I have no idea what to do with it."

Alex forced a smile. "Gotta keep you guessing." He laughed pathetically and started walking back toward the subway station. "Come on, let's go."

Logan caught Alex by the elbow. "What the hell is wrong with you?"

Alex ripped away. "Stop grabbing me! Seriously, you've been dragging me everywhere since we got here."

"Only because you'd fall apart if I didn't!" Logan huffed. "You'd still be a frozen statue at the subway station in Queens if it weren't for me! I've helped you every step of the way, and now you're getting mad at me for it? What gives?"

Alex looked down at his tennis shoes and shrugged. "I don't know," he grumbled, knowing Logan was right. He looked up. "Sorry. You've helped me a lot, but this is something you can't make me do, okay? I'm not ready."

"Why not?"

Looking down at his shoes again, Alex thought about the time he'd gone into his first audition when he was a junior, how nervous he'd been, with Ina's words stuck in his head: *Life's too short not to chase after dreams.*

He supposed Ina had been the one dragging him into that audition. Had he ever done *anything* on his own? Then he thought about all the work he'd done for the warehouse, for his family, for his father, and his heart swelled with the need to be back there, to be where he was needed, where he was comfortable. Everything he'd ever done for his family had been from the very heart of who he was. Nobody had ever made him do any of that. *That* was where he belonged right now.

He looked up at Logan again. "Because my family needs me. Ina needs me." He waved a hand at the conservatory. "I can't walk through those doors until everything else is taken care of. It's just what I have to do."

Logan's expression twisted into frustration. He looked over at the school and let out a long sigh. "Okay, man. I don't understand it, but okay."

Something tugged at Alex's emotions. Maybe it was guilt. Maybe it was heartache. Whatever it was, it hurt. He looked at the conservatory then turned away as quickly as he could. "Let's go," he muttered. "I've got a plane to catch."

* * *

Alex slid into the front of seat of his parents' LeSabre and took a deep breath of peppermint and freshly oiled leather. It smelled like home, like comfort and safety. He imagined his father oiling the leather, humming to the radio as he worked.

"So there's something you should know," Alex's mother said as she slid into the driver's seat and fastened her seatbelt. She had met Alex at his gate and led him out of the airport and to the car in a nearby parking garage. So far, all they had talked about was his flight and a few other pointless things.

"What should I know?" he asked. "Is it something about Ina? Is she okay? Or is it Dad? Did he hallucinate again?"

His mother started the engine and maneuvered the car into reverse. "No, your father's fine. He was fine the whole time you were gone. And Ina . . . she's okay . . . for the most part."

Alex tensed in his seat. "What do you mean 'for the most part'? What happened?"

"Nothing bad!" She tapped her thumb on the steering wheel as she backed out of the parking stall. "After your phone call last night, I asked Everett to help me make sure Ina didn't leave the warehouse just in case she got past me. After I fell asleep in the living room, she did sort of try to leave. Everett stopped her and they ended up talking. After that, she and Everett woke me up and we all decided it'd be best if Ina talked to Dr. Huang, so we—"

"Whoa!" Alex interrupted. "You're going way too fast!"

His mother pulled out of the garage and onto a road leading out of the airport. "Okay," she said slowly. "I'll explain this better. You were right about Ina. She isn't . . . well, something is wrong with her. But she came to terms with that last night and asked if there was a doctor she could talk to. So we called Dr. Huang this morning, and he came right over. He and Ina decided it would be best if she stays somewhere else for now, somewhere more controlled, where she'll feel safe and cared for. The warehouse is not that place. I'm too busy and there's too much going on."

"Where is she?" Alex wasn't sure how he felt about this new development. He was still completely confused as to what exactly had happened to make Ina "come to terms" about her mental condition.

"She's at River Meadows," his mother answered. "Dr. Huang sometimes sends patients there instead of Boise. Not that he's sending her to Boise. Nothing like that."

"How bad is this?" Alex asked shakily. "What happened? I mean, is she like . . . did she start doing stuff like Dad does?"

"No, nothing like that. Dr. Huang said it's trauma. He's certain he can help her through it, whatever it is. She's just had some strange behaviors develop because of it, and she's finally admitting that to herself."

Alex knew he should be relaxing at such news, but he was tensing up even more. A knot started forming at the base of his neck, and he reached up to rub it. "I don't understand," he whispered. "How did she just admit that to herself? Something must have happened."

"She talked to Everett. I don't know what he said, but she opened up to him."

Alex's eyebrows knit together. Why would Ina open up to Everett and not to him? Sure, Ina had told Alex things through email, even over the phone, but she had never opened up to him in the way his mother was implying. Why Everett? Alex knew it shouldn't bother him, but it did.

"Well, I can't wait to see her," he said. "I *can* go see her, right? I've waited too long to meet her. I can't—"

"Of course you can see her!" his mother laughed. "She's not under lock and key. She can come and go as she pleases. It's just a place she can stay until she feels well enough to move on. Dr. Huang is already trying to find a good doctor for her in New York."

Alex cringed at the thought of Ina flying back to New York. He knew she would at some point, but he hoped she stayed for a little while, at least. "Take me straight there, then," he said.

"Of course, Alex. Anything you want." His mother gave him a sidelong glance, her expression softening. "I'm so happy you're okay, honey." She reached over and squeezed his hand. "So, so happy you're okay."

"You called me a million times, Mom. You knew I was okay."

"I know, but it's not the same as having you here." She let go of his hand and focused on the road again. The tension and worry in her voice didn't escape Alex. She needed him more than ever, and he wasn't about to leave her again. Not for a long time. Not as long as she was like this.

Looking down at his lap, he noticed a worn spot in the left knee of his jeans that would probably rip the next time he bent down too fast. His life felt worn like that, he realized—so worn and thin it seemed useless to patch it up.

# Thirty-Three

"She's in Room 36," Leslie said as soon as Alex approached the front desk at River Meadows after his mother had dropped him off. "You're here for Sabrina Sanchez, right?"

It was strange to hear Ina called by her full name. Alex nodded. "Yeah, how did you know?"

Leslie smiled. "She said she hoped you'd come by."

"I can just go in?" Alex asked, his heart starting to pound. He was about to see Ina! After all these years, all the buildup . . . and it was here. It wasn't how he had imagined it would be, but that didn't matter. It was here.

"Sign in on the clipboard first then go right down that hall." Leslie motioned toward the left wing and turned back to her computer. "Let me know if you need anything."

A minute later, Alex was standing in front of the closed door to Room 36. He lifted his hand and knocked softly.

"Come in!"

He turned the handle and opened the door.

And there she was—as *Ina* as Ina could possibly be—sitting at a desk near the bed, dressed in sweatpants and an oversized royal blue sweatshirt. She swiveled her chair around to face him. She had honey-brown skin and dark chestnut eyes so intense they seemed to pierce right through Alex's heart. But it was her hair that stood out the most. It was just as she had described: big, curly, and frizzy. She had pulled it up into a messy bun, barely contained. For some weird reason, Alex wanted to touch it. He shoved his hands into his pockets, forcing himself to keep his eyes on her instead of looking at the ground. He didn't want to look too nervous.

"You're just like I imagined," Ina said. A smile broke across her face. She had nice, straight teeth.

Alex opened his mouth, struggling to find the right words. "You're . . . you're . . ." He wanted to say, *You're really hot*, but knew better. Instead, he fumbled like a fish gasping for water. Finally, he blurted, "Your nose is *not* big!"

Ina leaned forward, her smile widening into an all-out grin. "But my forehead is," she laughed, pointing to her head.

Alex raised an eyebrow. "No it's not. You're really pretty, Ina. I mean it."

Her grin softened into a grateful half-smile. "Thanks, Alex. You're not so bad yourself. You've come a long way since that picture hanging in your living room."

"Oh no," Alex groaned, his cheeks growing warm. "You saw that? I hate that picture."

"You were adorable."

"That's the last thing any guy wants to hear."

Ina motioned for him to come farther into the room. It was small but nice, with a bed and armchair in one corner and a kitchenette in another.

"Have a seat," Ina said, pointing to the armchair. She looked nervous, her eyes even more intense than before. "Or do you think it'd be weird if I hugged you? I mean, I wanted to hug you the second you walked in here, but . . . I don't know . . ." She looked down at her lap. "Everything's been so crazy the past few days, and I keep worrying about what you'll think of me." She looked up again, tears glistening in her eyes. "Thank you for everything you've done."

Ina's words reverberated through Alex like drumbeats. He felt everything she said because they were the same words in his own heart. "I don't think it'd be weird," he said, his voice almost cracking. He took a step forward, and Ina jumped out of the chair and rushed into his arms. He didn't know what she smelled like, but it was a good smell. She smelled like Ina, like eccentricity and honesty and pain, like a hand he wanted to hold forever. Her hair was soft as it brushed against his cheek.

He wrapped his arms around her, realizing she was just as she had described. Thin but not skinny. Just the right curves and just the right height. He tried not to hold her too tightly. The last thing he wanted to do was give her the wrong impression, even though he had to admit he was very attracted to her, physically and emotionally. She turned him on in a way someone like Emily couldn't. Still, he was her friend first and foremost, and that was how it was going to stay unless she indicated she wanted more. Even then, he wasn't sure what the right thing to do would be. There was still so much to figure out.

"Thank you, Alex," she sighed against his shoulder. "I don't know how much your mom told you, but thank you for understanding me. Thank you for always being there." She took a deep breath and pulled away.

Alex looked her in the eyes. "Are you okay?" he asked. "My mom explained a little bit about what happened, but she was pretty vague. What's really going on?"

Ina took a step back, her eyes widening as she shook her head. A soft sob escaped her throat, and she raised a trembling hand to her mouth. "This is all my fault. I never actually called you." She turned away from him. "I made it all up in my head. I pretended to call you. It wasn't your father I talked to. It was *myself.* I knew it wasn't real, but at the same time, I didn't know. It felt real. It was the only excuse I could find to get out of New York and get away from Jake. I've done it before—made up calls like that in my head. I even act them out. It's not normal. *I'm* not normal. I mean, who does that? Who panics so hard they make up seeing people in their head? I never really saw Jake all those times. Or maybe I did, but not here. I—"

Alex spun Ina around and pulled her close. "It's okay," he said, holding her tight. "It's okay, I promise." He released his hold on her enough to look her in the face. "There's nothing wrong with you. Dr. Huang would know. He's a great doctor, and my mom told me he said it was just trauma from your past. That can be fixed. *Anything* can be fixed, okay?"

Ina blinked. "Yeah, Dr. Huang talked with me for a long time this morning. It must've been two hours. He took all kinds of notes, asked me a million questions, had me take a test. He said I shouldn't worry, but he wanted me to feel safe and suggested I come and stay here for a few days while we do some therapy and stuff. He said this place has a security guard at night, and the nurses can get me anything I need, and if I feel like I'm getting out of control or scared or something, they can help. They're trained for that sort of thing." She looked up at Alex. "It helps me feel better to be here. I do feel safe. I feel even better now that you're here and I can explain stuff to you."

Alex frowned. "What do you have to explain?"

"That phone call," she sighed, stepping away from him again. "And seeing Jake here in town. I mean, you said you met with him yesterday morning, so how could he have found me here so fast, right? Seriously, you must think I've totally lost it. Just like Jake does."

Alex sighed. "I don't think you've lost it. We're talking normally now, aren't we? You're not crazy, and anything else that makes you feel like you're crazy is stuff Dr. Huang can help you with. Trust me, okay?"

Ina nodded, her curls bouncing up and down in her messy bun. "I know, I know. I just feel bad. There's so much I'm trying to figure out. I don't know why I am the way I am. I thought I had it all figured out, but Dr. Huang helped me see I really don't. There's something more, something I'm not remembering."

"Dr. Huang will help you," Alex said soothingly. "I think there's some stuff you should know about, though. Me and Emily and Logan went to see your boss."

Ina's eyes widened. "Philippe? Why?"

Alex shrugged, suddenly nervous. He wasn't sure how much Ina remembered about her night with Vincenzo Conti. Perhaps nothing. If so, she needed to know everything he and Logan and Emily knew. He started pacing the room, finally deciding it would be best to sit down. He went over to the armchair. Ina sat down in the office chair, her expression worried as she waited for him to talk.

"I don't want you to worry about this," Alex explained. "And maybe you can add more to the story. Maybe you remember more than Emily thinks you do. It's about the night you emailed me and told me you saw Jake. You said you were emailing me from a stranger's computer. That stranger was your Italian client, Mr. Conti, right?"

Ina sat up straight. "How do you know about him?" She paused for a moment. "You mean, you went to see Philippe about that?" She sat up even straighter. "Did Vincenzo tell him what happened?" Panic edged her voice.

Alex lifted a hand. "It's okay, I promise. How much do you remember?"

Ina shook her head. "Hardly anything. It's such a blur. I panicked that night, and then I woke up at home." Her hands balled into tight fists. "Did he hurt me?"

"No," Alex said quickly. "No." He relayed the visit to Philippe's office as he remembered it, giving all the details Vincenzo had given. As he spoke, the panic in Ina's expression melted away. Her hands relaxed in her lap.

"Oh," she said softly. "I must have forgotten a lot of it because of the drinks and the sleeping pills. The panic attack, though . . . that's not normal. I don't know why I panicked like that. It's like I have no control when I get like that." She let out a shaky laugh. "See? Crazy."

Alex frowned. "You are not crazy, Ina. Please don't say that."

Ina tilted her head. "Do you say that to your dad too?" she asked. "How do you talk to him about his condition?"

Alex sat back in the armchair and shook his head. "We're honest with him," he answered firmly. "Completely honest about what happens. We don't tell him he's crazy, though. He's not crazy. He's perfectly sane most of the time. It's just when he slips into a hallucination that he loses control."

Ina narrowed her eyes for a moment, studying Alex in a way that made him shift in his chair. It was surreal to have her look at him like that—like she knew him better than anyone—when they'd only been in the same room together for twenty minutes.

"I believe you," she finally said. "But you can't sit there and tell me it's easy and his illness doesn't bother you. You've told me in your emails how you really feel—that you're the one who's been left to take care of him. He *does* need help, and you're the one who has to help him."

Alex nodded. "Yeah, that's what I'm here for."

Ina chewed on her bottom lip for a moment. "Do you feel like *I* need help?" she asked.

Alex paused, worried about where this conversation was going. "I–I thought we talked about that," he said slowly. "Dr. Huang is going to—"

"Let me rephrase that," Ina interrupted. "Do you feel like *you* need to help me like you help your dad? Is that why you wanted to fly out to New York so bad?"

Ina could read him like an open book. He shook his head. "I care about you," he said, meeting her gaze. "I care a lot about you. If I was in trouble, you'd want to help me too."

"Yeah, I would."

"Do you feel the same about Everett?"

Ina narrowed her eyes. "What?"

"I'm just curious why you opened up to Everett and not to me." He rolled his eyes to the ceiling. "I sound like a jerk just asking that."

"I barely know Everett," Ina explained. "His own problems made me see things differently, that's all. You mean way more to me than him." She stood up and crossed the room to Alex. "Now, I mean this in the nicest way possible, but I'm seriously tired and need to sleep. Come back tomorrow and we can talk some more, okay?"

Alex stood up to face her, holding back from embracing her again. "I still can't believe I'm here," he said, giving her a soft smile. "But I'm glad I am, and I'm glad you're okay."

Ina smiled warmly. "I'm glad you survived New York," she laughed as they headed for the door. "Emily made it sound like you were gonna die."

Alex looked away, embarrassed. "I don't know how I'm ever gonna go to school there," he muttered. "I'm not used to a big city like that."

Ina stepped closer, still smiling. She looked hesitant, like she wanted to get even closer, but was holding back the same as he was. "I'll be there," she said. "I'll help you."

Clearing his throat, Alex nodded. "It'll happen. Next year."

"You sound just like your emails, Alex Winzelberg."

Alex laughed as he opened the door a few inches. "Gotta make sure I'm not some imposter."

Ina leaned up to kiss Alex on the cheek. A thrill ran straight from his head to his toes. He almost let go of the door, but held on to the handle to keep his balance.

"Thanks again," Ina whispered. "See you tomorrow."

Alex opened the door all the way, looking over his shoulder before stepping out into the hallway. "You too, Ina. Peace out."

Ina laughed. "Peace out."

# Thirty-Four

It was almost midnight. Tossing and turning, Alex couldn't get Ina out of his head. Finally, he got out of bed and walked to the window. The blinds were open, showing a dimly lit view of the empty warehouse parking lot.

A soft rap at the door made him spin around. "Yeah?"

The door opened and his mother stepped inside, her expression distraught. "Alex, it's—"

"Let me guess," Alex sighed. "Dad, right?"

She nodded. "He's down in the warehouse. I couldn't stop him. He wants to find Christmas decorations. He thinks Christmas is tomorrow morning, and he's upset we haven't decorated or bought any gifts."

Alex followed her down into the warehouse. He shivered when his bare feet hit cold concrete. It was unsafe to walk down here without shoes; there could be broken glass or nails the push brooms had missed. Alex didn't care. All of the lights were on, and the sound of his father's loud, booming voice echoed through the warehouse. Alex couldn't understand what his dad was saying.

"Sounds like he's down the holiday storage aisle," Alex said as they walked farther into the bowels of the warehouse. "I guess it'd make sense he'd go there."

"Not really," his mother sighed. "You know we store all of our Christmas decorations in the house, not down here. I tried to tell him that, but he insisted on coming down."

They rounded a corner and Alex stopped short at the sight of his father climbing up the pallet racking. It was warehouse law: never *ever* climb the racking. And yet there was Daniel Winzelberg, climbing up the racking like a newbie employee who didn't listen. He was almost to the top rack.

Alex took a deep breath to shout at him to come back down, but his mother put a hand on his arm. "Let's head over there and wait out whatever he's doing."

Alex watched his father scramble to the top rack. He stood up between two wrapped pallets of boxes and started ripping at one of them with his fingers. Only a few feet above him, the warehouse lights shone brightly on his head.

"I'll go get a ladder," Alex said. "Try to keep him up there until I get back."

His mother nodded, and Alex sprinted toward where they kept the ladders. His head was starting to pound. His heart hurt with something he couldn't pinpoint—grief or anger. Maybe it was both. There would never be an end to this. His father might get better temporarily, but there was no cure for his condition.

Ina's questions echoed through his mind: *Do you feel like you need to help me like you help your dad? Is that why you wanted to fly out to New York so bad?*

Alex reached the extension ladders and hefted the tallest one onto his shoulder. It was heavy and awkward, but he'd done it enough times it was second nature. He started back to the holiday aisle, more focused on Ina's questions than the current situation. She was right, he realized. He *did* feel like he needed to help her like he helped his dad. It *was* the reason he'd flown out to New York. But shouldn't he want to help her? Shouldn't he want to help his parents? Nobody else was going to do it. Nobody could care like he cared. Nobody could replace him.

He finally rounded the corner to see his mother craning her neck to look at her husband. She was now in a spot that if he toppled off the edge, he'd crush her. Alex hurried to her side, nudging her away from the danger zone, and maneuvered the ladder into position. He extended it until it reached the top rack, and secured the feet to the floor. His father didn't seem to notice at all.

"Should I go up there?" Alex asked.

She shrugged. "He doesn't even know we're down here. I haven't said a word to him. He just keeps tearing away at the pallet wrap."

"I'll go up. It'll be easier to convince him to climb down."

"No, I'll do it," his mother said firmly, stepping forward. "Just stay down here in case anything—"

"No way." Alex grabbed her arm. "I'll do it."

She glared at him. "Honey, if you fell . . ."

"If *you* fell, I'd never forgive myself."

Something burned in her eyes. Maybe it was stubbornness. Maybe it was something else. But Alex knew there was no way he was going to let her go up there. He knew she'd been up to the top rack before—everyone had—but never with her husband when he was hallucinating. Who knew what could happen up there.

Taking a deep breath, Alex let go of his mother's arm and started climbing the ladder. When he reached the top, his father looked down at him and smiled. "They've gotta be in here. The ornaments. They're in here."

Still gripping the sides of the ladder, Alex glanced at the boxes to read the text along the sides. "Yeah, those are Christmas ornaments," he replied, surprised. "They're supposed to ship out in September."

"But it's December," his father scoffed. "We've gotta get some out to put on the tree! Is it snowing yet? I love it when it snows on Christmas Eve, don't you?"

Alex's heart sank in his chest. His father looked so happy. How could he crush that happiness and tell him none of this was real? "Yes, I do love snow on Christmas Eve," he finally answered. "Let me help you get the ornaments, then we'll climb down the ladder, okay?"

Alex climbed the rest of the way up and instinctively reached for a box cutter in his back pocket before realizing he was wearing his pajama pants. Shrugging, he started ripping away at the pallet wrap with his father until they could free one of the boxes. Alex hoisted it down, placing it near his feet. There was just enough room for him and his father to crouch down between two pallets. "We won't need the whole box," he assured his father. "Let's just get one set out, okay?" If it came down to it, they could probably write off a set or two without upsetting the client.

His father clapped his hands together. "Yes! I want to see them. Get one out."

Alex peeled up the tape along one side and ripped it off the top of the box. Opening the lid, he pushed aside several sheets of bubble wrap and pulled out a smaller box. It was the size of a shoebox, the top of it covered with a thick, crinkly piece of translucent plastic so the delicate glass ornaments could be seen inside. Alex looked down at them, his eyes filling with tears. He'd always loved Christmas when his whole family was together. His father had never once hallucinated on Christmas. It had always been a good day, and Alex wanted to believe it would stay that way.

His father beamed down at him. "They're pretty," he said giddily. "I can't wait to see them on the tree. Can I hold them?"

Alex lifted the box up, and his father grabbed it. His eyes twinkled. It was a good thing this hallucination was a happy one. Those didn't happen often. They were usually accompanied by fear and anger. Alex would take what he could get. He rose to his feet and touched his father's shoulder. "Should we climb down?" he asked gently. "It's not very safe up here."

His father looked up at him, his eyes still twinkling. "Yes, yes, let's do that." Before Alex could stop him, he tossed the box over the edge. It hit the concrete floor with a heart-wrenching crunch.

"Alex!" his mother cried out. "What's going on?"

Alex watched his father carefully, panic rising in his chest as he waited for a reaction. "D–Dad, are you okay?" he asked gently.

His father blinked a few times, the twinkle in his eyes fizzling out. He stared at the racks across the aisle, as if they'd appeared out of nowhere. He took a shaky step back and looked at the drop below. Grabbing on to the edge of the ornaments pallet, he finally looked at Alex and took a deep breath. "I'm so sorry," he whispered. "I'm so sorry." He started rubbing his arms. "It's not really Christmas Eve, is it?" he asked, his voice strained.

Alex shook his head. "No, Dad."

"What day is it?" he asked urgently, clearly trying to grasp hold of reality.

"It's June 26th." Alex glanced at his watch. "Well, technically it's June 27th now."

His father nodded slowly. He kept hold of the pallet and carefully lowered himself to his knees. "I could have killed myself," he muttered. "And you . . . you're up here with me. You could have been hurt, Alex." He stared down at his knees as tears rolled down his cheeks.

"Dad, this is good," Alex said as relief flooded through him. "This one didn't last that long. You came out faster than you usually do, and you weren't angry. You were happy."

"Silver linings," his father chuckled. He looked up. "Where's your mother?"

Alex jerked his thumb toward the ladder.

"Let's get down," his father said, rising to his feet. "I'll go first. You be careful, okay?"

Alex nodded and backed out of the way so his father could slide past him. When he'd disappeared down the ladder, Alex followed him. His hands shook around the ladder, but not because he was nervous. It was adrenaline finally leaving his system. His father was safe. Everything would be okay.

For now.

* * *

"That's it, I'm coming out there as soon as I can get a flight," April said sternly over the phone. "This can't keep happening, Alex. Something has to change."

Alex leaned back on his pillows and put a hand to his forehead. Maybe it had been a bad idea to call his sister at 1:00 in the morning, practically in tears. He just hadn't known what else to do or who else to turn to. Besides Logan, April was the only other stable, reliable person in his life right now. She had answered the phone, groggily at first, but once Alex had told her everything that had happened since she'd left, she sounded wide awake.

"Please don't fly out here," Alex groaned. "That's not why I called. I just needed someone to talk to."

"You clearly need me there *with* you," April growled. "Mom and Dad are being so stupid. Why haven't they hired someone? You need to go to school! I mean, you made it all the way out to New York and survived! You have to go now."

Alex scrunched his brow. "I thought you wanted me to stay here for another year. It was your idea."

"I'm an idiot," April muttered. "Don't listen to me. The second I'm off the phone, I'm getting online to book a flight. I'll call and let you know what time."

Alex sat up on his bed. "Seriously? April, you can't just drop school for this! It's not that important. I'll go to New York next year. I'll—"

"It's not about that," April interrupted. "Why are you so blind?"

Alex rolled his eyes. "Because I'm just a dumb teenager," he replied sarcastically. "I don't know anything. Oh, except for how to run WFS and keep Mom from freaking out and Dad from hurting himself, right?"

"Yes, Alex, of course. Keep telling yourself that. See you tomorrow. You'd better be at the airport. Don't send Mom. I'll call you back in a few minutes with the time."

She hung up, and Alex turned off the phone and tossed it to the foot of his bed. So much for talking things through. Now he was more irritated than distraught. His sister was good at that.

# Thirty-Five

## Ina

"Tuesdays are the best days," the old lady sitting across from Ina said loudly through a mouthful of dry toast. She had to be at least eighty-five years old, but she looked pretty great, with carefully styled gray hair and perfectly applied makeup. "That's when they make silver-dollar pancakes."

Ina smiled. "Every Tuesday, huh? Too bad it's Sunday."

"Yep, too bad." The woman took another bite of toast and eyed Ina with a suddenly suspicious gaze. "You're new here," she said slowly. "Aren't you?"

Ina nodded. "Arrived yesterday. I'm one of Dr. Huang's patients. I probably won't be here very long."

The suspicion in the woman's eyes faded away. "What's your name, dear?"

"Ina."

"I'm Elvira. Don't hear that name anymore, do you? Must be a reason, eh?"

Ina laughed politely. "No, you don't hear it anymore, but that doesn't mean it isn't pretty."

Elvira took another bite of toast. "Well, you can eat breakfast with me as long as you're here. I always sit at this table. 9:30 every morning."

Ina looked down at her watch. It was 9:45 now, which meant Dr. Huang would be arriving soon. She looked around the dining room. It was pretty high-scale for such a small town. The round tables were set with crisp, white linen and fresh flowers in vases. Warm sunlight spilled in through the open-draped windows. The room was half full, occupied mostly by elderly people clustered in small groups.

Ina lowered her eyes to the remnants of her scrambled eggs and toast. The food wasn't half-bad either. She hadn't eaten scrambled eggs in a long time. She looked up to see Elvira finishing off her toast and staring out one of the windows with a look of longing. "Do you always eat alone?" Ina asked.

Elvira tore her eyes away from the window. "Usually," she said lightly. "I, uh . . . I forget things. It's difficult to make friends when you don't remember them from day to day. I'll probably have no idea who you are tomorrow. Hope you don't take that personally, dear."

That made Ina smile for some reason. She reached across the table and placed her hand on top of Elvira's. The woman's skin was soft and loose around her bones. "Nobody's perfect," Ina said gently. "I'll just introduce myself to you again, how's that?"

A hand touched Ina's shoulder, and she looked up to see Dr. Huang smiling down at her. "You ready for our session?" he asked.

Ina nodded and said goodbye to Elvira. She followed Dr. Huang out of the dining room and back toward the main lobby area. He nodded hello to the two girls working the front desk and then continued on to another hallway filled with glass-walled rooms. They looked like conference rooms, except for one fairly large room that contained a piano, a coffee table, and several couches. Dr. Huang opened the door for Ina.

"Have a seat," he said, motioning to the couch closest to the piano, and set his briefcase on the coffee table. He was dressed in slacks and a white button-down shirt. No tie.

Ina did as he said and watched him take a seat at the piano. It was a baby grand. The lid was closed. "You're going to play the piano?" Ina asked, confused.

"I sure am. We'll talk as I play. I've found it an excellent tool for getting through tough sessions. Trust me."

Ina realized her eyebrows were scrunched together, clearly showing her doubt. She relaxed her face and nodded. "Sure, okay."

Dr. Huang smiled at her and began to play without even looking down at his hands. Ina immediately recognized the tune: Beethoven's "Moonlight Sonata." Not the most upbeat thing to play, but she liked it anyway. It was soothing.

"How was meeting Alex?" Dr. Huang asked. "You said he was going to come by last night?"

Ina nodded. Her cheeks felt warm. "It was awesome to finally *see* him, you know? He's so, so nice, and he didn't freak when I told him about the phone call stuff . . . and how I might . . . you know . . . have issues to resolve."

"If anyone will understand you, it's Alex," Dr. Huang said, smiling. He kept playing as he spoke, every note soft and fluid as it melted into the haunting melody. "I was just over there early this morning, actually, and Alex asked me to say hello."

Ina raised her eyebrows. "What were you doing over there?"

Dr. Huang shrugged. "I'm sorry, I can't discuss that with you."

Ina wondered if Alex's father had been hallucinating again. "I wish Alex understood everything will be okay. I think he feels like everything will fall apart if he leaves."

Dr. Huang smiled. "Let's talk about you. We had quite the talk yesterday, but let's dig a little deeper today, shall we? Tell me more about this nightmare you've been having."

Ina shuddered. "It's stupid," she sighed. "It's not really anything specific, only a feeling I get that someone is after me. I don't remember any of the nightmare, just that I wake up from it and feel like someone is in the room."

Ina stopped and looked down at her hands. They were trembling. She pushed them under her thighs and leaned forward. Dr. Huang was looking at her when she finally lifted her eyes to him. He was still playing, but his notes had become softer and more delicate. Almost reverent. "What happens after that?" he asked. "How quickly do you realize that it's not real?"

Ina shook her head. "It's different every time. My roommate told me sometimes I scream for the person to leave me alone. Sometimes I'll wake up and feel like I can't breathe."

Dr. Huang's playing slowed a little. "Could you maybe describe who this person might be? Is it a man? A woman? A child?"

She thought for a moment, realizing she'd never tried to figure out the person's identity. "I don't know. I guess I've just assumed it was a man."

Dr. Huang nodded. "Did you ever ask your mother about it? She might remember something that frightened you when you were growing up."

Ina's eyes widened. "No, she's in prison now. I told you that. I don't talk to her."

Dr. Huang's playing slowed even more. "That's right. You said you used to call her, but many of those conversations weren't real, correct? You made them up."

"I must have," she said. "I never looked up the number. I know I don't have it memorized. I just picked up the phone, exactly like I did when I pretended to call Alex . . . and my boss, Philippe. I pretended to call him after I got here in town. I forgot about that until just now." She looked up at Dr. Huang, her voice shaky as she asked, "Do you think I could still do something like that now that I know what I've done? Do you think I could still do it and not realize I'm doing it?"

"Anything's possible," Dr. Huang answered, seemingly unconcerned. "The question now is do you think you'd be open to a real conversation with your mother? Perhaps in person? She might be able to help us get to the bottom of this nightmare." His playing sped up a little. "Or, simply speaking to your mother about the issue may trigger something in your memory."

The thought of speaking with her mother made Ina shift uncomfortably across the couch cushion. "I guess so," she said softly.

"Okay, let's move on. Let's talk about Jake."

Ina shifted again. It was a good thing Dr. Huang was playing such soothing music, because she was beginning to feel panicked. "I don't know what to think about him," she said. "Have I really been seeing him everywhere, or am I making that up too?"

Dr. Huang shook his head. "It's hard to say, but my guess is both. You did see him the first time—that was confirmed by a witness—but perhaps the shock of seeing him again is what triggered you to think you were seeing him those other times. The mind is very powerful, Ina. Alex's father sees people who don't exist. To him, they are solid and real. I'm not saying you suffer from schizo-phrenia, but your mind is just as capable of conjuring up images that seem real, even if it's just a temporary out-come of mental trauma. Your panic attacks, for instance."

Ina leaned forward, frustration gnawing at her. "Then how can I trust anything I see?" she asked angrily. "If I'm not really in danger, I'm going to do stupid things like fly across the country to escape someone who isn't really after me! I can't live my life like that. You give Alex's father medication for his condition, right? Is that something you can do for me to make me stop seeing things?"

Dr. Huang kept playing, as if nothing she said or did could stop him. "We'll discuss the possibility of medica-tion at a later time," he assured her. "Now, back to Jake. What initially made you not trust him?"

"He turned on me," Ina growled, leaning back into the couch again. She folded her arms. "He hit me and told the police I was insane."

"What exactly happened when he hit you?"

Ina tightened her arms around herself and stared down at her lap. "It was when he came into the hotel room," she muttered.

Dr. Huang continued to play, filling the silence. "Go on," he urged her.

She swallowed a lump in her throat and continued. "I told you about it before. I was in a hotel room with a man—a client. Things were okay until he . . . well, he wanted me to do something that made me uncomfortable, and I told him no. He got mad and I panicked. Then Jake was there. I don't even know how he got in or why he was there. The man pulled me in front of him and told Jake to let him leave or he'd hurt me. Jake came at us. I remember him looking at me like he wanted to kill me. That's when he punched me in the head. I fell down to the floor and tried to get out of the way, but the room was spinning. Someone kicked me. The police came a little bit after that. Jake kept telling them I had mental problems, that I was insane and needed special care. It was the way he said it that hurt the most . . . like he was embarrassed . . . like my problems explained everything that was going on. They arrested all of us and put me in a cell by myself. I never saw Jake after that, not until he came to the restaurant last week."

"I can see why you'd want to stay away from him," Dr. Huang said. "But it also sounds like you need some closure there."

"Yeah, I guess I do. I need to know why he told the police that I'm crazy."

"You are not crazy."

Ina looked down at her lap again. "I know."

"You don't sound so convinced."

She looked up. "You honestly believe there is nothing wrong with me? You think a sane person makes up phone calls and sees people who aren't there?"

Dr. Huang stopped playing. It was abrupt, and the room fell oddly silent. "All right, then," he said firmly, holding her gaze. "Tell me you're crazy. Say it loud. Convince me."

Ina stared at him. Her heart was pounding. She stood up from the couch, balling her hands into fists. "I'm crazy," she said shakily. Then, a little more loudly, "I'm crazy!"

Dr. Huang didn't blink. Instead, he started playing again, his eyes still on her. "You still don't sound convinced," he said softly. "Let's keep talking until we find something of which you *are* convinced. Maybe then we'll start getting to the bottom of things."

# Thirty-Six

Ina stared at the empty canvas in front of her. Alex and his sister, April, had come to visit her only a few hours earlier. They hadn't stayed long, but it had been a great visit anyway. The best thing was that they had brought painting supplies, even an easel. Ina hadn't known what to say, and had given Alex a hug and another kiss on the cheek. He'd blushed and stuttered. At that moment, Ina knew she had to be careful. She liked Alex, and she had to admit she was attracted to him, but there was no way anything could happen between them. Not with her past hanging over her. It was difficult to imagine herself in any sort of serious relationship right now.

Taking a deep breath, Ina turned to the supplies sitting on her bed. She was eager to paint something. She needed to feel a brush in her hands, the stiffness of a canvas against the bristles. Painting helped her get lost in another world, and right now that sounded amazing. She needed to get Dr. Huang and all of the things he'd urged her to talk about out of her head. He hadn't pushed her too hard, but nothing had been resolved by the end of the session. Ina felt frustrated knowing another person knew all the dark things in her head and nothing had changed. No pieces had been put together. No relief had come.

"Here's a list of psychiatrists in Jackson Heights," Dr. Huang had told her as he'd handed her a folded sheet of paper. "Any of them should be able to help you, but be prepared to test out a few in case they don't work out."

She looked down at the paper now sitting on her desk. She hadn't opened it yet. Part of the problem was money. She had health insurance, but it wasn't very good, and who knew how much all of this with Dr. Huang was going to end up costing—if her insurance would cover it at all. Her stay here at River Meadows alone was going to cost more than she should be spending. At this rate, she would never make it to the art school in Brooklyn.

"It's okay," she whispered to herself. "You can go later. Your health is more important, Ina. Don't be stupid."

She started unpacking the painting supplies, and within half an hour she had a makeshift studio set up near the window. She had two canvases. Luckily, Alex had done his homework and made sure they were pre-primed. The only problem now was what to paint.

Finally, she picked up a small palette and started mixing colors. She dipped one of her brushes into the paint, mixing more and more until she had the color she wanted. Something was itching at the back of her mind: an image of a face. She'd never thought her portraits were very good. They always came out looking haphazard and wild.

But anything was better than painting that stupid teddy bear again.

Touching the brush to the canvas, she let the image in her mind take shape. She painted basic shapes one on top of another until it was obvious it was a portrait from the shoulders up. She painted a strong jawline, eyebrows, hair. She noted places she'd want to add details to in a second wet-on-dry layer tomorrow or the next day. For now, she sat back and stared at the portrait, her emotions detached. She still had to do the initial stages of the eyes. She picked up a new brush and mixed a few more colors until a bright, almost luminescent blue stared up at her. It was perfect. She used a different brush to first shape the eyes, and then dipped another brush in the blue to begin the irises. When she finished, she sat back and realized her heart was hammering in her throat.

This was Jake.

Why was she painting Jake?

She had forgotten how well she knew his face. He stared back at her, a soft smirk on his lips. She wanted to paint over that smirk, but her hands felt frozen in her lap. He was always looking at her like that, like he knew something she didn't. It unnerved her. Maybe *that* was what had bothered her for so long, not the fact that he'd hit her and called her crazy.

The question was: *what did he know?*

Ina stood and paced the length of floor by the bed. She glanced at the phone on the desk.

She couldn't call him.

She paced some more, all the while glancing at the unfinished portrait. It was a good start. The mere fact that she'd been able to paint him at all was surprising. She just had no idea what it meant.

Was Jake really dangerous?

She curled her hands into fists. Of course he was! He'd been stalking her, hadn't he? But what did he want? It had to be more than just wanting to protect her, as he'd told Alex and Logan. Now that she finally felt like she was in a safe place, she had to know more.

With one last glance at the portrait, she marched to the desk and sat down. She opened one of the drawers and pulled out her planner. Flipping to the correct page, she found Jake's cell number and picked up the phone. If he truly wanted to speak with her as badly as it seemed he did, he would accept a Collect call. She dialed the necessary numbers, waiting impatiently as the Collect service connected to his number and he finally answered.

"Ina!" he said, his voice filled with relief. "I thought you would never call me. Are you okay?"

She glanced at his portrait, her mouth going dry. Was this another phone call she was making up in her head? She looked down at her knee, pinching it with her free hand. It hurt. She looked back at the phone, noting that the little screen showed an active call in progress. This was real. She wasn't crazy. She wasn't making it up.

"What do you want from me?" she finally asked.

"Oh, Ina, I'm so sorry I've frightened you. Your friend Alex told me you're scared of me. He said you think I'm trying to hurt you. You have to know that's not true."

"Why are you being so persistent?" she pressed.

"Because I'm worried about you!" he said, his voice strained. "Do you still think I hit you on purpose? It was a mistake. I was aiming for Gino—that asshole who had a hold of you. Francesca called me after you left with him. She wanted me to pull you off the job because Gino was into some sort of S&M crap she didn't think you could handle. She was right, wasn't she?"

Ina looked down at the desk. "Yeah, he wanted me to choke him. Like, it was super weird. He said it turned him on, and I don't know . . . I tried, but I just couldn't do it—not for real—and I panicked."

"Right. Francesca was really worried about you, so that's why I came by, and good thing too. You were not in your right . . . everything must have seemed so intense to you. I've only ever tried to protect you. Please believe me."

Ina squeezed the phone in her hand so tightly it felt like her fingers might break. "I was not in my right *what*, Jake? My right *mind*? You told them I was crazy. Do you have any idea how they treated me after that? Even if it's true . . . even if you . . . what right did you have to—"

"*That's* why you're trying to get away from me?" He took a deep breath and let it out again. "We need to meet face-to-face. I can't talk to you about this over the phone. It's too important. We can meet anywhere you want, however you want. I don't want to frighten you. What can I do to help you trust me?"

Ina's hands started to tremble. "I don't know," she said, tears spilling down her cheeks. "I–I don't know, Jake. You were right. I *am* crazy. I've realized things in the past few days, things I just couldn't see before. Something is wrong with me and I don't know why. You know something, don't you? Something that'll help me figure this out?"

Jake was quiet for a moment. "I can't promise what I know will help you, Ina, but I would like to try. Can we meet?"

Ina took a deep breath and held it for a long moment. "Yes," she finally said, everything inside of her feeling tense and uneasy. "I don't think I'm going to get better until we talk it through."

"I agree. Tell me where you are, then."

Ina looked at a little booklet sitting on the desk by the phone. It was filled with information about River Meadows: meal times, a map of the building, activity schedules. And an address.

Taking a deep breath, Ina read the address aloud. Her voice shook. If she hadn't believed she was crazy before, she believed it now, because everything inside of her was screaming that trusting Jake was wrong. But she couldn't help it. Looking at his portrait, she felt the same sense of loyalty to him she'd felt since the day she'd first met him.

It was time to find out why.

# Thirty-Seven

## Alex

"You can't live your life waiting in the wings," April said as Alex bent down to pull the milk out of the fridge. "You're an actor. Don't you want to be on the stage?"

Alex shut the refrigerator door and set the milk jug on the counter near the sink. He didn't know what to say to April. Ever since she'd arrived yesterday, she'd been harping on about him moving to New York. She'd bugged him about it when they'd driven around Boise looking for an art store to buy supplies for Ina; she'd nagged him about it all the way back to Anniston; she'd even mentioned it at dinner in front of their parents. It was too much. He turned around to face her. She was at the table eating toast and a couple of hardboiled eggs.

"Why is it so important I leave right away?" he asked. "You've skipped your classes, risked getting kicked out of school . . . to what? Push me out of the house? Why?"

April picked up her second egg and cracked the shell against the edge of the table. "I don't know. Maybe it's because Dad keeps getting worse. None of his medications seem to be helping. It just made me realize nothing is getting better."

Alex leaned against the counter and folded his arms. "Well, wouldn't that mean I'm needed here more than ever, then? I can't leave them, April. So, unless you're volunteering to quit school for good and come back to live here, I'm not going anywhere. Do you have any idea how scared I was for Dad when he climbed up to that top rack? I thought that was it. He was gonna fall and die, and Mom would never recover. It hurts me just as much to see her deal with this as it does to watch Dad go through it."

April lifted her eyes to his as she set her half-peeled egg back on her plate. "It hurts me too, Alex. I feel guilty every single day, but it's not right for you to stay here. They didn't raise any of us to take care of *them*. They want you to have your own life, and it's really important for you to start school as soon as possible. Broadway is hard to break into. You need the best start, and as much time as you can get. It's the same thing for me. I'll be lucky if I can land even one of the smallest positions in a prestigious kitchen. It's a tough world, and so is acting."

"I get that," Alex replied, filling a bowl with cereal and milk before heading over to the table. "I get it, but one year will not make that big of a difference."

"Maybe not, but you never know what could happen in a year. It might turn into longer. You should start making plans to leave. I'll take care of *this*." April waved her arm around the kitchen as if it represented their entire mess of a family.

"I can't let you do that," Alex growled, slamming his bowl onto the table. Milk and cereal sloshed over the side, dangerously close to the edge of the table. "You won't go back to school. You'll end up staying here and sacrificing everything you've—"

"No I won't. I've already found someone to help Mom and Dad." Eyeing Alex's mess on the table, she picked up the egg and continued peeling it. "It will work. I just need to talk to Dr. Huang about it. You said he's going to be with Ina when you visit her today?"

Alex stared down at the spilled milk and cereal. "Yeah," he sighed. "I'm taking Ina to lunch as soon as they finish her therapy session." He headed back to the sink to get some paper towels. "Wait, you already hired someone?"

"Not yet. He's the most affordable, but he's not a live-in caretaker, so I wanted to talk to Dr. Huang about what exactly would be best for Dad. Does he think Dad needs someone here all the time? Or just someone Mom can call when things take a turn? That kind of thing."

Alex sat down at the table with a wad of paper towels and dabbed at the mess around his bowl. "You think you can fix this, but you can't. I've gotta stay until Dr. Huang gets Dad's meds working better. That could take months, which puts me past the start date for the Marion Conservatory, which means I'll need to wait until next July anyway. That was your idea in the first place and I'm gonna stick with it." He picked up a spoon and shoveled cereal into his mouth. "It's not the end of the world," he muttered. "Seriously, it's not."

"It is too. It's a huge deal to sacrifice your dreams."

Alex looked away. He knew she was right. Still, something inside of him resisted. It was the same thing that had been in his way since he'd found out he had been accepted to Marion, the same thing that had kept him from crossing the street the other morning in New York.

Was it fear? Maybe.

No, it was more than that. What did he have to fear, anyway? He wasn't afraid of the stage. He wasn't afraid to move to New York since Logan would be there to help him. He wasn't afraid to leave his parents as long as he knew they were taken care of. So why did he keep resisting?

April finished eating her breakfast and stood up to carry her plate to the sink. "I'll go visit Ina with you," she said. "Don't worry, I won't get in your way. I just want to talk to Dr. Huang. I wouldn't mind seeing Ina a little more either. I really like her." She turned around, a smile on her lips. "Do you think you two will . . . you know . . . get together?"

Alex picked up his bowl to drink the rest of the milk at the bottom. "I'm not sure." His heart beat faster at the thought of him and Ina together. He set down his bowl. "I really like her, but she has issues she's gotta deal with. I'm going to try to help her as much as I can."

April walked over to the table and patted his shoulder. "Of course you are," she said, her voice almost sad. "Let me know when you're ready to go."

* * *

"Ina is with Dr. Huang in the art room," Leslie said as soon as Alex and April entered River Meadows. "Dr. Huang said you're welcome to meet them in there." She pointed down the left hallway.

Alex nodded, and he and April continued past the front desk and down the hall. They rounded a corner and came to the art room. One wall was entirely made of glass with a set of double doors leading inside. The room was quite large, filled with desks, pottery tables, and easels. Only a third of them were occupied.

Ina and Dr. Huang were in a far corner near a window overlooking the front lawn and parking lot. Ina was sitting behind an easel and canvas, her face hidden, but her curly hair still visible. Dr. Huang was facing her, his back to Alex and April as they opened the doors and stepped inside.

"Are they in the middle of a session?" April asked as they approached. "I don't want to interrupt."

"Leslie said it was okay," Alex said. He was eager to talk to Ina again. Yesterday's visit hadn't been nearly long enough.

Dr. Huang turned around as they approached. "Hello!" His smile brightened as he caught sight of April. "What are you doing here, April? I thought you were off to school in California."

"Just visiting for a few days," she said. "Can I talk to you for a minute, if you have time?"

Dr. Huang looked over at Ina as she slid her easel to the side. "Sure, I think we're done here anyway, right, Ina?"

Ina looked up at Alex, a warm smile on her lips as she brushed some hair off her forehead. Her hands were smudged with paint. "I think so," she answered, looking over at April. "It's nice to see you again," she said politely. "Did Alex drag you here?"

April laughed. "No, I made him bring me so I could talk to Dr. Huang about our father. Just trying to figure out a few things."

Ina nodded and turned back to Alex. "You ready to get some lunch?"

Alex smiled down at her, noting how pretty she looked in the afternoon sun spilling in through the window. He wanted to be close to her. It was a need inside of him he couldn't ignore. "If that's okay?" he asked. "Are you sure you don't need to finish up things here?" He glanced over at the easel and canvas she had pushed away. It was facing the wall, but he could see a corner of it. All he could make out was black paint, still wet and glistening.

*Wait a minute . . .*

He blinked a few times, stepping forward to see more of the canvas. Sure enough, nearly the entire canvas was black. Several shapes peeked out from between some of the black streaks, but he couldn't discern what any of them were.

"Hey, I saw the same sort of thing . . ." He couldn't finish. Ina was looking at him with confusion plastered across her face.

"What's the matter?" she asked, glancing at her painting.

Alex looked over at Dr. Huang. He and April had moved over to a table several feet away, speaking in low tones. "Nothing," he said. "Let's go get lunch. What are you in the mood for?"

She stood and began untying the white apron fastened around her waist. It was splattered with dried paint. "Is there any good pizza around here?"

Alex grinned. "If there's one good thing here, it's the pizza place."

"Awesome," Ina laughed as she picked up a jar of brushes. "Let me clean these real quick, then we can go."

* * *

"I hope you like it," Alex said as he held the door open for Ina. "It's mine and Logan's favorite place."

"You're forgetting I was born and raised in New York," Ina said as they both walked inside. "Not sure anywhere in Idaho can beat a slice of real New York pizza."

Alex shrugged. "Guess we'll see."

They found a booth and ordered as soon as the server arrived. Ina sat back against the booth and looked out the window. "It's hard to imagine growing up here," she said, playing with the wrapper from her straw. "It's so small."

Alex looked out the window too. It faced the busiest road in the entire town, the one that fed into the road leading to the Interstate, but it was nothing compared to New York.

"What was it like where you grew up?" Alex asked.

Ina looked down at the wrapper and crumpled it into a little ball. "It was a quiet neighborhood," she said, seeming distant all of a sudden. "Nothing small like this, though. We had a nice house on Long Island. It was two stories. I had a bedroom with a balcony. I even had my own bathroom. After Dad died, it was only the two of us living there, but it was the house they bought when they got married, so I guess Mom didn't want to leave even after he was gone. And maybe I begged her to never make us move out." She gave a little laugh, still staring down at the wrapper she was squeezing between her fingers.

Alex took a sip of his water. "Do you mind if I ask what your mom did for a living? Or did she not work?"

Ina looked up. "We were one of those opposite families. Mom always worked and Dad was the one who stayed home. She was kind of a badass. She was an investment banker for some big firm in Manhattan. Not a lot of women in that world, y'know? But she was always at work. When she was home, she spent every second with me, so I guess that's worth something, right?" She furrowed her brow. "One thing I don't understand is why she was embezzling money. I looked into what her salary must've been, and it was a lot more than I'll ever make. I mean, why wasn't what she made enough?"

Alex leaned forward, curious. "You said your dad died when you were a kid?"

"Yeah, it was a car accident. I was there too, but I don't really remember it."

"How old were you?"

"Eight, I think?"

Alex sipped his water. "Man, that must've sucked. I can't imagine losing a parent like that. I mean, me and my parents have our issues, but if one of them was just suddenly gone . . . that's sad."

Ina nodded. "You're lucky to have both of your parents, even if things are hard with your dad. You know he loves you, right?"

Alex took another sip of water, thinking back to the moment when his dad had told him to go to New York for the week. "I know he loves me, yeah," he said. "I'll never take that for granted."

Ina kept her eyes on his. "I have no idea if my mom loves me. I know she did at one point, but we hardly ever talk now. Anything she needs from me comes through her lawyer."

Alex's heart sank. "You don't deserve that, especially after losing your dad. Everyone deserves to be loved by someone. There are people who care about you right now."

Ina's expression warmed as she looked at Alex. She dropped the wrapper between her fingers and reached up to pull her hair away from her face. "Thanks," she said. "The only other person who's ever seemed to care as much about me was Jake. I guess that's why it was so hard when I felt like he betrayed me."

"I'll never do that to you," Alex promised. "You know that, right?"

Her expression softened even more. "Of course I do."

Their server approached the table. "One plain cheese New York-style pizza," he said, setting the pizza down in the middle of the table. "Can I get you guys anything else?"

"Nope, we're good," Alex answered, and watched Ina's eyes widen at the sight of the 18-inch pizza.

"That is huge," she laughed. "It definitely *looks* like a New York pizza. I'm just used to seeing them in slices, not the whole thing."

"Me and Logan polish off one of these, no problem," Alex laughed. "Four slices each. Sometimes, if we're super hungry, we order two."

"*Two*? I would love to see that."

"Well, maybe when I move to New York next year you'll get to see it. You'd better dig in now before I eat the whole thing myself." He grabbed a slice and started eating.

Ina grabbed a slice, folding it in half length-wise, just like he supposed she would. Cheese oozed over her fingers as she took a huge bite. "This is really good," she said through her chewing. "I've heard the pizza in New York has a certain taste because of the minerals in the tap water they use in the dough. But this tastes pretty close."

Alex smiled. He loved that Ina didn't mind talking with her mouth full. He loved the way her hair fell over her shoulders, the curls bouncing every time she moved. "I know the guy who owns this place," he said through a mouthful of pizza. "It wouldn't surprise me if he orders special water flown in from New York. The dude is serious about his pizza."

Ina laughed. "Awesome." She polished off her first piece and dug into a second. "So tell me, Mr. Winzelberg, what was it like to play Romeo? I keep trying to envision it."

A blush warmed Alex's face. "Uh . . . what do you want to know?"

"Well, I read those emails you sent, even if I didn't answer them. You were so excited opening night, remember?"

"Oh, yeah," Alex said, moving to his next slice of pizza. "Yeah, I was, huh? It was my first play, and I was the lead, so it was pretty amazing. I guess it was an ego boost, but it was more than that. It just feels good to have everything come together with people you've worked with so hard."

"And you got to kiss Juliet, right? How was that?"

Alex swallowed a mouthful of pizza and looked down at the table. "It was awesome at the time," he said, "but Jennifer, the girl who played Juliet, ended up . . . well, we ended up together in real life, and then she dumped me and it sucked. Kinda bittersweet."

"Oh, wow, sorry."

"It's okay. I have loads of other memories from that show that are good. My two swordfights were seriously killer, and it was my first play, so it was like . . ." He set down his pizza and started playing with the end of a napkin. "This might sound stupid," he muttered.

"No, it won't. Tell me."

He looked up at Ina, nervous to be telling her things he'd never told another living soul. "Doing that play was like falling in love," he explained slowly. "Like, not falling in love with the play, or any of the people in the play, but falling in love with theater. I'd go to bed after rehearsals, and I'd be so high. I'd never felt like that before. I was obsessed. I kind of got the same thing when I was dating Jennifer and we were super into each other. But even then, theater was even more of a high. The best thing is that I can feel that way every time I'm in another play."

Ina's eyes widened as she listened. She set down her pizza. "That is not stupid, Alex. I feel the same way about painting. You're totally right. It's like falling in love over and over. I mean, who wouldn't want that?"

"Right?"

They started eating again, their conversation revolving around art and theater and how different New York was from Idaho. Finally, Alex stared down at the empty pizza tray, laughing. "Okay, you're right up there with Logan," he pronounced. He put his chin in his hand and watched as Ina wiped her mouth with a napkin.

She noticed him watching her and smiled. "Alex Winzelberg," she said, pushing her cup away. "I've decided something."

He lifted his chin from his hand. "Oh?"

Ina grinned. "I've decided hanging out with you in person is way better than emailing you."

"I agree," he laughed.

# Thirty-Eight

Alex and Ina stayed in their booth talking until their server started making loud throat-clearing noises every time he passed them. Alex didn't want the afternoon to end, but they couldn't stay here all day. It was time to go.

Ina let out a heavy sigh as they left the pizza place. "It feels twenty degrees hotter out here than when we went in."

"Yeah, it's definitely warmer. I wish we could've taken the car, but I didn't want to leave April without a way to get home if we were gone too long."

"It's fine." Ina kept lifting her hair away from her neck, muttering something about a hair tie.

"Maybe we can find a rubber band," Alex offered as they crossed a road toward a field they could cut across to get back to River Meadows.

Ina fanned her face. "I'll survive. Sometimes I think about shaving my head, though."

Alex gave her a sidelong look. "I think your hair is really pretty."

Ina grunted. "People tell me my hair is pretty all the time. It's kind of annoying." She lifted her hair off her neck again, twisting it up into a fat bun on the top of her head and holding it there with both hands. "It's like my hair is the only thing worth noticing about me, you know?" She looked up at the sky and let out a laugh. "I learned to put it up in some sort of a French twist or bun when I'm meeting with clients for a translating job. That usually hides it enough that people don't notice it."

Alex raised an eyebrow. "If you hate it that much, why don't you always wear it up?"

"Yeah, right!" she scoffed. "You know how heavy it gets pinned up like that? I'm good for four, *maybe* five hours, and then I've gotta let it down." She let go of her hair and it fell down to her neck again, as big and curly as ever. Alex had to admit it did look like it would be very uncomfortable in the heat. He still wanted to touch it, but resisted.

They were entering the field now. It was similar to the fields behind the movie theater, packed with weeds and grasshoppers. Ina seemed to cringe every time one jumped anywhere near her face.

"You okay?" Alex asked as they picked their way along the thin trail.

"I'm fine. It's just when I rode your bike through some fields the other day, the grasshoppers got caught in my hair. It freaked me out!"

Suddenly, an idea came to Alex and he stopped to face Ina. She stopped short, looking surprised as he stood there, studying her hair. "Would my hat work?" he asked.

Ina shrugged. "Yeah, sure. Hand it over."

Alex pulled his baseball cap off his head and held it out to her. She took it and twisted and shoved her hair through the hole in the back to make a sort of loose, thick ponytail. She rolled her eyes to the sky. "Such a pain," she laughed. "But thanks. It's a little better."

"The brim will keep the sun off your face too," Alex said, grinning as he took a step forward, his hand brushing hers. She didn't pull away. "By the way," he said softly, looking into her eyes. "I think anyone who only notices your hair is missing out on a whole lot of Ina. There's so much more to you than that. So, so much more."

Taking a step forward, Ina leaned up to press her lips to his. A surge of surprise nearly froze him in place, but he pushed it aside and wrapped his arms around Ina in order to kiss her better. The hat brim bumped against his forehead. Ina giggled and reached up to push it out of the way, kissing Alex even harder. He pulled her closer, moving a hand up to the side of her face and then into her hair. It was soft and thick and felt nice, but her lips were even better. He'd never felt like this, not even during his best times with Jennifer when they'd done a whole lot more than kissing. Ina melted Alex's emotions into a complete and utter mess. It was a beautiful mess.

Ina pulled away a fraction of an inch, her breath warm on his lips. "I like you, Alex Winzelberg," she whispered. "I like you a lot, but I . . . I don't want things to go too fast with you. Sometimes I panic when I get too close to someone, and I never want you to see that. Ever."

Alex moved his hand down to her cheek, keeping his attention on her eyes. "My opinion of you wouldn't change even if I did see it," he said firmly. He leaned in for another kiss, but just then a huge grasshopper landed on Ina's neck. She jumped, batting at the insect with both hands.

"Get it off!" she laughed, but it was long gone by then.

"Let's go," Alex urged, and grabbed her hand. He started running up the trail through the field. "Hurry!" he yelled as Ina ran behind him, still holding onto his hand. "Before they attack us!"

"You're acting like we're ten years old!" Ina laughed at the top of her lungs.

Alex glanced back at her. She was breathing hard. Her eyes sparkled. He might as well be ten years old, he realized. Because that seemed to be the last time he'd ever felt so free and alive.

* * *

Alex spent the rest of the day with Ina at River Meadows. They played chess and then watched *Singin' in the Rain* in the lounge with a bunch of the other residents. Alex kept looking around at them, wondering if his dad might be better off living in a place like this, but he just couldn't envision it. His dad was too young and independent. A place like this would be safer for him, but it would kill him in every other way.

"Let's go to my place for dinner," Alex suggested as he and Ina sat in the lounge. The movie had ended a few minutes earlier and the residents were slowly filing out to the dining room.

Ina scooted a little bit closer to Alex on the sofa. She took his hand and squeezed. "I like that idea. Do you need to call April to come and get us?"

"Yeah, I'll go do that."

"It's weird living in a place without public transit," Ina remarked. "I mean, do you even have a taxi service here?"

"Not that I've ever seen, no."

"Buses?"

Alex shrugged. "Not any that go around town. There are ones that stop here from other places, though."

Ina shook her head. "Weird."

Alex squeezed her hand and then let go as he stood up. "I'll be right back."

Leslie was at the front desk when Alex entered the lobby. She smiled at him as he approached. "How's it going? Was the movie good?"

"It was great."

Leslie leaned back in her chair. "You need to use the phone?"

Alex nodded and Leslie handed him a cordless. He started dialing home.

"How is Ina doing?" Leslie asked as she leaned forward to type something into the computer in front of her.

"Good. I think she would've been fine staying at our place, but I guess she's more comfortable here."

Leslie nodded. "She told me she's leaving soon—I guess back to New York? You're moving out there too, right? That's what Mrs. Edwards said."

Alex rolled his eyes. Raven's mother was unbelievable. "I won't be going for another year," he muttered, wondering why nobody was answering the phone. It was probably close to switching over to the answering machine.

"Hello?"

It was April. Alex stepped away from the front desk. "Hey, can you come and get me and Ina? We want to eat dinner there. What's Mom making?"

There was the sound of water running in the background. "I'm the one making dinner, so I'll send someone else to come and pick you up. I'm making pappardelle Bolognese."

"Parpa-what?"

"It's spaghetti, okay? Kind of. Just hardly any tomatoes. You'll love it."

"Okay."

April hung up and Alex handed the phone back to Leslie. "Thanks."

Leslie gave him a concerned look. "Why are you staying another year?"

He rubbed a hand along his scratchy jaw, remembering that he hadn't shaved that morning. He hoped he hadn't scratched Ina's lips too badly when they'd kissed. That was something Jennifer had always complained about.

"I don't know," he said. "It's complicated with my dad, that's all."

"April offered someone the job this afternoon. He lives in Boise."

Alex's eyes widened. "She hired him? She told me she found someone, but I didn't know she'd hired him already."

"Well, he's great, trust me."

"I guess we'll see. Thanks for the info."

"No problem."

Alex left the lobby and found Ina sitting where he'd left her. The room was otherwise empty. Her back was to him.

"Will it be okay, do you think?" Ina asked.

Alex took another step forward, opening his mouth to ask her what she meant, when she started speaking again. Only, this time it was in a different language. It sounded like French, and Ina lowered her voice as she spoke. She kept her eyes cast down to her lap. She was perfectly still.

"Okay, then," she said, her tone normal again. "If you say so. I trust you."

Alex waited for another string of French, but Ina didn't speak again. She lifted her arms as if she was letting out a long yawn. Turning, she spotted Alex and a smile lit up her face. "Is someone coming to get us?" she asked.

Forcing a smile, Alex nodded. "Yeah, let's, uh, go wait in the lobby. My mom will be here in a bit. April's cooking dinner."

"Oh yeah? What's she making?"

"Some Italian dish. Parpa-bologna-something."

"Pappardelle Bolognese?" she asked in a beautiful Italian accent. "That sounds great."

"April's an amazing chef, yeah."

They walked out to the lobby and sat down in a place where they could see the parking lot. Alex tried to forget what he'd seen, but there was no way he was going to be able to let it go. Was Dr. Huang aware of Ina talking to herself? What if it was schizophrenia like his father's? Maybe it wasn't anything to worry about, but he found that hard to believe. He stared down at his hands, his thoughts swirling. He wanted so badly for Ina to be okay. He didn't want her to suffer from mental illness or anything like it. She deserved so much better.

"Are you okay?" Ina asked, running a finger up Alex's arm. "You seem distracted."

Alex looked down at her finger on his arm. He should tell her what he'd seen. She had talked freely enough about the made-up conversations she'd had on the phone, and he knew from experience that it was better to talk about these things openly rather than try to hide them.

"I heard you talking to yourself in the lounge a minute ago," he said, meeting her eyes. "In English and in French. Are you okay? Is that something Dr. Huang knows about?"

Pulling her hand away from his arm, Ina looked down at her lap. "I–I told you," she stuttered. "Things I do make me look crazy. I was talking to Philippe, just figuring out some stuff in my head. I do it out loud, and maybe that's not completely normal, but it helps me. Don't you ever do that? Talk yourself through problems?"

Alex looked away. "I guess everyone does it, but I try not to do it out loud. Not since my dad's diagnosis, anyway. People would read too much into it."

"Like you're reading too much into what you just heard?" She took a deep breath. "How much did you hear?"

Alex studied her face. She seemed okay, as if she knew exactly what had happened and accepted it. "You asked if it would be okay, then you said something in French, and then you said 'I trust you.'"

Ina's expression stayed relaxed. "That's right," she said nonchalantly. "You don't need to worry. Everything is going to be fine. I have it all figured out."

Alex furrowed his brow. "You have what figured out?"

"I'm going to find out what's wrong with me, and then everything will be how it's supposed to be."

"Dr. Huang is helping you a lot, then?"

Ina's relaxed expression faltered for just a moment. "Yes, of course he is." She smiled, reaching out to drag a finger across his stubble, her smile getting brighter. "Thank you for worrying about me."

"That's my job," he said gently. He opened his mouth to tell her he would always be there for her no matter what, but just then a pair of headlights swung into the parking lot. It was his parents' LeSabre.

"Let's go eat," Ina said, urging Alex to his feet. "I can't wait to try your sister's cooking."

"It won't disappoint you, I promise." He followed her out to the parking lot. His mother was behind the wheel of the car. She looked frazzled, as usual. Alex wondered if April had told her about hiring someone yet. He doubted it. If he knew his sister at all, he was pretty sure she was making a big, fancy dinner so she could drop the news as they were eating. Alex could only hope spaghetti didn't end up on the walls this time.

# Thirty-Nine

## Ina

"Alex wasn't kidding about your cooking," Ina said after swallowing another mouthful of pasta. It tasted so good, she was already on her second helping.

April raised an eyebrow. "Oh yeah? What did he say about my cooking?"

Ina smiled, surprised at how comfortable she was eating dinner with Alex and his family. They were all so nice, and eating dinner like this was something she'd only ever done with the Yuhns, the foster family that had taken her in after her mother had gone to prison. She still missed that family, but for the first time, she felt like that gaping hole was being filled—at least for the moment.

"Just that I wouldn't be disappointed," Ina answered, throwing a smile at Alex, who was sitting next to her. Marsha was next to April across from them, and Daniel was at the head of the table. He'd been quiet since Ina had arrived. He smiled at her every now and then, but mostly concentrated on his food.

"Well, that's good to hear," April said. "Alex *does* talk me up all the time." She flashed him a smile. "But only because I deserve it."

"Of course," he laughed as he shoveled another forkful of pasta into his mouth.

"Oh, you deserve it," Ina replied. "I've eaten at some of the best restaurants in New York, and this is right up there."

Daniel looked up from his plate. "How do you afford to eat at those kinds of places?" he asked bluntly.

Ina took a sip of her water. "Oh, *I* can't afford to eat at places like that," she explained, lowering her glass. "My clients pay for it. I'm a translator, and sometimes that's where the job takes me."

Marsha's eyes widened. "A translator? You speak other languages?"

Ina nodded, growing a tad uncomfortable.

"She speaks five languages," Alex chimed in, his voice thick with pride.

"Wow, really?" April asked. "What do you speak?"

Ina shrugged and gave everyone a half-smile. "It's really . . . *really* not a big deal," she answered, rubbing the edge of the table with her thumb. "I speak English, obviously. Spanish, Italian, French, and some Korean. Mostly Romance languages, so not that big of a deal. Korean is the hardest for me." She let out a laugh, trying to make it sound as carefree as possible.

But as she looked from one person to the next, she knew her words were falling on deaf ears. Everyone was looking at her with admiration, even Alex. As if her knowledge of other languages was like a magical gift. She needed to get off this subject, fast. The last thing she wanted was for everyone to dwell on *her*. Disappearing into the background was where she was most comfortable.

"So," she said, clearing her throat. "Do any of you know Elvira? She lives at River Meadows. Sweet woman who can't remember anyone? I've kinda made friends with her. She remembers me, for some reason."

Marsha's expression melted from curiosity to sadness. "Oh, poor Elvira," she sighed. "Yes, we all know her. Her husband died of cancer fifteen years ago. She's never been the same since."

"She used to babysit the three of us when we were super small," April said, getting the same sad look on her face as her mother. "She made the best cookies. She doesn't even know me now."

Ina raised an eyebrow. "The three of you?" she asked, looking from April to Alex.

"Oh!" Alex said, laughing. "I never really talk about Aaron, do I? He's my older brother. Middle child. He's always complaining about us forgetting him. He's kinda right."

"Oh, right, you've mentioned him before," Ina said, and then she remembered that there had been another sibling in the family picture hanging in the hallway. "Where is he?"

"Backpacking across Europe," Daniel muttered through a mouthful of pasta. "Got it in his head he had to 'find' himself before he decides what to do with his life."

"Don't start, Daniel," Marsha sighed. "Aaron is using his own money, and he wasn't much help around here, anyway. He was too antsy to get out into the world. You can't blame him."

"Wait a second," Alex said, dropping his fork on his plate. "Why are you all of a sudden defending Aaron packing up and leaving and not me? How is that fair?"

Ina shifted in her chair, sensing the tension in the room getting thicker. She suddenly felt in the way.

"Because you're the last one left," April said, spearing her mother with an accusing stare.

Marsha glanced guiltily at April and then looked at Alex, her breaths quick and huffy. "That is *not* why—"

"It is too!" Alex growled at her. "I'm the last one left to help take care of Dad. Even *he* says he's okay with me leaving. He told me that before I left for New York! But you won't even *look* at that list of caretakers I gave you. Well, guess what? Your stalling won't work, because April's already hired someone."

Marsha snapped her attention to April. "You *what*?"

April rolled her eyes. "Alex, I wasn't going to say anything until—"

"You already hired someone?" Daniel cut in. "Don't I have any say in this?"

April rolled her eyes again. "Of course you do, Dad, but I—"

"Is *that* why you're here?" Marsha interrupted, glaring at April. "It's not because of a school break?"

April looked down at the table. "No break. Alex called me and told me about Dad climbing the racking the other night, and I thought it'd be best if I came up here and fixed everything."

"You're skipping out on school?" Marsha gasped, as if this was the most horrifying thing she'd ever heard. "If you fail your classes, you will never be able to afford to get back—"

"I KNOW, MOM!" April yelled, standing up so fast that her chair teetered precariously for a moment and then fell over with a crash.

Nobody batted an eye except for Ina. She felt as if she was caught in a crossfire, almost like she should duck under the table. Instead, she sat stone-still, morbidly fascinated and frightened of the argument exploding around her. Was this what being in a real family was like?

"This isn't worth you dropping out of school!" Marsha yelled, standing up to face April.

April put her hands on her hips and leaned close to her mom's face. "I have not dropped out. This family is way more important than school. I'm missing a few days, and I explained to my professors why. They're working with me on it. It's fine. Would you chill out for one damn second?" She took a long, deep breath, and when Marsha didn't respond, she backed up and looked around at everyone else still sitting at the table, watching. "I hired a nurse from Boise," she continued. "He's already got a place to live in town. He will be here four days a week for ten hours a day, and he'll be on call the rest of the time. And best of all, he's not as expensive as—"

"You hired a *man*?" Daniel interrupted. He stood up and slammed a fist into the table, leaning forward, his lips curling back. "I will *not* be babysat by a grown *man* who works as a *nurse*."

"Do you think a woman could physically handle you if things got rough during one of your episodes?" April shot back. "Yes, grown men can be nurses, and that's a good thing! Get over it. Seriously." She pinched the bridge of her nose. "Sometimes I don't know why I bother," she sighed.

Ina almost jumped when she felt Alex's hand touch her knee. He looked at her with a mixture of pity and embarrassment, leaning close to her ear to whisper, "You can leave if you want, but this is kinda normal. It'll die down in a sec."

Ina nodded, trying not to dwell too much on how good Alex's hand felt on her knee.

"I'm sorry," Daniel muttered, casting an almost embarrassed look down at his plate. "I just don't think being a nurse is a very appropriate thing for—"

"Oh, don't even go there," April snapped. "If I get one more person telling me men and women belong in certain roles, I'm going to scream. Do you have any idea how much crap I get for wanting to be a head chef? Apparently, women only belong in the kitchen if it's not a professional one. Why is that, huh? Why does it matter if it's a man or a woman preparing your gourmet cuisine?"

"I don't know," he muttered. "You have a point."

"Okay, that's enough," Marsha said, sitting back down in her chair. "If we haven't scared off Ina yet, I don't know what will." She threw an apologetic look at Ina. "I'm so sorry. Please forgive us. These are just . . . touchy subjects."

Ina tried to keep the grin off her face, but failed. "It's fine," she almost laughed. "This is the first family fight I've seen in years, so don't worry about it. I'm kind of fascinated."

April picked up her chair and sat back down.

"So, tell us about this nurse you've hired," Alex said quickly as he squeezed Ina's knee reassuringly.

April picked up her glass of water and took a sip before speaking. "His name is Benjamin," she said. "He's had a lot of experience with in-home care, and he's got a minor in psychology. He . . ."

Ina tuned April out and looked at Alex, placing her hand over his on her knee. "I like your family," she whispered.

He laughed, leaning closer as he whispered, "I kind of like them too. Thanks for sticking around."

* * *

Ina struggled to fall asleep. After dinner, Alex had brought her back to River Meadows, giving her a kiss before she went inside. She'd thought her fears about getting too close to him would be what kept her up, but it was some-thing entirely different. Instead, she couldn't stop thinking about the worry in Alex's eyes when he'd told her he'd overheard her talking to herself. She'd known she was doing it; she'd known Philippe wasn't really there, but pretending to talk to him made her feel better, just like all those pretend phone calls had made her feel better. It was her coping mechanism. That was what Dr. Huang had told her.

"I'm not too worried about the phone calls," he had said, stroking his chin as Ina had sat painting in the art room. "I want to get to the bottom of whatever trauma you've experienced in the past. Those phone calls are a coping mechanism for you to deal with that trauma."

She had stopped painting at that point, her brush poised over the canvas. She'd been painting the child standing in the middle of a room, holding a teddy bear with a red bow on its head.

"Why are you so sure this is all from trauma?" she'd asked.

"Well, I've thought about several things you've told me," he'd said as Ina had resumed painting. "The recur-ring nightmare, the panic attacks, this image you said you paint over and over." He'd pointed to her canvas. "The fact that you and your mother don't have a close relation-ship anymore."

Ina had lowered her brush. "What are you saying?" she'd asked.

"I think you experienced something traumatic as a child, and your mind shut it out in order to protect you. Only, now it's starting to come back so you can deal with it. This is quite common, Ina. I've helped many patients through similar struggles. It's never easy, and it's never the same story, but one thing that must happen is for you to accept that it is going to be painful. You may discover things that change the way you view the world and everyone you think you know and trust. It will not be an easy journey."

Ina had stared at him, confused. "What kind of trauma?" she'd asked.

Dr. Huang had shrugged. "I can't make heads or tails of it yet. Are you able to give me more information than you have already?"

"The only trauma I can remember was the car accident when my dad died," she'd said, looking down at her lap. "Even then, I don't remember much of it. Dad was driving. I was in the back seat. Another car hit us. I guess I felt neglected after that because Mom worked so much, and Dad wasn't there anymore."

Dr. Huang had nodded. "And your father was never abusive?"

Ina had shaken her head. "No, I don't think so. Every memory I have of him is good."

"And your mother?"

"No, unless you count not being around very much as abusive. She was always there for me when she *was* around, though."

"And what about your foster families? Could any of them have harmed you in any way?"

"I guess it's possible. I had two foster families, but I only have good memories of living with them."

Dr. Huang had rubbed his chin again. "And at the group home? Anyone there?"

"No. I feel like I would remember anything that might have happened there. I was older then. Wouldn't I remember?"

"Possibly."

"So what do we do?" Ina had asked as she turned back to her painting. She'd stared at the little girl with the fuzzy teddy bear dangling from one of her hands.

"We keep up with your sessions," Dr. Huang had answered. "Or, if you feel you need to move back home, you start sessions with another psychiatrist until you get to the bottom of everything."

Ina had kept painting. "After a painful journey," she'd muttered sarcastically. "Wouldn't it be easier to keep it all buried? I was fine before. Why try digging it all up now?"

Frowning, Dr. Huang had sat back in his chair and folded his arms. "I don't think you've really been 'fine,' Ina. Trust me, the longer you put this off, the more it's going to eat you up inside. Think about how much happier you could be by resolving what has clearly been affecting you for years."

"I guess so." She'd looked at her painting again, irritated as the same sense of fear and restlessness came rushing at her.

"Everything okay?" Dr. Huang had asked as Ina set down her brush and grabbed a tube of black paint.

"I'm fine for now," she'd grumbled. "But you're right; this painting proves it. I hate it, and I know it's because of what I've buried." She'd squeezed paint onto her palette and grabbed a new brush, keenly aware of Dr. Huang watching her every move. She had never painted with someone watching her like that before. Surprisingly, it hadn't bothered her. She'd dragged her brush across the canvas, leaving a heavy black streak across the little girl.

Now, sitting up in bed after hours of restlessness, she switched on the bedside lamp and stared at Jake's unfinished portrait on the easel across the room. Why hadn't she painted over *him*? Just the thought of him put her on edge, but it wasn't enough to want to erase him, apparently. She glanced at the clock. It was 5:00 a.m.

"I'm waiting," she said aloud. "I know I'm talking to the air right now, but I need you to help me. I think you're the only one who can."

It wasn't until the words left her mouth that she believed them. Lying back down, she reached over to switch off her lamp and closed her eyes, remembering the time Jake had held her in his arms after her panic attack with Raphe.

"I'm here, Ina," he'd whispered. "I don't know why you're acting like this, but you're safe now."

She had collapsed against him, her tears soaking through his sweater. Jake had stroked her hair, whispering over and over she was safe and that he would take care of her. Finally, Ina had stopped crying.

"Why?" she'd asked.

He had kept stroking her head. "Why what?"

"Why are you always here for me?" She'd pulled away enough to look him in the eyes. He had been crying too, it seemed. His eyes had looked red and wet. "I–is it because you like me?" It was a question she had wanted to ask for so long.

Jake had blinked a few times, looking surprised. "Oh, Ina," he'd said sadly as he lifted a hand to brush away some hair that had stuck to her wet cheek. "Don't worry about things like that right now. I just want you to know as long as I'm alive, nothing will ever harm you."

He had helped her to her feet after that, and taken her inside. Ina remembered feeling a surge of gratitude for everything he had done for her. Now, as she fell back asleep almost a year and a half later, she realized how Jake had dismissed her question. He hadn't answered it at all, and she still didn't know the truth. He'd never once acted like he was physically attracted to her—only like he cared for her.

Not that she wanted Jake to be attracted to her. She liked Alex. The problem was her physical attraction and affection for Alex only seemed to surface when he was nearby. When he was away, it was as if her feelings for him became cloudy and muddled. She was too preoccupied with other things. He wanted to help her, but she wasn't sure he could do more than he'd already done. In fact, she was sure if he got any closer to her, something bad might happen. What if she panicked like she had with Raphe, or the client in the hotel room, or Vincenzo? He might decide she wasn't worth it at that point, especially since he already had to take care of his family.

"I'm sorry, Alex," she whispered into the darkness. "I'm so, so sorry."

# Forty

June 29th, 1999

Alex,

You probably know by now that I've left River Meadows. Please don't be mad. If I know you at all, I know you'll understand. All I ask is you believe me when I say how much I care about you—and yes, I mean I like you when I say that. I like you a lot.

Right now, I have to figure out what's wrong with me. Dr. Huang thinks it has to do with childhood trauma. I'm not sure if I believe that yet, but I think there's one person who has the answers. Jake. He flew into Boise early this morning and took a cab to Anniston to meet me. I'm not sure where we're going or how long it'll be before I see you again, but I promise I'm okay. Jake isn't dangerous like I thought. He's here with me right now as I write this in the lobby.

You're my best friend, Alex. I know it might be hard for you to understand why I'm leaving with Jake after everything that's happened, but Jake has never actually hurt me on purpose. He also admits he never should have told the police I was crazy.

Thank you for everything, Alex. Peace out.

Love,

Sabrina Mae Sanchez
(just don't ever call me that to my face, Mr. Winzelberg)

# Forty-One

## Alex

"This can't be happening," Alex groaned as he finished reading Ina's letter. "Why did you let her leave with that man? Couldn't you see how shifty he was?"

Leslie looked up at Alex from across the front desk. "We couldn't legally stop her from leaving," she answered stiffly.

"Is it policy to let *anyone* in here, then?" Alex growled, immediately regretting how rude he was being. He tried to soften his voice. "I thought you had security guards." His frustration reached a whole new level as he stared down at the letter in his hand. It was Ina's personality, no mistaking that.

"Look, she came out here to the lobby on her own with her bags packed, like she was expecting him. I tried to talk some sense into her, but she wouldn't listen. She kept saying she was fine and she needed to do this. I called Dr. Huang the second they were gone. Then I called you."

Alex got a hold of his emotions with some difficulty. "Thanks for calling me. Did they leave in a cab?"

"Yeah, about half an hour ago."

Alex pushed a hand through his messy hair. His mother had dragged him out of bed at 5:00 a.m. to tell him she and April were driving into Boise to meet with the nurse

April had hired, and that he and his father would be in charge of the warehouse until that afternoon. Alex had been fine with that until the phone rang and Leslie told him Ina had left suddenly with a man.

"What did Dr. Huang say when you called him?"

"He said he wants to read Ina's letter, with your permission. He's on his way over here. He sounded pretty worried."

"What if he took her straight to the airport? How are we going to find them?" Alex started pacing in front of the front desk, his heart pounding. Jake had finally gotten to Ina. What did he want with her? And how could Ina have gone from being terrified of him to running away with him in just a few days?

"I don't think they were going to the airport," Leslie said, stopping Alex in his tracks. "I overheard the guy saying something about a flight not leaving until tomorrow."

Alex chewed on his bottom lip. "Maybe they're going to stay somewhere in Boise," he thought out loud. "I still don't know how to track them down, though." Then a thought occurred to him and he stepped up to the front desk. "I forgot he has a cell phone. Maybe I should try calling him. If he doesn't want trouble and he really wants to help her like he said, he shouldn't have a problem talking to me, right?"

"It couldn't hurt to try."

Alex looked at the cordless phone Leslie was holding out to him. He waved it away. "I don't know the number off the top of my head . . . ugh, I can't remember Emily's number now either. Or Logan's." Then he remembered he had Emily and Ina's apartment number in his email. "Do you have a computer I can use to get online?" he asked.

"I'm not allowed to let you get on these computers, but Dr. Huang just drove up. Maybe he can help?"

Alex looked out the door to see Dr. Huang's car pulling into a parking stall. "I'll go talk to him, thanks."

"See you, Alex. Good luck!"

Alex hurried out the doors. Even though it was summer, the early morning air felt deathly cold.

"Alex!" Dr. Huang said, stepping up the curb. He was dressed more nicely than usual, in a suit and tie. "I'm so sorry to hear about Ina. Leslie said she left you a letter?"

Alex pulled the letter from his pocket and handed it over. He shivered in his T-shirt, patiently waiting as Dr. Huang read the contents. The doctor frowned and started rubbing his chin as he read.

"How much did she tell you about Jake?" Alex asked, unable to wait one more second. "Do you think she's in danger?"

Dr. Huang kept his eyes on the letter. "She told me a bit about him," he answered slowly. "Honestly, I'm not sure what to make of the man."

Alex nodded as Dr. Huang handed the letter back to him. "I met him once. He kinda scared me. I mean, he just got out of prison. In fact, it's probably illegal for him to even be here since he's on parole. That's a red flag right there, isn't it?"

"It sure is."

Alex started folding Ina's letter into a square. "Jake told me and Logan he thinks Ina needs help, but he made it sound like he was the *only* one who could help her. Why would he think that?"

Dr. Huang pushed his hands into his pants pockets. "I don't know. Like she said in the letter, I think she's dealing with a form of post-traumatic stress. That can do some scary things to the mind if it's not addressed and dealt with. I'm a little concerned that Jake thinks he can help with that sort of thing on his own. Perhaps he has good intentions, but he could end up doing her harm without even realizing it."

"How do you mean?"

Dr. Huang shrugged. "Let's just say Jake wouldn't be the first person I've seen who has tried to play doctor. Ina is in a very fragile state right now; she needs a specific kind of therapy."

"Then we have to find her," Alex said, his anxiety rising again. The first thing he had to do was get home and try to get Jake's number. He relayed this to Dr. Huang, who quickly agreed.

"Grab your bike and put it in the trunk," he said.

Once they were on the road, Alex began to relax a little.

"Thanks for helping me out," he said, placing his elbow on the edge of the door so he could rest his head against his hand.

"No problem, but I won't be able to help you try to track Ina down. I have an important conference in Los Angeles this afternoon. My flight is in a few hours, so I have to leave for the airport as soon as I drop you off."

Alex's heart sank to the floor. "Oh."

Dr. Huang gave him a sidelong look. "It'll be okay. Ina may have some problems, but she can take care of herself. Perhaps you should try to track down Jake's parole officer and let him know what's happened. That's a start."

"Leslie said she overheard Jake say there's a flight leaving tomorrow. I don't know if that means a flight for him or both of them. What if he came here to hurt her and then run away?"

Dr. Huang laughed, and Alex couldn't blame him. He *was* being overly dramatic.

"Do you really think that's Jake's plan? He came here without trying to hide. He let Leslie see him. They apparently spent some time in the lobby while Ina wrote that letter. I don't think he plans on hurting her. Let's get you home so you can try to contact him, okay?"

Alex nodded slowly as he used all his strength to tamp down his rising anxiety. Dr. Huang was right, and being a lot more level-headed than himself. He had to follow that example. He just wasn't sure how at the moment.

"I wish you weren't leaving," he said dejectedly as they pulled into the warehouse parking lot. "My mom and sister left for Boise a few hours ago. They won't be back until this afternoon, so it's just me and Dad running the warehouse. If he hallucinates while I'm trying to deal with this, I don't know what I'll do."

Dr. Huang put the car in park and looked sternly over at Alex. "You're starting to sound like your mother," he scolded. "Now promise me you'll get it together and take charge of this, okay? Your father is a lot more competent than you're giving him credit for." He reached over to put his hand on Alex's shoulder. His eyes were pleading. "Trust him, Alex. He's fighting harder than you know."

Alex nodded, remembering the night before when April had told everyone about hiring the male caretaker. Everything had been a mess for a few minutes, but it had blown over pretty fast, and Alex's father had ended up handling it just fine.

Alex came back to the moment. "Thanks for your help," he said, trying to sound as confident as possible.

"No problem. Keep me posted about what happens. I'll have my cell phone, okay?"

"Okay." Alex got out of the car, retrieved his bike from the trunk, and wheeled it over to the side door. Inside, everything seemed to be running smoothly. Employees were bustling around, talking on their radios. Some of them waved hello to Alex as he walked his bike toward the stairs. Then he spotted his father near one of the loading docks. He certainly looked okay. He was giving orders and marking things off on a clipboard.

Okay, so things were fine here. For now.

Alex left his bike beneath the stairs and went up to his room. The first thing he did was find Logan's number and call him.

"Hey, man!" Logan answered. "What's up? Thought you'd forgotten about me."

Alex rolled his eyes. "It's been three days, dude."

"Yeah, three days of me wondering how it was for you to meet Ina! Come on, man, spill it. How is she? Did you sleep with her yet?"

"*Sleep* with her? Dude, do you know me at all?" Alex sat back in his chair and let out a heavy sigh. "We made out a little yesterday, but something's happened and—"

"Awesome," Logan interrupted. "That's *some* action, right? So she's into you."

Alex tapped his fingers on his desk. "Something's happened. Jake found Ina, and she's taken off with him."

There was a long pause. "Wait, what?"

"She must've contacted him," Alex explained. "He flew out here this morning and she was waiting for him. I don't know where they went or what he's planning. I was hoping I could get Jake's cell phone number. Did you happen to put it in your phone?"

"Yeah, I think I did. But wait, he flew to Idaho? I thought the douchebag was on parole."

"Yeah, because Jake is the type of guy who follows *all* the rules."

"Yeah, yeah. Good point. Give me a sec and I'll get you his number." A minute later he read off Jake's number. Alex wrote it down and told Logan he'd call back later so they could catch up. They said goodbye and Alex immediately dialed Jake's number. He tapped his foot on the floor as he listened to the rings.

Nothing.

Finally, Jake's voicemail message began: *"Hey, you've reached the J-Man. Leave your message after the tone."*

Alex rolled his eyes. The J-Man? Who called themselves that? Then again, Alex had to admit he automatically hated anything Jake said or did. Maybe it was because he knew Jake had hurt Ina in the past, but he also couldn't deny the stinging jealousy he felt that Ina wanted Jake to help her instead of himself.

The tone sounded.

"Hey, Jake," Alex said, trying to keep his voice calm. "This is Alex Winzelberg. I'm trying to reach Ina, so please call me back." He recited the warehouse phone number and then hung up.

Alex set the phone on his desk and stared at it. He would have to wait here at the warehouse until Jake called back, which meant he couldn't go out looking for Ina. Not that he expected her to still be in Anniston. Jake was probably getting her as far away as possible.

A knock on his door interrupted his dark thoughts. "Yeah?"

His father opened the door and peeked in. He looked exhilarated, as if running the warehouse by himself had lit him up inside. "Can I come in?"

Alex nodded. "Sure. I'll be down there soon to help out. It's just all this stuff with Ina. If Mom and April had known, I'm sure they—"

"Don't worry about it!" He walked into the room and sat on the end of Alex's messy bed. "We have plenty of staff today. You do what you need to do." He folded his arms, concern filling his eyes. "So, what did you find out? Is Ina okay?"

Alex faced his father. He relayed everything that had happened and then let his father read the note.

"This doesn't sound good," his father said softly, lowering the paper. "Although I have to say it's great she seems to like you so much. That Jennifer girl was never good enough for you. She broke your heart and I'm still angry about it. I hope Ina doesn't end up doing the same thing."

Alex shrugged. "I'd rather be able to see her again and have her break my heart than never hear from her again." He gave his father a pleading look. "I'm really worried, Dad. Dr. Huang said he's not too worried about it, but I don't think I'll be able to sleep again until I know she's all right."

"I can understand that. Let me think for a sec."

Alex watched him carefully, realizing for the first time that perhaps his father's mental illness wasn't the only reason he wanted to stay home for a year. Maybe it was because he would miss his father—*a lot*. Was that what he was so afraid of? Leaving his parents? Missing them? It felt like a good explanation, but he wasn't sure it was the right one.

"Any ideas?" Alex asked after a few minutes. "Because I don't know what else to do unless Jake actually calls. How am I supposed to track him down?"

His father raised a finger in the air, signaling for Alex to wait a moment. Finally, he spoke. "I think I have a plan," he said, his eyes lighting up.

"Really? What?"

His father smiled. "Let's just say I'm happy I've spent so much time watching all those cop shows on TV. This might not work, but it's worth a try." He nodded toward the phone sitting on Alex's desk. "First, I need you to call the girl at River Meadows. You said she saw Jake pull up in a cab?"

"Yeah."

"Good. Get her on the phone. That's where we'll start."

# Forty-Two

## Ina

Ina dropped her suitcase on the bed and turned around to face Jake. He looked cleaner than she remembered. Maybe it was his clothes, or maybe he'd shaved closer than usual. He also looked stronger than she remembered, like he'd been working out a lot.

"Ina?" Jake asked. "Are you okay? I have my own room. Do you want me to leave now?"

She took a step back, but the bed got in her way. She stumbled, catching herself as she forced her breathing back to normal. "No, no, I'm just . . . old feelings, y'know? I . . . I trust you."

Jake stayed by the door. "I'll leave," he said gently.

"No, you can stay." She had to get a grip. Jake hadn't hurt her, and he wasn't about to. If anything, he looked more nervous than she felt. He was still holding tightly on to the handle of his suitcase and his shirt was rumpled from his plane ride. Ina realized he looked completely out of his element and she wasn't sure why.

"So the room is okay?" he asked, his stark blue eyes focused on her.

Ina looked around the room, a little weirded out that she was back at the Two Spoons, the same place she'd thought she had seen Jake on Friday. The décor was rustic, mostly bear-themed. It matched the feel of the café downstairs. "It's exactly what I would have chosen," she said, trying not to sound too nervous.

Jake smiled. "I'll be next door if you need me. We have the rest of the day to talk, and then you can decide if you want to fly back to New York with me in the morning. It's up to you."

She took a deep breath. "Yeah, I don't know. Maybe we should get some breakfast downstairs and talk? There's a pretty view of the forest." She pointed toward the window overlooking the same stretch of trees that she had seen from the café the other day. That was when she had remembered her panic attack with Raphe. For some reason, the memory was no longer disturbing.

"That sounds great." Jake stayed by the door.

She watched him for a moment, thinking about where he'd been since she had seen him last. "What was it like?" she asked.

"What was what like?"

"Prison."

Jake's expression melted into a grimace. "It was awful," he muttered. "I don't really want to talk about it." He tightened his grip on his suitcase. "I'm breaking my parole coming here to see you; I'm not allowed to leave the state."

Ina's eyes widened. She hadn't thought of that. "You shouldn't have come, then. I don't want you to get in trouble over me."

Jake took a step forward, his eyes filling with urgency. "You're worth the risk, okay? There are things you need to know. Now. Before anything gets worse."

Ina motioned to the door. "Let's go get breakfast. I have things I need to ask you."

Jake left his suitcase in his own room before they headed downstairs to the café. Caroline was sitting behind the register, just as before. She smiled at the two of them.

"Table for two?" she asked. "Inside or out?"

Jake looked at Ina. "Which would you prefer?"

"Outside, I guess."

"Excellent," Caroline said. "It's going to be a hot one today, but it's lovely right now." She grabbed two menus and led them through the café to a set of French doors leading outside. There was a wide porch overlooking the view of the forest and rising mountains. One couple was already seated, eating stacks of syrup-drenched pancakes. The air smelled like lilacs and pine.

Caroline led them to a table and left them with the menus.

"You chose a good place," Jake said. "If I'd known it was going to be this nice, I might've booked a few nights instead of just one."

Ina looked up from her menu. "Probably not a good idea if you aren't supposed to be here," she scolded. "How long does your parole last, anyway?"

Jake shrugged. "It depends. If my parole officer finds out I left the state, I'll probably have to serve some more time, and then my next parole will be even longer, if I get one at all."

"I have a question for you," Ina said, sitting back in her chair. Their table was shaded by an open umbrella, but a patch of morning sun was shining on Jake's face. Ina kept her attention there, afraid to look him in the eyes.

"Fire away," Jake said.

She shifted in her chair. "What did you want for me? The more I think about it, the more it seems your whole plan was for me to come and live in your house with the rest of your women." She folded her arms and gave Jake a stern stare.

He frowned. "I never wanted you to prostitute yourself. That wasn't my plan. I didn't even want you to be a part of the legal side of my business."

Ina tapped her fingers on her arm. "Okay, then what *was* your plan?"

He ran his finger along the top edge of his menu. "That's what I want to talk to you about. See . . . Ina . . . I knew you a long time before we met at Harmony House."

"What are you talking about? I would have remembered you."

"Well, it was a long time ago; I looked different back then." He pulled out his wallet and flipped through a few of the pictures before handing it over. "I still wore glasses back then, and I had the beard."

Ina took the wallet and stared down at the picture of a younger, hairier Jake. He was right. He *had* looked different, and also a little familiar. The glasses were what jogged her memory. Coke-bottle monstrosities perched over his nose. They almost hid his blue eyes, but they were still visible, piercing her. "Maybe . . ." she said softly as some memories filtered into the foreground. "I remember a guy like this . . . maybe someone I talked to after the accident?"

Jake nodded. "I should have told you this a long time ago, as soon as I recognized you. I used to be a social worker. I was one of the people assigned to your case when your father died."

A snippet of memory slid into Ina's mind: a mostly empty room with a sofa, the same room as in her painting, only there was a man and a woman there. The woman had long brown hair and was wearing a black blazer. The man had striking blue eyes behind thick glasses and was wearing jeans. He was handing her a teddy bear.

Jake leaned forward. "See, Ina, your car accident happened one year to the day after I'd lost my Anna." He met Ina's questioning look. "Anna was my daughter. She was four years old when she died from a seizure, and even though you were older than her, you reminded me of her. Even your names are similar."

Ina stared at him, surprised. "I didn't know you had a kid."

"I was only eighteen when she was born. Her mother left us when Anna was just two years old. After that, Anna was my whole world until . . ."

Ina's heart sank. Jake's past was something she had never wondered about. It made her feel guilty all of a sudden. Why hadn't she ever asked him about his life? She'd been so wrapped up in her own problems, she'd never even considered stepping outside of herself. "I'm so sorry," she whispered.

He blinked a few times, his eyes filling with tears. "When I saw you, I felt like you were my second chance. It was myself and another social worker who helped you that day of the accident. I can't even remember her name now. We met with you three times: once at the police department right after the accident, and twice at your home for follow-up visits. I loved those meetings because of how much you reminded me of my daughter.

"You were so frightened, Ina. You'd just lost your father. You were devastated. I don't blame you for not remembering much of anything from back then."

Ina shook her head. "I remember the accident. Mom went to the hospital with a broken leg . . . no, it was her ankle. I was . . . I was fine, and nobody was there to take care of me right after everything happened. The police came and one of them took me to the station."

"Right, and you were scared. I tried so hard to make you feel better, to get you to open up to me so we could work through your grief, but all you could do was cry and hold that teddy bear I gave you."

She froze as goosebumps popped up along her arms. The teddy bear . . .

Just then, Caroline approached their table, carrying a tray with two glasses of water and a basket of warm biscuits. "All right, you two!" she chimed. "Ready to order? What'll it be?"

Ina looked up at Caroline, her eyes filling with tears. She blinked them back quickly, hoping Caroline wouldn't notice. "I–I'll have the waffles," she said quickly.

"I'll have the same," Jake said, handing both menus to Caroline. "Thank you."

Caroline smiled brightly at them. "No problem. Your food will be out shortly." She walked away.

Ina waited until the older woman was out of earshot before she spoke. "I remember you giving me a teddy bear," she said in a strained voice. "Why would you do that?"

Jake shrugged. "Stuffed toys are comforting. I had a whole trunkful for cases involving kids."

She shook her head. "I keep painting a picture of a little girl holding a teddy bear with a red bow on its head. The girl is standing in an empty room. I've never known where that image came from, and I've never been able to finish it. I always end up painting over it."

"That's interesting," Jake said, his eyes softening. "Listen, Ina, I've wanted to talk to you about this for so many years, but it seemed too cruel to remind you of that time—to bring back all of those sad memories when you seemed to be doing so well at Harmony House. But then your mother . . . well, I took you to that retreat and you had that panic attack out by the lake, and things got worse from there. You . . . you . . ." He stopped and looked away, lifting his hands to his face and rubbing at his eyes. "You kept doing the strangest things, Ina. It scared the hell out of me. I minored in psychology, so I know a bit about mental disorders, and I knew I needed to protect you long enough to figure out what kind of help you needed."

Ina glowered at him, her emotions swirling into a vortex. "It was not *your* job to fix me," she hissed. "You never encouraged me to finish high school, never let me try to get a real job. I felt like you were the only way I could survive. Why did you do that to me? I'm still trying to get used to the fact that I'm in charge of my own life now."

Jake gave her a pleading look. "I didn't want you to have to worry about money or food or where you were going to sleep, and I honestly thought you weren't ready to finish high school." He looked down at the table. "I thought the stress might be too much." He looked back up at her, his eyes filling with anger now. "That's why I was so upset when I found out Francesca was helping you set up appointments with her own clients. I didn't stop you because I knew you would fight me, so I let you do what you wanted, even though I was terrified it was going to backfire on you."

Ina folded her arms. "You were right about that. That was not a world I wanted to be in, but the money was too damn good. I felt like it was the only way I'd ever be able to go to art school . . . or anywhere, really."

"I know, I know. You were in the same boat as everyone else. I can imagine what went through your head, seeing things like Julie paying for nursing school, and Evangeline supporting her son *and* her mother. I know none of my girls could have accomplished what they were doing without making the kind of money I was helping them make, but I guess it wasn't the best way."

"Damn right it wasn't."

"I thought it was at the time. There just aren't a lot of options for young women coming out of group homes like Harmony House."

Ina narrowed her eyes. "How did you end up working for Harmony House, anyway?"

"I was a social worker for NYPD for a long time, but it was too intense after a while, so I started working in different fields. I got into group home management."

"Was that before or after you started running the escort service?" Ina asked.

"Before." Jake cleared his throat and reached for one of the biscuits in the middle of the table. He held it in his hands for a moment. "How much do you remember about the car accident that killed your father?" he asked softly.

Ina tilted her head, taken aback by the change in subject. "I don't remember a lot of it, mostly what my mom told me about it later. We were driving on the freeway and a truck swerved from the other lane and hit us. The truck driver died."

Jake nodded. "And your dad. Did he die on impact?"

"I guess so . . . I mean . . ." Her voice trailed off as she closed her eyes, trying to remember. "There's . . . nothing," she whispered. Just . . . nothing. All I know is what my mom told me. There are no memories." She opened her eyes to see Jake staring at her with a curious expression on his face.

Just then, a server came to their table with a tray full of food.

"Here you go!" he said, setting plates heaped with waffles in front of them, along with a jar of syrup and a bowl of fresh-cut strawberries. "Enjoy." He left.

Ina didn't look down at her food. The rich smell of waffles wafted up to her, but they didn't smell appealing.

"I need to tell you something about your father's death," Jake said. "Is right now okay? It might be a bit of a shock, and I don't want you to feel like I'm isolating you. We can go back to River Meadows or find your friend Alex, if you'd like. Or—"

Ina shook her head. "No, here is fine. Just tell me whatever it is you need to tell me."

Jake looked down at his plate. "Did you know there was a big investigation into the accident?"

Ina's eyes narrowed. "What for? The driver who hit us?"

Jake cleared his throat again and took a sip of his water. "No, the driver was having a stroke when he hit you. That's what killed him, not the crash. The investigation was about your father's death. I had a lot of friends on the force back then, and one of them was in charge of the investigation. Larry thought your father's death looked suspicious, and he started doing some digging. See, your mom . . . well, she wasn't exactly faithful to your father."

Ina leaned forward, her eyes widening. "She had an affair?"

"Several. Do you remember ever seeing your mother with another man?"

Ina's heart began racing. "Mom was gone all the time for work. Nannies took take care of me after Dad died. I guess she could've been seeing someone else without me knowing." She lifted her eyes to Jake. "Do you think that's why she's refused to talk to me all these years? She was worried I'd find out she'd cheated on Dad? Seriously?"

Jake looked away from her. "I–I can't do this," he growled, pushing his chair away from the table and standing. "I can't do this to you—not here, not—"

Every muscle in Ina's body tensed. "You'd better tell me what happened," she demanded. "You can't stop there, Jake. You *can't*. You told me yourself this is the only way."

Jake sat back down and buried his face in his hands. "Okay, okay," he sighed. "Please . . . just promise me you'll stay calm, okay?"

Ina clenched her jaw, knowing she couldn't promise any such thing. She took a deep breath and said, "I'll try."

# Forty-Three

Jake lowered his hands from his face, but kept his eyes on the table. "As your caseworker, I was there when Larry questioned you about your mother. You didn't seem to remember anything, just like now. But, Ina . . . if you could remember what happened in the car right after the accident, if you could remember anything strange about your mother's behavior, I think it would help you get to the bottom of why you have panic attacks, and why you've been talking to yourself."

Ina narrowed her eyes. "What are you getting at?"

He took a deep breath, looking away for a long moment before finally meeting her gaze. "Larry suspected your mother of murdering your father right after the accident occurred."

"*What?*" A nervous laugh bubbled up from Ina's throat. "My mom wouldn't have—"

"Just listen for a moment," Jake interrupted firmly, keeping his eyes on hers. "Your father's injuries were serious but not life-threatening. The official coroner's report says that the force of the impact threw your father facedown into your mother's lap and he died of asphyxiation. Your mother claimed that she was afraid to move him and had no idea he couldn't breathe. Larry didn't buy her story. He didn't think she was acting like a grieving widow who'd accidentally let her husband die. She was too calm and collected. He believed that when your mother saw that your father was unconscious, she deliberately pushed his head down and smothered him with her skirt. But he couldn't prove his theory, and of course your mother denied everything."

Ina's mouth dropped open. It couldn't be true. Either Jake was lying, or his stupid detective buddy was just plain vindictive. She looked down to see Jake reaching across the table for her hand. She pulled away, suddenly feeling nauseous as the sweet smell of waffles and strawberries turned sickly. She pushed her plate away. "None of this is real," she whispered. "It's not real, just like those phone calls. It's all in my head."

But she knew it was real. She was starting to remember things. Memories that had been buried for years. The screeching tires, the blurry sky and broken glass. Her father slumped across the center console, his head in his wife's lap, facing away from Ina.

And her mother's hand grabbing a fistful of hair, turning his head, holding him down . . .

"Ina?" Jake's voice cut into her thoughts. "Are you okay?"

Ina snapped back to the moment, shaking her head. "I remember it," she whispered. "Why couldn't I remember it before? Why now? Why didn't I tell the police what I saw?" She wrung her hands together. "But I still don't know if what I saw was . . . *did I really see that*? If I did, why didn't I tell the police?"

Jake's eyes filled with pity. "I don't know, Ina. At first, you were in shock. After that you just seemed to shut down. They eventually closed the investigation, and your mother was off the hook." He shrugged. "Until she went to prison for embezzlement . . . but she never confessed to the murder. We'll probably never know what really happened." He gave Ina a look so sad that she thought he might start crying.

For some reason, that made her furious. "Why didn't you bring *any* of this up before?" Ina demanded.

He looked away. "I wanted to," he said gently. "I really, really wanted to, but you didn't remember me at all, and I decided you were dealing with enough already with your mom in prison and having to live in a group home with no other family to love you. I just couldn't do it."

"You treated me differently than the other kids," Ina said. "Like you cared about me more."

Jake gave her a half-smile. "I never stopped thinking about you, wondering if there was anything else I could have done to help you. You still reminded me of my daughter. You remind me of her even now. She had curly hair like yours. She was half Argentinian too." He fell silent for a moment, a haunted look in his eyes. "That was all it ever was, Ina: my infatuation with my own grief. You take away that pain every time I look at you, and all I've ever wanted to do is protect you and every other woman I see who is in trouble or in pain. You always insisted you were fine, but you buried your pain, didn't you? You buried it so deep it's killing you inside."

Ina looked down at her untouched food. It was cold now. "I don't know if I believe any of it," she said softly. She tried to swallow the growing lump in her throat. "I need to talk to Mom," she whispered. "I have to make her tell me the truth."

Jake leaned forward. "That's another thing," he said slowly. "Where do you think your mother is right now?"

Ina gave him a confused look. "In prison. Where else would she be?"

Jake took a deep breath and looked Ina in the eyes. "Your mother is dead," he said in a firm voice. He waited for a moment, as if he was expecting Ina to react. "Do you remember when she died?" he asked in a tone that sounded like he was talking to a five-year-old.

Ina stared at him. Everything felt cold. Numb. Dark.

"She committed suicide a year and a half ago," Jake continued, still using that gentle, patronizing tone. "Her lawyer came to Harmony House and told you. You refused to have anything to do with the funeral arrangements, and when the House counselor tried to treat you, you just . . . shut down again. That was part of why we took you on that retreat to the ski lodge. We were hoping it would help you, but then you had that panic attack out by the lake and everything fell apart after that. Every time I brought up your mother, you acted like she was still alive. The one time I tried to talk to you about it like I'm talking to you now, you had another panic attack. I decided it was best to let it go until you were ready to talk about it, so I've never mentioned it again."

Ina looked down at her hands resting in her lap. She didn't feel panicked, but everything around her was starting to get fuzzy and quiet. She stared at her fingers. They were shaking and she couldn't stop them.

"Dead," she whispered, suddenly recalling the meeting with her mother's lawyer, Gary Hammond. He'd come to Harmony House to see her. He had broken the news gently, and then said something about insurance and disposal of the body. *Disposal of the body*, like her mother was nothing more than a used tissue . . .

"Ina, listen to me," Jake's voice cut through her thoughts.

She looked up. "I kind of freaked out on Gary when he told me," she said shakily. "The counselor wouldn't leave me alone after that. I told her I was fine, and I . . . I *was*." Leaning forward, Ina gripped the edge of the table and looked Jake in the eyes. "I showed her I was fine. I showed everyone nothing was wrong so they would leave me alone."

Jake regarded her with a mixture of triumph and sadness. "So you do remember."

Ina nodded. "I do now. I think I always have. I just . . . I don't know what the hell is wrong with my brain." She reached up and squeezed a handful of hair.

"You were repressing too many memories," Jake said. "Too much grief. You're having a difficult time accepting your mother's death and what you saw her do. You made up phone calls with her to convince yourself she was still alive. You buried everything . . . and that's why I've been so intent on finding you. When I got out of prison, I just wanted to check on you and make sure you were okay. But that night at the restaurant, you looked so lost and scared. That's when I knew you still needed my help. I had to protect you." He reached across the table, holding his hand out to her.

Ina didn't make any move to take it.

"We'll go one step at a time," Jake said, pulling his hand back. "I understand it's—"

He was interrupted by a ringtone from his pocket. He looked down and pulled a cell phone out, his eyebrows scrunching together.

"What is it?" Ina asked.

"My parole officer," Jake muttered, and flipped the phone open. "I'm surprised I even have service here. If I don't take this, I'll be in even more trouble than I already am. I'll be right back." He stood and walked away from the table before speaking into his phone.

Slumping in her chair, Ina folded her arms and looked out at the line of trees across the meadow. She couldn't even begin to sort through her emotions and memories. She felt numb, but at the same time there was a battle raging inside of her—one she wasn't sure she had the strength to fight. She hated Jake for dumping all of this on her so fast, even though she'd asked him to. She wished she could bury the memories again, but how could she keep living without facing her past? This was what she needed, wasn't it? So that she could start to heal?

"I can't do this, Dr. Huang," she whispered. "Please make it stop." She started rubbing her eyes. "Make it stop." She looked up at the forest across the meadow. She wasn't really aware of leaving the table, but the forest was getting closer. Dark. Safe. A place she could bury her bad memories for good. She kept moving forward. The forest was even darker now, closing around her. When she looked back, Jake was nothing but a small speck standing on a wooden porch across the meadow.

# Forty-Four

## Alex

"Tapping your foot that hard isn't going to get us there faster," Alex's father said as the car bumped along the graded dirt road toward the Two Spoons Bed & Breakfast. "Everything will be fine, Alex. Think positive."

Alex threw a worried glance at his father in the driver's seat. He wasn't supposed to drive, especially while adjusting to a new medication, and especially not someone else's car. But the car they'd borrowed from Everett was a stick shift, which Alex was not experienced driving. Still, he couldn't stop thinking of how awful it would be if his dad started hallucinating at the wheel and crashed into a telephone pole—or worse, another car.

"*Think positive?*" Alex snorted.

His dad shrugged. "Worrying doesn't solve a thing. You think I got where I am today by worrying?"

"You worry plenty, Dad. I heard you talking to Maria in your bedroom, remember?"

His dad scrunched his brow. "You're right, I worry about you. A lot. I want you around, but I don't want to be the reason you aren't living the life you want. It's not fair to you."

Alex shrugged. "Well, maybe with hiring this new guy for you, things will be way better."

The car hit a particularly deep depression in the road, sending both Alex and his father up toward the roof and then back down.

"Maybe," his father sighed. "If I'm really the reason you've been staying."

Alex put a hand to his forehead. "It's not just you, Dad. It's Mom too, and the warehouse and all the stuff I do to help out. Even if you didn't have health problems, you guys would still need me here."

"We'll hire more people," his dad retorted. "That's not an unsolvable problem."

"It is when you're trying to save money. You don't deal with the finances. You don't know how much it'll cost to hire new employees and train them to do all the different things I do."

A smirk lifted his father's lips. "Okay, you win."

Alex glared at him, not understanding what he was getting at. "I'm not afraid to leave. That's not it at all."

"I didn't say you were afraid. I guess I'm wondering how you really see me. Has today proved nothing to you?"

Alex sat farther back in his seat, thinking about the past few hours. He supposed he wouldn't be here now, heading to the Two Spoons to find Ina, if it wasn't for his father. He had, after all, been the one who'd called Leslie at River Meadows to see if she'd noticed which cab service Jake had used. When she said yes, he'd told her about Jake's parole violation, and then asked if she'd call local law enforcement with the cab information so they could start to track him down. Then they'd borrowed Everett's car and driven over to Mark Pedersen's place.

Mark sometimes worked holiday shifts at the warehouse, and was also the self-appointed captain of Anniston's volunteer Search and Rescue unit, which was really just Mark, his hunting buddies, and their dogs.

Mark had ways of finding out anything important that was going on in town, like Benita but less chatty. The second Alex and his father knocked on his door, he was all over the news—he'd been listening to his police scanner—and the second he found out the Two Spoons was where the police might be headed, Alex and his father had jumped back in the car to drive straight there.

It was brilliant, really. Alex had been impressed. He was even more impressed now as he watched his dad drive the stick shift down the dirt road, as if he did it every day. In reality, he hadn't been behind the wheel in over ten years.

Alex folded his arms. "I guess it's proved I can still count on you sometimes. You ran the warehouse this morning while I was gone, you found out where Ina is, and you're driving without wrecking the car."

His dad raised a finger off the wheel. "I also made sure the warehouse is run properly while we're gone."

Alex nodded. "We have a good crew, yeah."

"It's not just that. I want you to trust me, okay? I can take care of myself."

Alex gave his father a sidelong look. "Where is this confidence coming from? You know as well as I do that your . . . you know—"

"My schizophrenia. Just say it."

Alex stared at his Dad. His father never said the "S" word. "Fine. You know as well as I do that your *schizophrenia* will always keep you from being independent. It can be dangerous."

His dad pressed his lips together and squeezed the steering wheel tighter. "Yes, I know," he finally answered. "But this new medication is really helping me, even after only a few days. I think clearer. I feel better." His face lit up for a moment as he glanced over at Alex. "This morning I had a pretty bad hallucination and *nobody knew.* I recognized it for what it was and just kept doing what I was doing. It just took Dr. Huang a little time to figure out the right meds for me, that's all."

Alex kept his eyes on the road. They were almost to the Two Spoons now. "Okay," he said. "I believe you, but I still think we should be careful. Meds take a long time to stabilize. Like, maybe I should drive home when we're done here."

"Think you can do that without stripping the gears?" his father said with a grin. He pulled into the parking lot and turned off the engine. "Come on. Let's go find Ina."

Alex stepped out of the car and headed through the parking lot. He'd been here dozens of times before since Raven's grandmother gave all of her granddaughter's friends a discount. Mr. Barringer held some of his wrap parties here. It was a familiar place that Alex associated with good times and comfort food. Today, something felt different as he and his dad walked up the steps and into the café. Caroline wasn't in her usual spot behind the register. In fact, nobody was in the café at all. Half-eaten meals sat on empty tables. Alex's stomach dropped to the floor. "Something's wrong," he whispered. "And why aren't the police here yet?"

Alex's dad pointed to the windows. Five people were gathered at the edge of the meadow, their hands lifted to shade their eyes as if they were searching for something in the distance. Caroline was out there too, pacing in front of the group. She was so small she almost looked like a child at that distance.

Alex brushed past his father to get out to the back porch, his father right on his heels. Caroline stopped pacing as soon as she saw them descending the stairs. She headed over to them, holding out her hands. "There's nothing to see here," she said, craning her neck to look them both in the eye. "Just go back inside." She turned to the others. "Everybody go back inside, please. I'm not gonna ask again. You already know the police are on their way."

The group reluctantly disbursed, looking over their shoulders at the forest. Alex recognized two of them, and nodded hello as they headed back into the café.

Caroline fixed a stern gaze on Alex and his father. "You too," she said. "Scoot."

Alex's father put a friendly hand on Caroline's shoulder. "We came here looking for Ina Sanchez. Any chance you know if she's here or not?"

Caroline shifted her feet and raised an eyebrow. "You know her?"

Alex stepped forward. "She's my friend. Do you know where she is?"

Caroline jerked a thumb toward the forest. "She ran in there 'bout twenty minutes ago." She shook her head and raised her hands in a prayer-like gesture. "Lord help her if she gets lost in there with that man after her."

"You mean Jake?" Alex asked, his heart beginning to pound. "He chased her into the forest?" It took all his willpower not to take off running toward the forest. He needed the whole story first.

"Yeah, Jake . . . uh . . . I've already forgotten his last name," Caroline replied. "The Chief called to tell me they're comin' right away to arrest him, but after I said they'd gone into the woods he decided to get Mark's rescue unit rounded up too. Guess the man's wanted in New York or somethin'. Didn't tell me much else, just to keep everyone away from the forest. I told him they'd better hurry or they'll never find him. Wouldn't take much to disappear in there."

Alex couldn't hold back for one more second. In a burst of energy, he broke into a run across the meadow, barreling straight for the trees. People had gone into that forest and never come out again. Hikers, campers, hunters . . . and those people had gone in *prepared*. Ina was scared and being chased. She wasn't prepared for anything.

"I have to help her," Alex huffed as he sprinted toward the trees. "I have to—"

A heavy weight slammed into him, driving him to the ground. He face-planted into tangled weeds and grass. The smell of dirt filled his nose. Twisting around, he saw his father hunched over him, a scowl on his face.

"Dad?" Alex grunted, trying to sit up.

His dad pushed him back down, pressing hard on his shoulders. "Alex, listen to me," he growled. "You are not going in there. This is not your day to save."

Twisting again, Alex tried to break free from his father, but he wasn't strong enough. "What do you mean?" he argued. "I'm trying to help Ina! Jake is after her. What if she gets lost in there, or hurt? What if—"

"The police will find her and Jake!" his father insisted. "They just pulled up. See?"

He let go of Alex, and Alex sat up to see several vehicles pulling into the parking lot: one cop car, Mark Pedersen's jacked-up Ford truck, and a rusty Dodge with dogs riding in the back. Mark must have gotten the call right after Alex and his father had left. He'd gotten a team together in record time. There were three of them today, with two dogs. All of them were heading toward Alex and his dad through the meadow. The chief of police, Randy Carlisle, and his deputy sheriff got out of the cop car and followed Mark's crew. They looked serious.

Alex started to get to his feet. "I'll go with them," he said, trying to free his left foot from a tangle of grass.

His dad shoved him back down. "No you won't."

"What is your deal?" Alex snapped as he rubbed his sore tailbone. "I want to help!"

His father sat back on his heels. His forehead was shiny with sweat and there was a smudge of dirt on his chin. He looked so determined. So sure of himself. Alex realized how strong his father actually was, and how easy it had been to think of him as a weak victim of mental illness for the past ten years.

Lifting his eyes to the group of men tromping toward them, Alex blinked a few times and then sat back on his hands. "I guess they couldn't have gone far," he said, referring to Ina and Jake. "Still, I'd like to help look for them. I need to know Ina is okay."

"I know, but you can't help everyone all the time, okay? You're not Superman."

Alex rolled his eyes. "Right, Dad."

"I mean it, Alex. You aren't."

"We got a problem here?" Chief Carlisle asked, his hand on the butt of his gun as he looked from Alex to his father. He was a tall man, taller and stronger than Alex's father, and that was saying something. He had a neatly trimmed beard that was starting to show signs of gray. "You go ahead," he said to the rest of the group, motioning toward the forest. The men filed past with the two dogs trotting behind them.

Finally getting to his feet, Alex narrowed his eyes at Carlisle's hand that was still on the butt of his gun.

"No problem, Chief," Alex's dad said, slowly getting to his feet. He backed up to stand next to Alex. "I was just stopping my son from heading into the forest. I've explained to him that you've got everything under control and there's no need for him to try to be a hero."

Carlisle nodded. "Good call, Mr. Winzelberg. Head back to the Two Spoons, please."

"Sure thing."

Alex and his dad started back toward the Two Spoons, Alex dragging his feet the entire way. He felt defeated, as if he'd lost something, but he had no idea what that something was. He was still worried about Ina, but at the same time, he was sure she'd be found soon. She couldn't have gone far.

"I'm glad they're going to arrest Jake," he muttered. "At least she'll be safer that way."

"Is that what's most important to you?" his dad asked gently. "That everyone is safe?"

Alex scrunched his brow. "Huh?"

His dad brushed a hand across his forehead. He looked exasperated as he searched Alex's face. He put a hand on Alex's shoulder. "I think moving to New York is exactly what you need," he said confidently. "Not for me. Not for your mother. Not for Ina. For *you*. Think about it, Alex. Let me know when you're ready to buy your plane ticket. I'll book it myself."

With that, his father gave his shoulder a squeeze and headed up the steps. Alex watched him go inside the café, his heart sinking as he tried to make sense of what his dad had just told him. Was he kicking him out of the house? It felt like it. But maybe he had a point. Maybe Alex wasn't Superman. And maybe he didn't need to go to New York for anyone else but himself.

He turned around to face the forest, wondering where Ina was at that very moment. His heart ached for her. He wanted to make everything better for her. What good was he if he couldn't help her? If he couldn't help his family? If he couldn't *fix* things?

*You're not Superman.*

It was true. And that was what he had lost: the delusion that he was responsible for everyone's safety, that he could fix everything for everybody else. Walking away from the forest and leaving it up to Mark and the police to find Ina made him want to scream. He felt as if the truth was finally staring him in the face, but he still couldn't see what it was. It was so close he could almost touch it, but then it slipped away and his tears broke free. He swiped at them, embarrassed. He was not weak. He would not cry.

*You're not Superman.*

And that had been the problem all along.

* * *

Alex knew he couldn't do anything until the search party emerged from the woods, so he sat on the porch steps. He fixed his attention on the line of trees, every minute feeling like an eternity. At some point, his father came out with a Styrofoam cup in his hands.

"Still nothing?" he asked, sitting down next to Alex.

"Nope. I hope it's soon."

"Me too." He shifted on the step. "Listen, about what I said . . . I didn't mean to make it sound like I don't want you around."

Alex kept his eyes on the forest. "I think I know what you meant. You're saying I need to focus on me, not everybody else."

His dad took a sip of coffee. "So, you do understand."

Alex shrugged. "I'm not a hero, like you said. I can't save everyone." Alex glanced over at his father, his heart aching as the truth hit him. "What if I can't do that? What if I can't help *myself*? It's so much easier to help everyone else. You know, like when you got sick and all of a sudden everything changed and you weren't there for us anymore. We were there for *you* . . . and that's . . ." He focused on the forest again. "That's all I've known for so long."

His dad set his coffee cup on the bottom step and leaned forward, his face in his hands. "I know, but that broke you. I finally saw it yesterday. April said something that hit home for me. I can't even remember what she said, but it made me realize how much you've struggled over the years." He lifted his face from his hands and looked over at Alex. "You get so anxious and depressed over the smallest things, and you haven't tried to fix it because you've been too busy helping me and your mother, and now Ina. Nobody has ever taken the time to see that you might have something *you* need help with."

Alex raised an eyebrow, surprised that his father had noticed that about him. He'd thought he had hidden it so well. Sighing, he settled his elbows on his knees. "Logan has always been there to help me with that stuff," he said. "Kind of ironic, huh, since you can't stand him?"

His father grunted. "Okay, maybe he's not so bad after all. I was wrong." He sat up straight. "Is that someone coming out of the forest?"

Alex saw Chief Carlisle and his deputy emerging from the trees. "Looks like they have Jake," he said, standing to get a better view. He shaded his eyes from the sun, scanning the edge of the forest. "Where's Ina?"

His dad stood too, pointing. "Right there, to the north."

Sure enough, the rest of the search party came into view with Ina in their midst and the two dogs trotting proudly behind them. It was difficult to see if she was okay. She was walking, at least.

"Looks like they've arrested Jake," Alex's father said. "He's handcuffed."

Alex frowned at his dad. "You're not gonna try and stop me if I go out there now, are you? I just want to make sure Ina's okay."

His father shrugged. "Do what you need to."

Alex took off, his heart thumping. The Chief and his deputy were already to the parking lot now, putting Jake in the patrol car. Ina wasn't paying attention. She was walking beside Mark and his two buddies, still only halfway across the meadow. Her head was down, her jeans ripped on one knee and smeared with dirt. She looked up just as Alex stopped in front of the group. "Hey," he huffed, nodding hello to Mark. "Can I talk to Ina?"

Mark shrugged. "Chief wants her to come to the police station for some questions, but I don't see why not." He raised an eyebrow at Ina. "That okay with you?"

Ina nodded. "He's my friend, it's fine."

Mark nodded. "We'll tell Carlisle to wait for you," he said before he and his buddies left. Their dogs bounded behind them.

Alex stepped closer to Ina, studying her face for any clues of what might have happened. She looked like she'd been crying. Her skin was splotchy in places, a smudge of dirt across her jawline. It was her eyes that worried Alex. They looked empty, as if a light had gone out inside of her.

She met Alex's gaze, her expression blank. "I'm fine," she said flatly.

Alex frowned. "Did Jake hurt you? Is that why you ran in there?"

"No, it was because he told me things about my past and I panicked. I got a little lost, but those men found me and helped me snap out of it." She forced a smile. "I told you my panic attacks are the worst thing ever."

"What did Jake tell you to make you panic like that?"

She looked at the ground. "Dr. Huang was right. Something bad happened when I was a kid . . . and my mom . . . Jake helped me remember that she's dead. She died in prison." She looked up, fear filling her eyes. "I was trying to deny everything. I couldn't deal with it, and I . . . I don't know how I'm going to deal with it now. I need to go back to New York. I need to find a doctor who can help me." She gave Alex a shaky smile. "I'll be fine. I needed Jake to tell me those things. He got in trouble just for me."

Alex couldn't stop himself from rushing forward and taking her into his arms. She felt limp, like she might collapse any second. "I was so worried about you," he said, holding her close, but it must have been too much for her because she stiffened. He let her go and took a step back. "Ina, please . . . I want to help you, but I—"

"You can't help me with this. Jake can't either. I don't want to make you worry anymore. I don't want to make *anyone* worry. Not you or Emily or Jake or Dr. Huang." She put a hand to her chest. "This is my problem and I have to deal with it now that I know what it is." Glancing back at the forest, she sniffed and swiped a hand across her cheeks to wipe away her tears. "That's what I figured out in there when I was on the ground, crying and panicking. I need time to figure all of this out." She took a deep breath and let it out slowly. "On my own."

Alex nodded, his resolve stronger than ever now. "It's funny you say that, because me and my dad were talking about fixing some of my problems too." He let out a nervous laugh.

Ina wiped away some more tears. "I'll see you around." She started to walk toward the parking lot, her shoulders drooping.

"Ina," Alex said, hoping she'd stop. It was like a huge hole was opening up inside of him, swallowing everything happy and hopeful and sunny that Ina had always made him feel. It killed him to see her cry, to know she was in pain and there was nothing he could do.

She turned around to face him. "Yeah?"

"Email me when you get back to New York? Please? And maybe when you figure all of this out? I'm going to miss you."

A soft smile lifted her lips. "I will," she said. "And I'll miss you too."

# Forty-Five

From: Ina <ina.artgirl1979@hotmail.com>
To: Alex Winzelberg <winzwarehouse5@hotmail.com>
Date: July 1, 1999
Subject: Touching Base

Just letting you know I got home okay. Jake bought me a first-class ticket in case I wanted to go back to New York with him. It was weird sitting next to his empty seat, though. I have no idea when or how he's getting back to New York, or what will happen to him since he broke his parole. One of the officers told me he'll have to serve the rest of his sentence.

Sorry for how down I was when I left you. I hope you understand. I just have to focus on finding a doctor who can help me. Dr. Huang left a message on my machine after you called him. Thanks for letting him know what's up. He told me we can keep doing sessions over the phone until I find someone else to take over.

Are you moving out here for school or waiting a year?

From: <winzwarehouse5@hotmail.com>
To: <ina.artgirl1979@hotmail.com>
Date: July 2, 1999
Subject: Re: Touching Base

I'm glad you got home okay, and I'm glad Dr. Huang isn't going to leave you hanging. I called the Marion Conservatory this morning and they said it's too late for me to go this year since I already gave them notice I'm not attending until next year. I was worrying and going back and forth on deciding what to do … for nothing!!! Ugh, what a waste of energy.

But, be prepared to be shocked … I am thinking of moving out there in a few months even though I won't be going to school yet. Look at me being all proactive and courageous like a real adult. Seriously, though, the whole plan is making me sick. Excuse me while I go puke my guts out.



From: <winzwarehouse5@hotmail.com>
To: <ina.artgirl1979@hotmail.com>
Date: July 6, 1999
Subject: Missing you

I understand you might not be answering my email because you need space. You can ignore it, and any others, until you feel ready to read them. It just makes me feel better to write to you.

The caretaker my parents hired came by today. His name is Ben and Dad actually gets along with him. They're a lot alike. I'm worried how the warehouse will run without me, but I guess they'll figure it out.

So yeah, I'm still making plans to move out there. Logan says I can move in with him. He found a place in Greenwich Village by the Marion Conservatory. I think he did that on purpose so I'd feel more comfortable moving out there. He can't afford to live there alone for longer than a few months, so it's kinda important I get out there soon and get a job.

I miss you. I hope things are going okay.

---

**From: <winzwarehouse5@hotmail.com>**
**To: <ina.artgirl1979@hotmail.com>**
**Date: July 10, 1999**
**Subject: Still missing you**

I broke down and tried to call you yesterday. Sorry. Emily answered the phone and said you've been working a lot and you're hardly ever home. She said you found a new doctor, so I hope that's working out.

My dad had a really bad hallucination yesterday, and Ben handled it great. It was hard to watch because I felt like I needed to do something. It's really hard to stand back and let someone else take over.

---

**From: <winzwarehouse5@hotmail.com>**
**To: <ina.artgirl1979@hotmail.com>**
**Date: July 20, 1999**
**Subject: Finally Happening**

I miss you. Everything is good here at home, but work is crazy busy. Seriously, nobody can do all the stuff I do. I feel like things will fall apart when I leave, and my mom is worried it will too. But I have to stick to my plan, so I finally booked a flight into LaGuardia on September 4th. It gets in at 4:00 p.m. your time. Logan's going to meet me, but if you happen to read this and feel like meeting up, let me know.

# Forty-Six

## Ina

"I want everything to go away," Ina said as she bent forward and buried her face in her hands. "I want the memories to go away. I want the past to go away. I even want the people I care about to go away. That's why I haven't emailed Alex. I just can't do it. I can't."

She looked up at Dr. Ingraham—or Beth, as she insisted Ina call her. She was thin and blonde and young and nothing like what Ina had imagined she'd be when she was trying to find a new psychiatrist. She had tried four other doctors before finding her, but it had been worth it so far. Beth specialized in trauma and PTSD therapy. Right now, she was sitting across the room in a leather office chair, her eyes cast down to a legal pad on her lap.

"That's perfectly normal," Beth said, looking up. "Are you upset that you feel like running away from your past?"

Ina folded her arms and leaned back into the sofa. They were in Beth's Manhattan high-rise office, in a posh little corner decorated to feel like a living room, complete with a fireplace. Outside the large window was a view of Manhattan and a bank of gray clouds. A strong wind splattered rain across the glass. It was the middle of July, yet it felt like January. That was how Ina felt inside too.

Cold.

Dark.

Empty.

"I don't know," Ina sighed as she settled deeper into the sofa and stared out the window at the rain. "But it doesn't feel good. It happened forever ago. I know I should try to contact Jake's detective friend, but a part of me doesn't even care. I know what I remember; I'm pretty sure Mom meant to kill Dad, and maybe she felt so bad about it she killed herself. That's probably why she never wanted to talk to me or see me, so does it really matter *why* she killed Dad? It's in the past. It's over."

Out of the corner of her eye, Ina could see Beth writing something down on her legal pad. "Let's think through this logically," she said gently. "You should move on, yes. But not before resolving your feelings. You need to face them head-on. You need to deal with them. Accept them. I still think getting more information would help you do that. Do you still feel like it won't?"

Ina shook her head. "Maybe one day, but not right now."

Beth frowned. "I want you to understand I'm not suggesting you need to contact Jake's detective friend, or start digging up police reports. And I'm not saying you need to start visiting your traumatic memories like old friends. I'm just asking what you think burying your emotions will accomplish. How do you see that panning out?"

Ina closed her eyes. It was a mistake, she realized, but it was too late. She was back in the car where her mother killed her father. She went back fifty times a day, it seemed. She had finally realized that her mother had somehow felt threatened by her husband. Maybe she'd feared he would find out about her affairs, or maybe he'd discovered her embezzling. Maybe he had abused Ina and she couldn't remember it, or maybe her mother had abused her and he'd found out. There were too many horrible possibilities to contemplate, and that was why Ina wanted to bury her emotions. Getting the entire truth might be too painful, if it was even possible.

"Ina?" Beth said, cutting into Ina's thoughts. "Step away from what you're thinking. Open your eyes. You're safe right now, okay? Listen to me."

Ina opened her eyes, realizing her breaths had become rapid and shallow. "I'm sorry," she gasped. "It's just too much to think about."

"Don't apologize. You're not in trouble. Look at me."

Ina met Beth's gaze. She had kind, understanding eyes.

"Good," Beth said gently. "Let's go back to the question. What will burying your emotions accomplish?"

"I can pretend I don't hurt inside," Ina whimpered, realizing how illogical it sounded when she said it out loud.

Beth shook her head. "You're an intelligent woman, Ina. You know as well as I do that you're going to hurt no matter what. It's just hidden temporarily. If a patient comes to me with a fear of dogs and we trace it back to a traumatic event in their childhood where they were bitten by a dog, do you really think avoiding dogs for the rest of their life is the answer? Is trying to forget that event the answer? What's the true issue, do you think?"

Ina chewed on her bottom lip, not sure what to say.

Beth set her pen down on the legal pad and leaned forward. "The issue is the *avoidance*," she said matter-of-factly. "Not dogs or the traumatic event. The patient is afraid of dogs because he avoids them. Now, the answer might be to put the patient in a room with a bunch of dogs, but maybe not. Maybe the answer is more simple than that. Maybe the patient needs to learn some problem-solving skills for when a dog happens to show up unexpectedly. I can't cure the patient's fear. I can't take away the trauma. What I *can* do is tap into his well of strength and resilience because I know it's there. I know it's there in you, too, Ina. You can beat this. You don't have to run away from it. You don't have to face it head-on. All you need to do is find strength to acknowledge it and learn how to adapt. Let it change you. It's okay to change."

Ina opened her mouth and closed it again. "How do I reach that strength you think I have?"

A soft smile lifted Beth's lips. "We find a way for you to reach it." She tilted her head. "You mentioned in our last meeting how much you love to paint. Tell me more about that teddy bear picture you kept painting."

Ina shook her head and looked away. Something dark inside of her twisted into a knot, making her feel nauseous. "I never want to paint again," she muttered, remembering all the black-painted canvases. Painting would forever remind her of her father, of her past, of how it had all gotten so warped inside her head until it had literally driven her crazy. Her greatest love was ruined.

Beth leaned forward, concern filling her eyes. "I'm sorry to hear you say that," she said sadly. "But maybe you shouldn't give it up quite yet." She lifted her pen and tapped it on her chin. "In fact, I have an idea, if you're up for it."

Ina lifted her eyebrows. "Oh?"

"It won't be easy, but think about how you've always gone back to painting, how it has sustained you through everything up until now. Why not let it take you those last few steps into a new life? They will be difficult steps, but worth it."

Ina's eyes filled with tears as she thought about the possibility of stepping past the pain and anger and fear she kept reliving day after day. "I'll consider it," she said softly. "I'll consider anything."

# Invitation

**THE BROOKLYN VISUAL ART LEAGUE**

and

**THE STUART ART GALLERY of BROOKLYN**

Cordially invite you to attend a reception introducing:

*Down the Line: A Visual Journey of Healing*
Paintings by Sabrina Mae Sanchez

Saturday, September 4, 1999

6–8 p.m., Open House
@ The Stuart Art Gallery of Brooklyn, 21 Grant St.

# Forty-Seven

## Alex

Alex looked up from the invitation Logan had shoved into his hand the second he'd stepped off the airplane.

"I don't understand," he said as Logan nudged him out of the way of departing passengers. "Ina has paintings in an art show?"

"Yes, and you have exactly one hour to get there. I don't know what's going on. She just showed up at my apartment yesterday and gave that to me. All she said was she'd really like it if we could both be there."

Alex furrowed his brow. "She knows where you live?"

"Where *we* live now, and yes, I gave her the address the other day when she called me."

Alex stopped in the middle of the terminal. "She hasn't answered my emails or phone calls for two months. The only reason I know she's alive is because I talked to Emily."

Logan shrugged and gave Alex a little push in the direction of the baggage claim. "Don't ask me to explain anything, man. You said she told you she would need space, so that's what you're giving her."

"Yeah . . ." Alex looked at the invitation again. "Guess we should head straight to Brooklyn so we're not late?"

"We have time to swing by the apartment real quick to drop off your luggage. We'll take a cab."

Alex thanked him and focused on the signs leading them to the baggage claim. He tried to ignore the growing anxiety in his gut. He was proud of himself for flying here all by himself, but he felt like he had a long way to go before he wouldn't feel like he was going to hurl every ten seconds.



"Do you see her anywhere?" Alex asked as he and Logan walked into the gallery showcasing Ina's artwork. They had been greeted in the lobby by some of the people running the event, but Ina hadn't been among them.

Logan kept walking, turning in a full circle as he did so. "Nope," he said, shrugging. "Maybe we should look at the exhibit first."

They stopped at the first painting just as a woman in a yellow cocktail dress approached them. "Are you Alex?" she asked, smiling warmly. "Ina said she was hoping you'd come tonight."

"Yeah, I am."

Logan introduced himself and she shook both their hands. "I'm Beth, Ina's psychiatrist. It's nice to meet you."

"Nice to meet you too." Alex looked around the gallery. It was open and airy, the walls covered with pieces of art illuminated by bare lightbulbs hanging from the ceiling. "Is Ina here?"

"She's here. I'll try to find her for you. In the meantime, maybe you should start viewing Ina's paintings. They go in order."

"Like a story?" Alex asked.

Beth nodded. "I don't know how much Ina has told you already, but when she and I connected, we decided the best way for her to work through her trauma was to paint. She told me about her wish to see her paintings in a gallery someday. I happened to know a few people who could help make it happen." She flourished a hand at the first painting on the wall. "Ina named her journey *Down the Line*, alluding to an event in her past that has followed her into the present. The idea is that everything catches up with us at some point."

A pang of emotion hit Alex in the gut. He didn't know what it was; he just knew it made him want to find Ina and hug her. The name of her collection was perfect. Everything did catch up to a person eventually, just as it had with him and his parents. They had finally realized how tightly they had been holding on to him, and he had finally realized how he had convinced himself that they couldn't survive without him. When all of that caught up to them, he'd been able to step free. That was how he was here. All he needed now was to see Ina.

Logan tilted his head. "What kind of trauma did she go through?" he asked.

Beth gave them a small smile. "I'll leave that for you to discover. Start here and make your way to the end. I'll go find Ina for you."

Beth left them standing in front of the first painting. Alex took a step back, his heart pounding. He didn't know why he was so nervous.

"She's really good," Logan said, stepping back to stand next to Alex. "I mean, I already knew that from looking at her paintings in her apartment, but these are even better."

Alex nodded as he studied the painting in front of them. It was a portrait of a woman who looked a lot like Ina, but subtly different. Her clothes seemed dated by a couple of decades. Her head was tilted down, her eyes on the dark-haired infant she held in her arms. Both were gently smiling at each other. The painting was titled *Burned*. Alex remembered Ina telling him about her mother burning a bunch of her dad's paintings. Was this a re-creation of one of those paintings?

"Is that her mom?" Logan asked.

Alex knitted his brow. "I think so? I'm not sure."

They moved on to the next painting, a portrait of a man Alex guessed was Ina's father. He was dressed in jeans and a T-shirt, his eyes sorrowful. Ina had positioned him so that he seemed to be looking in the direction of the first painting of his wife and daughter.

Next was the family standing together in front of a beautiful white house. Ina's mother was in a pantsuit, her posture stiff. Ina's father, dressed in jeans and a T-shirt, also looked stiff. He and his wife were smiling, but their expressions looked fake. Ina, a small child, stood between them, holding both their hands. Her smile was genuine.

The next painting was a slight variation on the same subjects, and so was the next. The smiles changed in each painting. Sometimes Ina's mother's smile looked genuine. Sometimes it was her father's. Not one version showed them all smiling genuinely. The effect was a bit creepy, but Alex figured that was Ina's intention. In all of the pictures, the house behind the family was crumbling bit by bit. By the time they reached the last one, it was a pile of rubble.

Then there was a series with Ina's mother on Wall Street. She looked viciously powerful in each one, beautiful but not necessarily happy. One painting was surrounded by snippets of actual news articles that mentioned Ina's mother, Reina Sanchez, and the incredible things she was doing in the financial world back in the early 1980s. Some of the articles had an angry streak of red paint slashed through them.

The next series of paintings was all black and white except for an occasional splash of color. The effect was almost chaotic, and Alex took an instinctual step backward to try to make sense of it all.

"It's a car wreck," Logan said after a moment. "Wow. That's kinda awesome."

Alex nodded in agreement. One painting depicted the actual crash: a large pickup truck smashing into the driver's side of a small sedan. Only the yellow lines on the road were in color. Another depicted a car on its side with only a few splashes of red blood on broken glass. Another was inside the car, showing the same family, broken and battered from the accident. The father was literally broken into shattered, glass-like pieces, as if he was a puzzle that needed to be put back together. The most eerie thing of all, however, was Ina's mother's expression. She was smiling. Ina, probably only about eight years old, had a confused look on her face. Ina's body was painted in two extremes—one side in light, the other in shadow. Alex stared at the painting for a long time.

"That is seriously creepy," Logan said. "Why is her mother *smiling*?"

"I don't know." Alex stepped over to the next painting. They had moved to a different wall now. Alex looked around the room, hoping to catch a glimpse of Ina, but couldn't see her. There was now a steady line of people looking at the paintings in order.

Focusing on the paintings in front of him, Alex saw that there were two duplicates side-by-side. One was streaked with black, just as Alex had seen in Ina's living room and at River Meadows. The one next to it was completed: a small girl with wildly curly hair. Her back was to the viewer, a teddy bear hanging from one hand, a red bow on its head. She was in an empty room. Next to these two paintings was a portrait of Jake. It was almost Picasso-like in its composition. The brightest spots of color were Jake's blue eyes. It was stunning.

Logan grunted under his breath. "Why isn't there a picture of *you*?" he asked, sounding upset. "Why Jake?"

Alex shrugged, silent as they continued on. There were paintings of New York, then of a house that was titled *Harmony House*. There was a painting of a ski lodge next to a lake, a girl lying in the snow, crying, and then the paintings got darker and darker from there. One depicted Ina in what Alex could only describe as a brothel. She was in a bright purple cocktail dress, surrounded by men and women. It was disjointed, painted in sharp-edged triangles. If Alex stepped too close, the triangles were too geometric, erasing the image as a whole. The painting was not graphic, but it screamed pain and fear and desperation. It was titled *Forget*.

Alex and Logan looked at the painting for a long time and then moved on to the next one. It was more disjointed than the last. Alex wasn't sure what it was until Logan pointed out the shapes of two caskets. The whole scene was dark, like it was underground. It felt smothering. The portraits gradually lightened, each one telling another part of Ina's healing journey, including meeting Alex. She'd painted a picture of him and her running through a field holding hands, their faces smiling and happy. It was the brightest picture in the entire set.

"I was hoping you'd like that one," a voice said from behind.

Alex spun around to see Ina. She was in a bright blue dress, her hair down and as curly as ever, but devoid of frizz. It shone under the gallery lights. She was wearing makeup, and her eyes sparkled.

"Ina," Alex whispered, unsure of how to talk to her after trying to reach out to her for so long. "You look amazing. And your paintings. I had no idea . . . this whole thing . . . it's—"

"I've been waiting for you to see that one," she interrupted. "I'm sorry I had to hide from you." She looked over at Beth, who was talking to a group of people at the other end of the room. "My doctor is a good guide for me. She knew exactly what I needed, and I hope . . . I hope you understand why this was something I needed to do without you."

Alex nodded. "Of course. You've been through a lot. I hope you can talk about it now? No more panic attacks?"

Ina grinned. "I feel better than I ever have. No more panic attacks. By the way, I read your emails. I'm glad your dad is doing better and things are working out at home."

Alex smiled. "Yeah, it was rough for a while, but he's doing a lot better."

"That's great." She rushed forward and wrapped her arms around him. He wrapped his arms around her too, and squeezed. It felt incredible to have her want to be near him. She pulled away enough to look him in the eyes. "How are *you*? I've been through hell and back the past few months, but what about you? Are you really here to stay? Because that is *huge*!"

Alex laughed softly, leaning forward to brush his lips across hers. "Yeah, I'm here to stay, but I think things are just starting for me."

Ina broke into a smile. She moved her arm down Alex's side until her hand closed around his. "Then let's start together."

Alex's heart warmed at the hope sparkling in her eyes. Strangely enough, it felt good to know that while he had played a part in her healing journey, he was not the one who had healed her. She'd done that on her own, just as it had needed to happen. "You got a deal," he said, glancing back to see that Logan had left them to go look at the rest of the paintings. "Want to show me the rest of your collection?" he asked.

Ina nodded enthusiastically. "Let's go, Alex Winzelberg."

"Sure thing, Sabrina Mae Sanchez."

It was the first time he'd ever said her full name aloud. He waited for her to punch him in the chest, but instead, her smile widened into a grin. "You know," she said softly, "that's the first time I've ever liked the sound of my name. And you know what else I just realized?"

He raised an eyebrow in question.

"You don't look like you want to run away and hide. We're standing in the middle of Brooklyn, at night, with a large group of strangers, and you're fine."

He looked around, realizing he didn't feel nervous at all. "Maybe it's because of you?"

She squeezed his hand and started leading him to her next painting. "Maybe, Mr. Winzelberg. Or maybe you just took your first step on that new journey of yours."

Alex let out a sarcastic laugh, but deep down he knew she was right.

# Author's Note

Thank you for reading *Down the Line*. This story was born out of my deep respect and personal experiences with mental illness and the effects it can have on not only those who suffer from it, but those who live with others suffering from it. Mental illness takes on many forms, as this story shows. If you, or someone you know, suffers from mental illness in any form, and it has not been treated or addressed, I strongly urge finding help in the form of a trained psychiatrist, psychologist, or other trusted medical professional.

Also, please consider leaving an honest review of this book on Amazon.com, Goodreads, your blog, or another form of social media. Reviews can dramatically boost visibility for a published book, effectively increasing sales and allowing an author to continue their craft—and you to continue reading.

# Also by Michelle D. Argyle

A Fine Line *(Down the Line #2) Forthcoming*

The Breakaway *(contemporary suspense)*
Pieces *(The Breakaway #2)*
Unbroken *(The Breakaway #3)*

Streets of Glass *(a thriller)*
If I Forget You *(contemporary women's fic.)*
Out of Tune *(contemporary women's fic.)*
Monarch *(a romantic spy thriller)*

Catch *(a novella)*
Bonded *(a grown-up fairy-tale collection)*

*True Colors & Other Short Stories*

See **michelledargyle.com** for more details

# About the Author

MICHELLE D. ARGYLE lives and writes surrounded by the Rocky Mountains, where she finds every excuse possible to go hiking and be outdoors. Michelle mainly writes contemporary fiction, but occasionally branches into other genres.